QUEEN MOTHER

✦ ANGEL SWORN ✦

WALL STREET JOURNAL BESTSELLING AUTHOR

JEFF WHEELER

OLIVERHEBERBOOKS

Queen Mother 2025 © Jeff Wheeler

Cover Art by Drazenka Kimpel

Published by Oliver-Heber Books

0 9 8 7 6 5 4 3 2 1

ALSO BY JEFF WHEELER

Your First Million Words

Tales from Kingfountain, Muirwood, and Beyond: The Worlds of Jeff Wheeler

The Invisible College

The Invisible College

The Violence of Sound

The Dresden Codex

Doomsday Match

Jaguar Prophecies

Final Strike

The First Argentines Series

Knight's Ransom

Warrior's Ransom

Lady's Ransom

Fate's Ransom

The Grave Kingdom Series

The Killing Fog

The Buried World

The Immortal Words

The Covenant of Muirwood Trilogy

The Banished of Muirwood

The Ciphers of Muirwood

The Void of Muirwood

Whispers from Mirrowen Trilogy

Fireblood

Dryad-Born

Poisonwell

Landmoor Series

Landmoor

Silverkin

To Tyler

The man implored her to eat of the fruit of the tree and learn for herself good and evil. Yet she refused and would not partake. And the man's eyes were opened, and he understood the nature of all things, both good and evil. So she drove out the man, and the Oldknow placed to the west of the garden of Clairvaux an angel sworn and, of flame, a sword, whirling to guard the way to the Gallows Tree.

— ORIGIN, THE TALE OF THE QUEEN MOTHER
OF CLAIRVAUX

ONE

Edelweiss

There was no place in all the world as beautiful as Clairvaux. Rugged cliffs rose on either side, forming a wedge-shaped valley between them. Waterfalls cascaded down their speckled faces. Some large and fierce. Some hardly more than a trickle. There were seventy-two waterfalls in all. Cimree had counted them and knew each one. And where the valley stretched to its widest, there loomed snow-peaked mountains showing a change in the weather was coming. Honeysuckle, purple catmint, blanched aspen, and meadows of wildflowers provided colors that dazzled the eye, and combined with the ever-present soothing noise of the waterfalls, they created an impossible beauty and feeling of serenity. Every morning, choirs of angelic voices sang from the upper heights of the cliffs. This morning had been no different. Why did she feel she didn't belong there?

Cimree knelt in the tall meadow grass, watching bees dart from within the violet flowers of a catmint bush. She brushed dirt from her trews as she knelt there, her cloak snug against her shoulders as she observed the hive's activity. Their droning noise made her nervous, but she'd been working to tame her fear. When she was little, she'd shriek if one lit on her, for even though she knew the insects were harmless, they terrified her. But they shouldn't. If she was going to be a healer in the valley, it would be to her benefit to befriend the creatures. Not that she could ever become a true Beesinger, *that* was asking too much of herself. But honey was nutritious and could sustain a life. Bees were hardworking and industrious—as she was supposed to be herself. The breeze tousled her hair and she sighed, trying to summon her courage. She slipped the distaff from her belt and held it in her cupped palm, her gaze on an individual bee foraging the blooms.

Cimree bit her lip and focused. Grafting magic was the birthright of the angel sworn. It allowed them to join, temporarily, with beast, bird, or insect and claim an essential part of their power to combine with their own. Every person had a natural affinity for some creature or other, and it was up to the individual to discover what that was. That natural affinity made the grafting easier and last longer. Otherwise, a creature's resistance to any bond which caused discomfort, pain, or weakness meant the magic lasted only a short while. But for those who shared an affinity to that animal, there was a mutual acceptance.

The distaff in her hand—about the length of her forearm—she had inherited from a previous angel sworn. Distaffs were broadly used to wind wool or flax. Their particular shape made it easy to gather wool or flax to twist it into yarn or thread. Every inhabitant of Clairvaux made their own clothing. But these wands, when made of ancient scionwood, were also used for the grafting magic, so every angel sworn carried one with them.

She gazed at her solitary bee and began coaxing the magic. She didn't compel the bee. She coaxed it. The distinction between telling and asking made all the difference. The magic sent a shiver down her spine as she felt it connecting her to the tiny insect. She was looking for edelweiss flowers, a hardy variety that grew in the cliffs. It was incredibly rare and had the very interesting properties of a double-star formation and white woolly hairs. It was helpful for stomach pangs and breathing illnesses, and it was good for the heart. She thought of its distinctive shape as she joined her mind with the insect's tiny one. Bees ranged far and wide to collect their nectar. Had it seen any edelweiss flower yet?

The grafting released as the bee tugged away its thoughts, but not before she'd glimpsed the flower she sought up in the mountains on the northern face. Cimree felt a tingling sensation in her fingertips and her nose, a small consequence of the magic she'd used. She rose from her knees, brushed off her trews again, and continued to hike through the wildflowers in the direction the bee had indicated.

Her teacher, Milena, would be pleased to know that Cimree had tamed a bee to help her find the plant. She passed several of the smaller falls as she ventured deeper into the valley. The majority of the inhabitants of Clairvaux lived in the village at the head of the valley. She'd never felt comfortable there, preferring solitude to talkative neighbors. Being a healer in training meant living in the hinterlands. Spread apart. Separate. Every person was different, though they shared certain similarities, or so the Queen Mother taught. Some people preferred solitude to company. Some preferred confrontation to attack problems head-on and others demurred. Cimree would never be a leader in Clairvaux, not with her shy if slightly rebellious personality, not when social hierarchy was modeled after the Queen Mother's virtues.

As she neared the narrowed part of the wedge of the valley, she took a footpath to the cliffs and began to climb. Some angel sworn would use their grafting magic to borrow the agility of a goat, allowing them to climb more quickly and with surefootedness. But Cimree didn't have an affinity for goats. Or for cows. Or a rare minx. Birds ignored her completely. Horses snorted at her. What if her affinity ended up being something loathsome, like snails? She knew one of the field-workers, a young man by the name of

Calvor, who was particularly fond of snails and liked to talk about them and how useful they were. No one liked talking to Calvor.

Cimree's legs burned as she scrambled up the trail to the higher reach. There were other smaller communities farther up the mountains, but the trek was difficult, and those who lived there had affinities for birds or climbing animals. She puffed out her breath and kept plodding on, feeling her muscles ache with the exertion as her brow dampened. It was a steep, challenging ascent, but she'd done it before. She was winded by the time she'd crested the rise, only to find more mountains looming above. Gazing back down at the valley, she admired the beautiful scene below.

"You're not supposed to be up here, Cimree."

The voice startled her, and she touched her chest and laughed. Of course one of the Morgarten would have caught her unaware. They were the guardians of Clairvaux, the expert hunters of the valley. The defenders of the Gallows Tree. She saw the mirror blade that rode on his hip, one gloved hand gripping the pommel. He had a bow strapped to his back and a quiver full of arrows. A long dagger was fastened to his thigh. His drab hunter garb helped him blend in with the rocks and scrub.

"There's some ... edelweiss growing ... near here," she panted. "A bee told me."

"I saw some yesterday," he replied. His name was Damion. The members of the Morgarten were quite memorable, and as they were so few in number, she'd encountered most of them over the years. Damion had hazel eyes and a rugged face. The training he and his cohorts went through was secretive, as was the initiation they endured. His narrowed eyes offered a little reproof, but then he shook his head. "I won't tell on you for wandering out of bounds, but be careful. You'll want to be off the mountain soon."

"Thank you, Damion," she said. She admired his physique as she wondered how many lifespans he'd already lived. Because of the fruit of the Gallows Tree, he could have lived for centuries already.

But everyone knew Cimree was a novice. She was in her first lifetime, a maggot in comparison.

She hiked farther up the steep slope, searching for evidence of the elusive edelweiss. It was colder higher up, and Damion hadn't been wrong. The clouds were coming down quickly, blotting out the sky. Soon they'd engulf the mountains and maybe even reach the valley floor. The weather in Clairvaux was often temperamental. In mid-spring a freak snowstorm could blanket everything in white only to melt off by the end of the day. That's why it was only sensible to wear a cloak and sturdy boots.

She continued her search, climbing so high she felt the brush of mist against her face. That added to her frustration, for it would make it more difficult to—

There!

Her heart thrilled as she recognized the star-shaped flower with the buttery core. Cimree knelt near an outcropping of rock and slid the dirk from her belt sheath. Along with a distaff, everyone carried a dirk for cutting cheese or meat, a short double-edged blade always kept sharp with a whetstone. Gently, she lifted at the base of the edelweiss petals and gently nicked the stem to separate it. A few others grew nearby, so she cut off three more and stopped. She slid the dirk back in her belt sheath and then smelled the petals of the edelweiss. A smile curved her mouth.

She opened her shoulder pack, gently wrapped the flowers in burlap, and stowed the bundle atop her other supplies. Then she hiked to a nearby stream and cupped some water in her hand to drink. The mist thickened around her. Better to get off the mountain in a hurry, before the way became too difficult to see. She backtracked down the trail, feeling an uneasiness creep into her stomach. There was no reason to be fearful. A snow lynx wouldn't be so close to the valley floor, especially at that time of year. They didn't typically prey on lost young women either.

The mist swirled around her, limiting visibility, and she began to regret her choice of seeking the flower. Her display of independence would be thwarted if she needed Damion to help her navigate back down to the valley floor. That would be embarrassing. But Milena would only tease her, not report her transgression to the high council.

A feeling of dread began to form a knot in her belly. Something was in the mist. Something was coming for her. This was not the fear of a potential bee sting. It was a much deeper fear, a primal fear. She'd walked the mountains hundreds of times and never experienced such a feeling before, not even when the mist came or when a lightning storm lashed the sky. The fear was compelling, full of danger and warning.

Run.

She found herself breathing faster and faster and not just from the pace. The impulse to flee grew stronger and stronger. But that was foolhardy. In the mountains, you couldn't run, or you'd risk tumbling off a cliff. She gazed ahead, trying to quell the irrational fear that had gripped her. She thought she saw a bulky shadow moving in the mist off to her right.

"Damion?"

She walked through the mist in the direction of the shadow but tripped over something lying before her and went down with a gasp of shock. She put her hands out and felt stiff leather beneath her fingers. Cimree quickly rose, about to utter an apology when she saw Damion's lifeless eyes staring fixedly at nothing, a grimace of fear frozen on his face. His hunter leathers were shredded and bloodstained, the gashes deep. Claw wounds. In a daze, she lifted her hands in front of her face and started shaking as she saw the blood there as well.

Cimree gazed at the hunter in abject fear. His mirror blade was still in its sheath. So were his daggers. He'd been attacked and savaged by a monstrous animal, and she hadn't heard a sound except for the breeze in her ears and the distant roar of the falls.

Damion was dead.

Impossible.

An angel sworn didn't just die.

She bent to touch his neck, feeling for a pulse. Nothing. She leaned over him, her ear next to his lips.

No breath.

And then Cimree saw the bulky shadow again, and fear locked her legs and gripped her throat.

Two

Clairvaux

As Cimree froze in place, rigid with fear, she heard a snuffling grunt in the mist and a noise similar to the whickering of a horse. Her heart raced, the feeling of danger growing more and more pronounced. Whatever creature had killed Damion was coming for her next. Instinct prevailed. If she did not flee, she would die.

Springing into action, Cimree fled from the creature in the mist. Uncontrollable whimpering ejected from her mouth as she raced to the trail leading down the mountain. She heard the snuffling noise again just behind her, and her mind went black with fear, leaving only a tiny corner that recalled that fleeing a predator tended to provoke it into attacking, but her legs only responded to the threat on her life by pumping. Mist swirled around her, obscuring the trail, and gasps came from her throat, intermingled with choking sobs.

Her downward plunge startled a black grouse into bursting from some foliage in a rocky crevice as it took flight off the edge of the cliff.

Cimree saw the chance to escape and immediately seized it. Whipping out her distaff, she snagged the grouse with a grafting spell, capturing its power of flight. It was an unwilling bond, which the grouse resisted, but Cimree's desperation overshadowed the bird's reluctance. She felt the magic join them together and took a running leap, launching herself off the edge of the cliff. Immediately she was soaring like the grouse, swathed in the misty cloud that had settled on the mountains. She felt it as a wet kiss against her face, her fear turning to thrill as she soared, leaving the stony ledge behind.

Pinpricks of pain riddled her toes up her legs and from her fingertips up her arms as the grouse resisted the grafting magic imposed on it. Cimree and the bird descended rapidly, tugging against each other for control. Her stomach fluttered with the sensation of the drop, and she worried that if the magic were severed, she'd plummet to her death. Gripping the distaff in her hand, she clenched her fist and wrung her will over the black grouse as the mist cleared and she saw trees rushing toward her.

She released a low moan of panic and held tighter to the tether. The grouse was trying to flap away from her but was yet drawn into the vortex of the unwilling bond. Cimree's hands and feet were totally numb at this point, and the needle pricks of pain were past her knees and elbows. Grafting was always painful, but she'd never experienced it to such a degree, had never forced a creature into sharing its power with her. The valley walls loomed in the distance, the colored bracken coming at her fast.

She slowed her fall the best she could, descending feet forward as she glided down the edge of the cliff. The intense dread and fear she'd experienced on the mountain edge was fading, replaced by a lesser spasm caused by the precipitous drop. The grouse seemed to realize her intent of landing and stubbornly acquiesced to her wish for control. She touched down in a field of meadow grass just past a cliff-hugging copse of silver birch.

As soon as her boots skimmed the grass, she released the grafting, and the grouse sped away from her, flapping its wings raucously. Her numb legs wouldn't bear weight, and she collapsed into the grass, panting and swallowing and feeling a giddy relief that she was even alive. The pain was intense, but slowly, feeling began to trickle back into her limbs as she huddled there silently.

She had never been so afraid in her life.

And just when her heart began to slow to a normal pace, she heard a distant roar from the mountain. A sound she'd never heard before in the valley of Clairvaux, which caused a shiver of fear to run down her spine.

⁂

CIMREE REACHED the small cabin she shared with Milena at the road's edge breathless. There was a lean-to with stacked lumber in preparation for the coming winter. Near it was a beehive that Milena tended. A rock trough with water from the well sat outside. Cimree, panting after the run, raced up the steps and flung open the door.

Milena was tending a young girl with a scrape on her arm, applying ointment. A little bloodied rag was on the table. Milena looked to be in her early thirties but she'd been in Clairvaux for centuries, and so her looks belied her age as it did for most of the angel sworn. Milena was soft-spoken, compassionate, and a gentle teacher. She glanced at Cimree's face and halted her treatment. Her dark brown hair matched Cimree's own.

"You look frightened," Milena observed, her brow wrinkling with concern.

Cimree was still panting, trying to catch her breath. Milena added a little linen wrap to the wound and then kissed the girl on her forehead. "Go back to Haleyna. You'll be all right."

The girl gave Milena a hug and then trotted past Cimree before bounding down the steps and taking the road toward the village.

Milena wiped her hands on a rag, giving Cimree a quizzical look.

"Damion is dead." Cimree finally got the words out. "He was attacked."

Milena blinked and then shook her head. "Damion?"

"Yes! I just ... made it back. Something *killed* him."

"What kind of wound did he have?" Milena approached Cimree and began examining her for injuries.

"I'm fine," Cimree said. "I think it was a bear. There were claw wounds on his chest. His shirt was soaked in blood. It happened so fast."

"Tell me everything," Milena said, coaxing Cimree to the chair at the table where the little girl had been sitting for her treatment.

Cimree quickly explained how she'd been looking for some edelweiss and had ventured higher on the mountain even though it was forbidden. Her admission provoked a disappointed look in Milena's eyes, but not a scolding came. She described the mist, the shadow she'd seen, and the unfamiliar sounds she'd heard.

"Did you take his weapon? His mirror blade?" Milena asked.

"I didn't even think of it," Cimree confessed. "I've never felt so afraid. If I hadn't startled that grouse, I might have jumped off the mountain anyway. I panicked."

Milena nodded and put her hand on Cimree's shoulder. "We need to tell the high council. Or Trinati."

Cimree clamped her mouth shut. Trinati was the authority in the valley, the one who fulfilled the Queen Mother's purposes. She was tall, powerful, and held the highest rank in the valley floor, archangel, and she was one who frequently visited the eyrie heights of the mountains. She'd be furious if she learned Cimree had disobeyed again.

"You're afraid of being punished," Milena observed, noticing Cimree's expression.

"Trinati isn't as patient as you," Cimree said. "She can be quite ... severe."

"But you knew that before you went up the mountain," Milena said. "As the Queen Mother teaches, when there is no law there is no sin. If there is no sin, there is no consequence. But this news cannot wait. She must be told. Let's go together."

"Do you think it was a bear? I've never heard such a noise before."

"I don't know," Milena said. "It may have been a snow lynx. Sometimes they come down from the mountains if they can't find food."

"But Damion had a distaff. It shouldn't have been a problem for him."

"True. But maybe he was surprised."

The mist might have obscured a snow lynx's approach. Those creatures typically roamed the higher passes of the Arvadin. They were long and sleek, with dark splotches on their pelts, and had long bushy tails. A snow lynx could rip out a massive red deer's throat in a single bite. Even wolves were reluctant to prey on red deer, but a snow lynx was bigger and more cunning. It could have caught the hunter unawares, as Milena thought. Just an unfortunate accident.

Cimree nodded and rose from the chair as Milena fetched her cloak and hurriedly put it on. Together, they left the cottage and started down the road toward the village at the edge of the valley. As they walked, Cimree asked about the girl and her injuries and was pleased to hear they weren't serious.

The mist had spread to cover most of the valley walls, but the noise of rushing water grew louder as they approached the village, where, on a clear day, there was a view of eight different falls. After about a mile, they crossed a rock bridge over the Silver River, which extended the length of the valley, fed by mountain snow. The waters were pure and cold and fresh.

The closer they got to the village, the more Cimree dreaded what was to come. It wasn't the same as what she'd experienced in the mountains, but facing Trinati was nothing to be enjoyed. When Cimree was younger, her indiscretions had earned her prompt rebukes, and she still chafed at the austerity sometimes.

Milena was like the river and allowed concerns to pass her by as inconsequential. Relationships were more important to her than rules. But Trinati led the high council and oversaw adherence to the Queen Mother's words. And her affinity for eagles allowed her to meld with one and quickly soar up the cliff walls to the domain of the Queen Mother on the topmost peak at a moment's notice.

The village was built at the mouth of the valley, a series of buildings and structures made from carved stone with timber roofs and shingles. Each dwelling was distinct and unique, a panorama of craftsmanship that rivaled each other for beauty. Longhouses, small cottages that intermingled with larger structures, hostels to house the angel sworn each time they returned from their journeys. The streets were clean and well tended, undulating up and down along with the terrain, and the noisy waterfall they'd already passed was on prime display. Cimree was grateful to share Milena's dwelling, which was cozy for the two of them and away from the larger population in the village. But her realization that angel sworn were all around them in the village chased away the dregs of her earlier fear, and she finally felt safe.

They reached the hall of the high council with its stone arches and elegant timbered roofline. There were no battlement walls in Clairvaux. It was not a fortress. The mountains themselves were the defensive barriers. Its secret location aided in its ability to camouflage itself. The angel sworn had fortresses elsewhere, where accessibility and the proximity to mortal men and women meant that sin and consequence were more common.

Milena walked confidently up the stone steps leading to the high council chambers and opened the heavy wooden door. Cimree swallowed and prepared herself for another scolding.

The high council was a body of angel sworn who represented the different cantons throughout their strongholds. The interests of farmers, weavers, and drovers all blended together so concerns could be discussed and decisions made. It was no surprise to find Trinati there at all hours, dealing with messengers from around the world, solving problems that were not of enough importance to bring to the Queen Mother's attention. Trinati was a hard worker and very diligent. She just wasn't very ... nice.

Milena approached one of the custodians, a balding man by the name of Wegner who oversaw the scheduling of the high council as well as construction within the village. He was an impressive architect as evidenced by the beautiful and functional structures even in the most inhospitable areas of the valley and mountains. She spoke to him in confidential tones, and his lips pursed in apparent concern before he nodded and walked away briskly, disappearing behind a door leading to the council chamber.

Milena went back to Cimree and stroked her arm, giving her a reassuring smile.

The council door opened and Wegner motioned for them both to approach.

Butterflies danced in Cimree's stomach as she followed her mentor through the open door to the high council. Thankfully, the council was not in session and Trinati was in the room with only one other person, who Cimree deduced was also a member.

Trinati always spoke with an authoritative voice. "I want the farmers to find a way of sharing pasture on the northern front. This bickering has gone on long enough. If *I* need to impose a solution, they will not like it."

"Yes, my lady," said the councilwoman. She glanced at the new arrivals and then bowed in deference and walked away.

Trinati turned and Cimree felt a surge of unwanted jealousy. Trinati was the epitome of womankind. Beautiful, flawless face, a look of keen intelligence in her eyes. Her body was honed for war, her voice meant for diplomacy, and she carried herself with an appearance of self-confidence that was intimidating.

"Well, well," Trinati said, sizing up Cimree with a look of contempt. "Let me guess. Our little foundling has broken another rule."

THREE

BLOODSTAINS

"She has, Trinati," Milena said softly, offering a small, reverent bow. "But this is not about an infraction. Damion is dead. I wanted Cimree to tell you herself."

At the mention of the hunter, Trinati's eyebrows furrowed with concern and, Cimree decided, disbelief. She approached the two with a commanding posture.

"Speak," she told Cimree curtly.

"I followed a honeybee, looking for edelweiss," Cimree said, feeling her throat thicken with worry. Usually the Queen Mother made the decision as to whether someone should be expelled from Clairvaux. But Trinati's condemnation could guarantee it.

"Edelweiss grows in the mountains," Trinati said. "That is out of bounds for you."

Rather than trying to justify her actions, she proceeded with her tale. "I encountered Damion on the way. The mist was coming down quickly, but he'd seen some of the flowers growing and allowed me to pass to collect them. I found some, cut a few stars, and put them in my bag. When I came back, I stumbled over his body. He'd been savaged by a beast. He was already dead when I got there."

Trinati frowned and folded her arms. "How long were you gone?"

"It's hard to say. But it wasn't long."

"Did you hear him cry out? Any alarm?"

"None. His weapons were still in their sheaths. The arrows in his quiver."

"You left a mirror blade up on the mountain?" Trinati asked incredulously. "You didn't think to bring it down? A token that you're telling the truth?"

"Cimree isn't deceitful," Milena said, momentarily interrupting the interrogation.

"Are you sure he was dead?" Trinati pressed.

Cimree gulped. "Yes. He had no heartbeat. He wasn't breathing. The wounds were savage and deep."

"Where was this exactly? Damion has a wide patrol. Can you be specific?"

"It was on the north side of the valley. The trail just past Little Quickening."

Trinati nodded. All the little waterfalls had names. The stern woman pursed her lips and then nodded. "You did right to confess this, Cimree. And so did you, Milena, for bringing her here. I'll dispatch hunters to investigate. Please stay in the village while I confirm your story."

Cimree's stomach began to unclench.

"Are you going to tell the Queen Mother?" Milena asked cautiously.

Trinati shook her head. "I want to see the evidence myself. And if what you've told me is true, Cimree, I'll take you with me to relate the tale in greater detail. Is there anything else?"

"I saw something. In the mist," Cimree said, her voice throbbing with remembered fear. "It was big and shaggy. It might have been a bear. I've never felt so afraid."

"Did it have a long tail?" Trinati asked.

Cimree shook her head. "I don't think it was a snow lynx. But I've never seen one."

"They have superior camouflage in the mountains," Trinati said. "They're not easy to pick out. But that's nothing Damion couldn't have handled. This is peculiar. Anything else?"

"Just the sound it made," Cimree said. "I heard it roar. I've never heard that sound before in Clairvaux."

"Interesting. Well, thank you for reporting what you found. Go have some supper at Milton's and stay there until I call for you."

"Yes, Trinati," Milena said with a bow. Cimree copied the motion, grateful she hadn't gotten a scolding this time. A feeling of relief washed through her at not being in trouble. But no, she couldn't count on not being in trouble. Especially if the Queen Mother found out.

❧✿❧

MILTON RAN an inn off the main village road called the Silberhorn. The shrouded mountains concealed the receding light of the encroaching dusk, causing the muted shadows to thicken around them as they walked up the steep side road to the inn. A stone-rimmed flowerbed displayed a colorful variety of mountain flowers nested in damp, rich soil. Cimree rubbed her palm along the edge of the wall as they climbed the road. They passed another stone trough of mountain water, and Cimree paused to scoop up a drink.

While she felt safer in the village after her ordeal, she was uncomfortable around so many other people. And, not surprisingly, they found the common room of Milton's quite crowded, although the smell of melting cheese and freshly baked bread was inviting.

Milton was a sinewy man with the lean body of an ardent walker. His hair had bits of gray in it, showing he was overdue for a bite of fruit from the Gallows Tree. The fruit was rationed and distributed equitably, each person getting their turn in time.

"Milena, so good to see you," Milton said with a hearty smile. "You rarely come by for dinner. Is this little Cimree? How you've grown. You were just a girl when I last saw you."

It had been a few years so she certainly had grown since she'd last been to the Silberhorn. Awkwardness gripped her throat so she only smiled shyly at him.

"Milena!" cried another guest, waving her hand.

Cimree's stomach shriveled. She usually had no problem talking to people, but being in crowds always made her feel ill. Her duties had her speaking with most of the people in Clairvaux at some point—a farmer who'd cut himself on a scythe, the blistered feet of people who had traveled long distances, even the occasional fever or sickness caused by bee stings. One on one, she was fine, but the overall noise at Milton's was making her more and more uncomfortable.

Milena responded to the wave. "Can we have a small table off to the side?" she asked Milton.

"I forget those of you living deeper in the valley don't like how friendly we are. Your loss, my dear. Yes, I can arrange it. How about that little table right there, hmmm?"

Milena looked over her shoulder at a little table by itself near the back corner. "That would be perfect. Thank you. Trinati might send someone to see us. She told us not to leave."

"Trinati? That's unusual."

Milena shrugged but didn't elaborate. Milton escorted them through the noisome bunch to the little table off against a wall.

"Some raclette to start?" Milton asked them eagerly.

"Yes, that would be nice. Thank you, Milton."

There were so many people talking at once that it was impossible to follow any of the conversations except in little bits. Cimree wanted to slink under the table and hide from them, but she wasn't a child anymore and such childish antics would be frowned on at her age. She'd be expected to act sensibly. She began to feel the edginess fade as she sat down on the wooden chair and propped her elbows on the table.

Milton returned shortly after with a small tray and began to unload it onto their table, first putting a wooden plate down in front of each of them. Next were a little dish with slices of raclette cheese and a bowl full of steaming vegetables, which he placed off to one side. Then he put two stubby candles in the center of the table, along with an unlit straw spill. Last, he put down two metal raclette stands, two trays, and two wooden scoops.

"We have some venison with huckleberries if you'd like some as well. Let me know what else you need. It's good to see you, Milena. Remember the time you sutured my hand when I cut it in the kitchen? Though that scar is gone now, I still think of it sometimes. I was so afraid I'd damaged my hand permanently."

Milena nodded and smiled and watched as Milton left. "Would you light the spill, please?" she said to Cimree.

Sighing, Cimree picked up the little stub of straw and maneuvered through the tables to the hearth where she knelt and lit it. Protecting the flame with her hand, she returned to the table and lit both the stubby candles before blowing out the spill.

Milena put her raclette tray on the metal stand over a candle and put a slice of cheese on it. While it began to melt, she scooped some of the vegetables onto her plate—small little potatoes, asparagus stalks, brussels sprouts, and beets.

"Did you know, Cimree, that inns such as this, far away, make people pay for rooms and meals?"

"What do they pay?" Cimree asked. "They don't exchange favors?"

"No, they don't. They have these little metal disks called coins. And each different size and metal has a different value. Some people hoard the coins or steal them."

Cimree's eyes widened. "So they can eat or sleep without doing anything for it?"

"It sounds strange, doesn't it? Here in Clairvaux, we're a community. You and I heal and cure people. Others grow food. The blacksmiths work metal. The hunters protect us and bring back meat. The drovers tend the herds. We all do our part. Everything has a purpose. The purpose of coins is greed."

"But how can a coin have its own motivation?" Cimree asked, wrinkling her nose.

"Not the coin itself. The people who use it to show they are superior to each other. To claim more than they need."

That made more sense. "How long have you lived out in the world?" Cimree asked.

Milena had a peculiar expression. "Several lifetimes on different occasions. To teach people how to heal. To learn remedies we don't know about."

"Doesn't the Queen Mother know everything?" Cimree asked, although it was an impertinent question.

"Oh, she does. But the best way to learn things is through exploring them. At our own pace. At our own willingness to learn. I'm glad you were able to graft with a bee today. But that didn't give you an excuse to leave the valley. Please don't wander away from Clairvaux. Stay within its bounds."

Cimree felt the gentle sting and was grateful, once again, that Milena had been chosen to be her teacher. Not everyone was as patient as her.

The cheese started bubbling, so they lifted the little pans by the handles and, with the wooden scrapers, dragged the melted cheese onto their plates. The seasoning for the vegetables was excellent, and the cheese only enhanced the flavor. It was made from the contributions of the many herd animals in the valley. Though making cheese was an art that Cimree hadn't learned, in another lifespan, she would.

Milton brought some bread during their meal and asked if

they wanted any meat. Milena didn't want any, but when Milton turned his gaze to Cimree, her anxiety awakened and her tongue began to defy her. She wanted more, but she felt embarrassed asking for it. Just at that moment, another angel sworn hunter entered the Silberhorn. Milton gazed that way and excused himself to greet the new guest.

"If you want some, ask for it," Milena said. "There's no need to be timid."

"I'm trying, Milena. It's just so noisy in here. I can't find my words."

Milena nodded and then her expression darkened. "He came to find us."

Cimree craned her neck to see Milton pointing toward their table. The hunter from the Morgarten came hurriedly to their table. Though she was surprised to not recognize him, his style of clothing and weaponry announced his position. He planted his palms on the table.

"Hurry and finish," he said. "Trinati wants you both to come before the high council. She's summoning them now."

Cimree felt a squeeze in her stomach. "R-Right now?"

The hunter nodded. He gave Milena a purposeful look. "Damion's body was right there. I've seen survivors of bear attacks. This wasn't that."

Milena reached over and gripped Cimree's forearm as she addressed the man. "What was it, do you think?"

"We don't know. It didn't leave any tracks."

"How is that possible?" Milena said in a concerned tone.

"Who can say? An animal doesn't conceal its tracks. But the wounds aren't the kind made by mortal or angel sworn. This is serious. Now come with me."

"I'm not hungry anymore," Cimree said, pushing away her half-eaten plate of food. How quickly the hunters had gone to the mountains. How quickly they'd returned with the news.

"You're the only one who has seen this thing, Cimree," the

hunter said. "We'll send more hunters out at first light to try and track it. But how do you track something that doesn't leave a trail?"

hunter said. "We'll send more hunters out at first light to try and track it. But how do you track something that doesn't leave a trail?"

The First Woman tended the garden granted her by the Oldknow. It was her dominion, her work, her legacy. She laid orchards in perfect rows. She carved stone into troughs, walls, and buildings. She tamed beasts, fowls, and fishes and gave them names. She protected the Gallows Tree and its precious fruit granting long life. The tree taught her the grafting magic, how to cut and splice, how to bind and tie. It gave her part of itself to do so, the first distaff of scionwood. Only those sworn to Clairvaux are granted their own distaffs of scionwood. For the grafting magic can unravel any living thing.

— ORIGIN, THE TALE OF THE QUEEN MOTHER
OF CLAIRVAUX

Four

High Council

Cimree had eight winters when she was first threatened to be brought before the high council for disobedience. At the time, her error had seemed grave indeed. She'd walked naked down the main road into the village because she'd bathed in the Silver River when the water had been too high, and as she had set her bundle of clothes too near the rocky edge, they'd been carried downstream. There was a rule about bathing in the river during flood tide, but she'd felt confident she could do so without consequence. It had felt like a foolish rule. She'd tried to catch up to her clothes, but they'd traveled away too swiftly. Not wanting to be caught in her error, she'd hoped they'd snag on something before reaching town. Only they hadn't. They were found by a villager, and she was left not only without excuse but also without her tunic and trews.

As Cimree walked with the hunter back to the high council chamber, her ears burned with the memory of her embarrassment. Many bathed in the waterfalls or in the bathhouses in the village—where the water was definitely warmer. Bodies were a stewardship from the Oldknow and must be cleaned. Indulging in too much food was a grievous thing. Refusing to eat, equally so. Every aspect of life in Clairvaux was in balance, in proportion, and had rules and consequences. When she was eight, she'd been considered as a potential hunter because she didn't mind long bouts of being alone. But it was decided that her defiant nature required more constant supervision. Many winters had passed, and she still hadn't lost that willfulness; it had brought her into the mountains earlier that day.

And it was bringing her before the dreaded high council.

There were no stars visible in the sky due to the mist laying over the valley. Sometimes the mist could last for days before it cleared, and she hoped, fervently, that it would pass in the night. The weather in the mountains was ever changing. One day, she could sweat from the walk to the village. The next day, she could shiver. Being prepared to handle the shifting moods of the mountain valley was a requirement of living there. She knew how to build a shelter if a blizzard suddenly came.

"Don't be nervous," Milena said encouragingly, touching her shoulder. "This meeting won't decide your future."

Oh, but it might, and that possibility terrified her. What if she were banished from the valley? Never allowed to return. An exile. What a horrid thought.

She climbed the steps leading to the building lit with rushlights. There was Wegner standing at the open door, and he nodded to her and Milena as they entered with the hunter, then he closed the door and drew a sturdy wooden crossbar over the tongues of metal. The entry was devoid of color and light, except for the rushlights burning in the high council chamber ahead of them. Cimree rubbed her arm, feeling the anxious twist in her stomach become more fervent.

The entire high council was gathered. She didn't know enough of them to recognize more than two or three faces. Trinati sat at the head of the table, her eyes fixed on Cimree's face as she entered.

"You will sit over there," Wegner said in a gentle voice, motioning to a bench along the wall that was framed in wood and polished to a shine. As soon as they did, he took his place in a chair directly next to Trinati's. Both Cimree and Milena removed their packs and set them on the floor.

"I've summoned the high council tonight because it could not wait," Trinati said, looking from face to face across the assembled group. Only three of the twelve were men. For some reason, Cimree had always supposed the numbers would be equal, but she'd never known the makeup of the council. Another man in hunter leathers stood in the corner by the door, so she hadn't seen him when she'd first entered. "Damion was killed today in the mountains. His body is being brought down right now."

Murmurs of surprise began to bubble within the room, and Trinati held up her hand with a look of annoyance. "Damion's body was discovered by Cimree, who you see has joined us with her mentor. She will tell you what she saw." She gestured for Cimree to approach her chair.

Cimree felt her stomach clench with agitation, but she obeyed and came forward, overhearing as she passed one of the council members whisper that the mountains were out of bounds for apprentices.

With everyone looking at her, she felt her heart quiver with nerves. "I was gathering edelweiss, for healing," she said in a small voice. "I'd seen Damian and told him what I was doing, and he let me. The clouds came down quickly, and it became difficult to see. I knew I needed to get down the mountain, but when I retraced my steps, I felt ... afraid. I tripped over his body. He'd been ravaged by claws. Then I saw the shadow of a beast in the mist and ran from it, fearing for my life." Her words had come out quickly, breathlessly, and when she had recounted all she could remember, she turned to Trinati with a look that asked if that were enough.

"What questions do you have?" Trinati asked, turning her attention to the high council.

"Were you injured, Cimree?" one of the women asked her.

She shook her head no.

"Didn't you try to heal him?" asked another woman. "That is what you are being trained for. You ran away from an injured man."

"He was already dead," Cimree said, feeling even more timid at the questioning.

"In your panic, you might have not noticed if he were still breathing? The fruit of the Gallows Tree would have revived him if—"

"I'd like to know why she was out of bounds," interrupted another woman, older than the others and looking displeased. "That is grounds for banishment."

"Let me intercede," Trinati said firmly. "She glimpsed the beast. Heard it. Felt a malevolence in its presence that caused her to flee."

"How did she escape it?" said the older woman, unconvinced. "What affinity does she have?"

"I w-was so afraid I jumped off the mountain," Cimree stammered. "And grafted with a black grouse to come to the ground."

More fervent whispers and exclamations came from this.

Trinati leaned against the high back of her chair. The wooden frame had been carved with reliefs of scenes from the rich history of the valley. "We have no other witnesses save hers. We have the evidence inflicted on Damion's body. A party of hunters led by Captain Jodocus of the Morgarten will go in the morning. I summoned Captain Jodocus to help investigate the matter further. Now, before any more questions, Cimree is safe but still frightened. I plan to bring her to see the Queen Mother tomorrow but will wait for further details from the hunters' investigation. No one else knows of this, and I would like it to stay that way. You would not be on the high council if you were not fully trustworthy. You must keep this matter to yourselves. Is that clear?"

There were murmurs of assent. Trinati nodded to accept them. "Good. Now, finish your questions."

"Captain Jodocus, what do *you* think killed Damion?" asked one of the women councilors.

His voice was deep and penetrating. "I won't hazard a guess at this point. I haven't seen the body."

"Were the injuries treatable? What if a more experienced healer had been there?"

Cimree felt a throb of anger at the insinuation.

"He was already dead when she arrived," Trinati said, waving off the question. "What else?"

"Why can't we tell the village what happened?" asked one of the men.

"Because it is my decision not to," Trinati responded sharply. "I've chosen to tell you so that if you hear something, something related, you will let us know at once. What happened has never happened before. Not in my memory anyway."

"Could it be lyssa?" asked one of the other women. "It is very rare, but it sickens some animals and turns them violent."

Trinati looked over at Milena.

"It is incredibly rare for lyssa to derange a bear. And even more uncommon for one to attack like this unless threatened."

Captain Jodocus stepped away from his spot in the corner. "It also doesn't explain the lack of prints in the earth. A frenzied animal would have left them."

"Oh, that's true," said the woman, slightly abashed.

Cimree knew about lyssa. If a person was bitten by an animal who was sick with the disease, the only way to save their life was fruit from the Gallows Tree, which would reverse the aging of the victim. There was no medicine or poultice that could cure it. Someone with lyssa would be aversive to water and act strange, even delirious. It could take months for manifestations of the disease to appear. Sometimes a person might forget they'd been bitten. She'd never seen any cases herself, but Milena had explained this to her.

There were more general and vague questions that were not

very relevant to the situation. After all had been exhausted, Trinati excused the council but gave Milena a hard look implying she wasn't supposed to leave. Again Cimree felt a little stab of jealousy at Trinati's favorable looks and countenance.

Several members of the high council came to where they were sitting and said they were grateful that Cimree hadn't been hurt. That she'd willingly jumped off a mountain earlier in the day suddenly seemed like a nightmare. Wegner escorted the others out of the room, and the noise of their talking began to die down.

"She's yours, Jodocus," Trinati said, looking and sounding fatigued.

Cimree started with surprise. The tables were arranged in a squared U shape, six chairs on the opposing sides, one for Trinati at the center and one on either side of her. Captain Jodocus walked around the chairs and stood in front of the bench. He folded his arms.

"I was told you were hunting edelweiss and found some. Can you show it to me?"

Cimree glanced at Milena, who nodded. Cimree opened her pack and drew out one of the star-shaped flowers and offered it to Captain Jodocus.

He examined it, smelled it, and then handed it back.

"Can I see your dirk?" he asked, holding out his hand.

"Do you think *I* did it?" Cimree asked, feeling another surge of anger.

"Did I accuse you?" he answered, holding his hand in front of her.

Cimree noticed Trinati's smirk, and it made her even more angry. But she slid the dirk from her belt sheath and handed it over.

Jodocus examined the blade carefully and then held it to his nose. He made an expression of understanding and said, "I can still smell the flower on the blade." He offered it back, hilt first, so she took it and slid it back into the scabbard.

"Stand up, please," he said.

Cimree felt another impulse to rebel but realized it was probably not ideal to challenge this person. As she stood in front of him, he examined her cloak carefully, even dropping to one knee so he could look at the hem. He studied her boots too, even the bottoms, and used his own dirk to scrape something from one, a little bit of mud, and held it to his nose before flicking it away. He tugged at her tunic belt, which felt very intrusive, then even checked behind her ears.

"Show me your hands," he said, holding out his palms like he wanted her to put her hands on his. She complied, begrudgingly.

"Your fingernails are dirty," he observed, lifting them closer to his eyes.

"I fled from the mountain, came to the village, and haven't had time to bathe," she said tersely.

"I'm glad you didn't," he replied. Then he turned to Trinati. "The amount of blood spilled would have left a trace. She has bloodstains on her knees and palms, but not under her fingernails, which would have been the case if she'd been the killer."

This was news to Cimree, and she quickly looked down at her pants. Sure enough, mixed with the brown of mud was a slightly darker color she hadn't even noticed.

Captain Jodocus turned back and tilted her chin slightly with a finger. "Her behavior is also indicative of her innocence. She's even angry. Offended. That's to be expected."

"Is that so, Captain?" Trinati said with a mocking smile.

Jodocus gazed intently on Cimree's upturned face. "You only saw a glimpse of the beast. Heard it make unusual sounds, including a roar. Another hunter said he was near enough to hear it as well. Said it made him fearful."

"You have another witness?" Trinati said, showing surprise at the news.

"I do. I'd like to take Cimree to Montheron. Have her describe what she saw to Azra. He's traveled farther than anyone else I know. He may know of such a beast as this."

Milena gasped at the mention of the man's name.

"Azra is rotting in the dungeon," Trinati said, her voice and her loathing look revealing she knew this man.

"He's been helpful before," Jodocus said. "This is too unusual to not consider seeking him out."

Cimree had never left Clairvaux before. The idea was frightening and exciting. She deliberately jerked her chin away from the captain's finger. It gave her a chance to see Milena's face.

Milena had turned white as chalk. She clearly knew the name Azra as well.

Five

Gardens

Despite lying awake worrying most of the night, despite the mist still shrouding the mountains and concealing the dawn, Cimree and Milena were kneeling in the herb garden behind their cottage at the break of day. Every inhabitant of Clairvaux awoke before the sun to the hymns of angelic choirs and performed the tasks and duties that were part of their daily routines. It was one of the Queen Mother's dictums. The angel sworn must be unwearying in diligence. The land and its animals and plants and trees were theirs to care for. And in return, they had access to the Gallows Tree and the magic of its fruit, which could extend life indefinitely. The hymns were a reminder of those promises.

Each row of herbs in the garden were multipurpose and functioned in healing. Cimree knew their names: peppermint, marjoram, hyssop, tansy, lavender, garlic, rock jasmine, sage, arnica, lemon balm. And she knew how to properly harvest them and prepare them for the sheds next to the cottage where the clipped plants were dried. As she worked, she enjoyed the feeling of manipulating the dirt with her fingers and the little tools in her belt that helped her in the work.

"Why wouldn't you tell me about the prisoner last night?" Cimree asked as she worked side by side with Milena.

"Because we don't talk of him," she answered.

"But why?"

Milena paused and wiped her brow on her forearm. "He betrayed the angel sworn, Cimree. That is all you need to know."

"But what did he do?"

"That one is ready for the drying room, I think," Milena said, pointing to one of the lavender stalks.

Cimree cut it off and laid it on the burlap sack they used to collect the readied pieces.

"How long has he been imprisoned?"

"A long time. He's refused to partake of the fruit of the Gallows Tree. The Queen Mother has offered him forgiveness if he submits to her authority again. But he's stubborn."

"Was he a hunter?"

"That's how he started, but he was part of the Long Patrol. He's roved far beyond the mountains. The Morgarten protect us here. The Long Patrol protect us from threats far away."

"But what made him turn away from the angel sworn?"

"I think we should talk about something else."

"But you knew him. It affected you."

"Cimree, we all know each other here in the valley. He was someone respected by everyone. He wasn't friendly. But we felt safe knowing he was protecting Clairvaux. When someone like that turns against you, against all you hold dear, it ... it hurts."

Cimree paused and wiped her hands on her thighs. "But wouldn't it make sense to understand why he did it?"

"Why are you so concerned about something that happened long before you came here?"

"Because I'm worried it could happen to *me*," Cimree said, fingers tightening on her thighs. "Because sometimes I don't feel like *I* belong here."

"Everyone feels like that at first, Cimree. It can take several lifespans before it all makes sense."

"You've felt this too?"

"I did. I came when I was fourteen years old. My parents were both sick with the plague, and I came to try and help them. To find medicine. The healer went back with me, but my parents had died while I was gone. My younger siblings had already succumbed to the plague. I was the only one left. The angel sworn healer had compassion for me and invited me to come and learn with her while she treated the community. Many more villagers got sick, and I was able to help. I was invited to join even though I was older than most supplicants usually are. I've been in Clairvaux many lifespans already. But in the beginning, I felt everything was so difficult, so foreign to the way life was in my village far away."

"I've no memory of my parents," Cimree said. "I was given as a supplicant while a baby."

Milena reached out from her kneeling position and gripped Cimree's shoulder. "What greater love and sacrifice for a parent than to offer their bone and flesh to a higher life? And now you get to choose whether or not to honor their choice."

Milena released her affectionate touch, and Cimree began to work again. She still didn't know why Azra had forsaken the angel sworn. Perhaps what he'd done was so awful it couldn't be talked about. But her curiosity had ebbed when Milena opened up. Cimree considered herself one of the luckiest to have been assigned to such a patient mentor.

"Do you ever think about what your life could have been?" Cimree asked.

"How so?"

"If you'd stayed in your village. Found a boy you liked and chosen him to start a family. I'm sure you could have had your pick in the village."

"That's kind of you to say, Cimree, but it is an honor being an angel sworn. A noble sacrifice. In Clairvaux, we neither choose to marry nor are given in marriage. That is the order of things. I don't regret that choice."

Cimree had wondered about marriage and what it was like outside the valley. It sounded ... awkward. More a necessity for survival in the harsh conditions outside the mountains.

Her knees were beginning to ache, so she stood and stretched, then walked to the water trough for a refreshing drink. As she sipped from the ladle, she saw an angel sworn coming down from the skies toward the cottage. The elegance and smoothness of the flight showed that there was cooperation with the grafting, not the struggle Cimree had encountered with the black grouse. As the person came closer, she recognized it to be Trinati.

"Milena," Cimree called out, putting the ladle back on the peg.

Her mentor gazed back and, noticing the descending figure, hurriedly rose, brushing earth from her hands as she joined Cimree at the stone trough. When Trinati touched ground, the look on her face showed deep concern and, if Cimree was interpreting it right, fear.

"We weren't expecting to see you so soon," Milena said.

"Three more hunters are dead," Trinati said curtly. "One was found higher up the slopes. The carrion birds gave away the location. It was Trumfel."

"Oh, no," Milena gasped. Cimree's stomach clenched with dread.

"He was dead before Damion, it seems. The two others were attacked this morning. Jodocus sent them into the mountain early to begin hunting in the area around where Damion was found, and both were immediately attacked. There was a third hunter in the area who heard some screams and came flying in with his bow, but the other two were dead before he got there."

"I am so sorry, Trinati," Milena said.

"I came to bring Cimree to see the Queen Mother. We need to sound the warning horns. Something dangerous is in that part of the mountains. Until we know what it is, we need everyone to be wary."

"There are a lot of cottages out here," Cimree said. "Would it be safer to bring—"

"I've already thought of that," Trinati interrupted. "Yes, after the alarm is sounded, we'll bring everyone into the village proper. Jodocus is sending word to bring in the hunters from distant posts. The Long Patrol will be gathered, but that takes time."

Milena nodded. "Can I come with you?"

Trinati shook her head. "Your skills are needed down here. You know what is happening, but you must keep it to yourself for now. Is that understood?"

"Yes, Trinati," Milena said, her gaze downcast.

Cimree's worry increased. She had supposed that when she saw the Queen Mother, Milena would be there for companionship. Trinati was even more brusque than usual, but since she was an archangel, her orders must be obeyed.

"Change your clothes," Trinati said to Cimree. "You can't go to the Queen Mother looking like that."

✦◦❈◦✦

THANKFULLY, Cimree had a clean pair of trews to wear under her more formal tunic, which was saved for fetes and special days of celebration. It didn't make sense to Cimree that she was dressing so formally on the occasion of a killing rampage, but she knew voicing her opinion wouldn't be appreciated—or tolerated—especially in such a fraught moment, so she hurriedly changed and met Trinati at the front door of the cottage, where the two began their swift walk to the intersection of the valley cliffs.

At first, the roads on either side of the Silver River were close enough to call across to any travelers opposite, and stone bridges straddled the waters in several places, but the closer to the valley head they went, the wider and more turbulent the waters were, and the more spaced apart the bridges became. The added distance and noise made such greetings impossible. The archangel offered no conversation on the way, and Cimree felt too uncomfortable to broach any herself, plus, she was finding it difficult to keep up with Trinati's pace. Her stomach ached with worry and fear, and she wished she'd had time for some peppermint tea beforehand to calm it.

At the fork in the valley, there sat a hamlet of stone guarding the trails that led higher into the mountains where the Queen Mother's citadel was. The small hamlet had been there for thousands of years, designed with dramatic buttresses to hold up the heavy stone walls. The main structure had been designed by Wegner if Cimree remembered correctly. His feats of architecture and planning were legendary, but Cimree preferred living in a simple cottage near the woods. However, the stone walls did project a sense of safety.

"Are we going inside?" Cimree asked as they approached.

"I guess we'll have to since you don't have any affinity toward birds. Do you?"

"Not really."

"Mm-hmm. You mentioned the grouse fought you for control, so we won't be flying up the mountain. A goat will have to do, and they have them penned inside. You're stubborn. Maybe that's where your affinity lies?"

Cimree had the distinct feeling that Trinati did not like her, judging by the comment, so she kept her thoughts to herself. She already knew she didn't have an affinity for goats, but why say so?

The sentinels on duty were startled to see Trinati approaching the fencing and hastily stood at attention. They gave curious looks Cimree's way, but no one asked a question, and they seemed nervous. Had they heard about the deaths in the mountains?

Cimree's stomach gurgled with hunger. They hadn't had time for breakfast yet, but she kept that to herself, not wanting to annoy the imposing angel sworn any further. Trinati led her to a paddock where animals of all sorts were kept, including some squabbling goats that bleated at each other. Their huge curved horns looked like they were made out of rock. She'd often seen these agile creatures going up what seemed like sheer portions of the cliff in order to nibble on vegetation growing in the seams.

Trinati removed her distaff and began the silent incantation. Cimree could have done it herself, but the leader seemed to prefer her own abilities than seeing what Cimree was capable of. Immediately, her legs began to tingle as if falling asleep, but then she felt the power of the animal as the grafting magic took hold. Energy and agility transfused into her. The grafting was painful, as she felt a resistance, and she couldn't keep the grimace from her face.

"Not comfortable? Hmm. Well, it won't take nearly as long now to climb up the mountain. We'd best get going." Trinati used her distaff again and drew a grafting between herself and one of the other goats. "Remember the Queen Mother respects those who are submissive and meek. Just ... do as you're told, all right?"

"I will," Cimree said, but she felt a surge of defiance in her heart. It did not feel comfortable or natural being bonded with a goat. What if snails were her fate after all? She abhorred the thought.

"Oh, and try to keep up, Cimree."

Six

The Queen Mother of Clairvaux

Knees throbbing, calves aching, breath panting, Cimree thought longingly of her unfortunately short-lived grafting with the goat. In addition to the incredible strength it had added to her legs, Cimree had been surprised at how surefooted she'd become despite the loose rock and gravel. The steep mountain trail and its switchbacks had proven to be more challenging and arduous than she'd imagined once the grafting failed, but finally they reached the upper shelf of the valley wall where a small village lay nestled in the mountains. Cimree paused, hands on knees, gulping for air. Trinati waited for her with an impatient look, not looking exhausted at all.

The view of the valley down below, however, was breathtaking in another way. The plunge of the cliff was steep, and there was a multitude of greens on the valley floor—the meadow grass contrasting with the darker fir trees, mingled with aspen along the edges. Then there were the splashes of color from the fields of wildflowers. The stark and beautiful Silver River cutting its way across the valley floor. And in the other direction were still higher peaks above them that were crested with snow year-round, and Cimree felt her heart ache with the beauty of the scene.

This upper village was even more isolated than the one on the valley floor and contained angel sworn who had participated in life beyond the vale and had earned a respite and the opportunity for the quietude of contemplation, a nearer proximity to the Queen Mother, and to join the angelic choirs.

"You should drink," Trinati suggested, imposing herself on Cimree's reverie. There was a stone trough just ahead, and Cimree walked there, although her legs trembled with the exertion. When she'd climbed the northern wall of the valley to seek edelweiss, it had not been so rigorous. But then again, she hadn't been trying to keep pace with anyone else.

After a refreshing drink, Cimree followed as Trinati led the way through the upper-mountain village, past beautiful stone cottages with steep rooflines—a design that prevented too much snow from accumulating during the winter. Because of the higher elevation and the corresponding cooler air, the people they passed wore heavier clothing than those below. Cimree was still panting as she walked, gazing from cottage to cottage, taking in the little details of handmade chairs, garden boxes attached to windows, and even herb beds. The village had a serenity about it, and Cimree wondered if anyone had heard about the attacks. But every face looked pleasant, and many offered words of greeting as they passed.

The road continued to ascend, and at the upper portion of the village was a beautiful grove and a shrine dedicated to the Queen Mother. Stone sculptures within the grove depicted scenes from the creation of the world and faced stone benches placed for visitors to sit in contemplation, but Trinati kept them walking past all of this, and the pace she set prevented Cimree from observing all the details she wanted to.

Beyond the grove, they came upon a footpath that led them even higher and that ended at the edge of a waterfall trickling from a cliff above. Trinati pulled out her grafting wand again and pointed the distaff at Cimree.

"We'll be flying the rest of the way up," she said. "There's no more time to waste."

Cimree sensed the sting of a rebuke in the comment, which caused a throb of anger. This was her first time coming up into the mountains, and she'd done her best, but still it wasn't enough. As the invocation was completed, she felt the prickles of magic begin to tingle, this time in her shoulder blades. The instinct to fly overwhelmed her senses. It didn't require any thought or concentration. Part of her essence had joined with a bird. Not just any bird, but a golden eagle. She felt its power, its predominance, and as Trinati began to rise, Cimree followed like a youngling.

A giddy feeling in her stomach turned to wonder as she began to ascend up the line of the waterfall, feeling the spray of its mist on her face. As Cimree gazed down to the valley floor, that feeling of giddiness bloomed inside her. Oh, to be an eagle! To be able to soar over the entire valley. The pinpricks of pain in her shoulders were nothing compared to the feeling of flying this way. It was easy —effortless even. It amazed her how her chest constantly felt full of air, even when she exhaled. Up they went, following the trail of the waterfall and its source, the melting snow higher up, which was mostly on the leeward side of the mountain. And then, to her astonishment, she saw a citadel built into the top of the mountain, a fortress so grand and beautiful it made her want to weep. There was a mountain trail leading up to it, but the slope and terrain were even more terrible than on the one to the upper-mountain village, and she had been sapped by that climb. Even on hands and knees she couldn't have managed a climb such as this.

At the end of the barely used trail sat a stronghold with towering stone walls and a steeply slanted spire in the middle, like a spike aimed to pierce the clouds. No part of the structure could be seen from the valley floor, the steepness of the cliffs and the angles of the architecture making it impossible. The fact that it was so cloistered gave her a sense of peace and calm. Yes, they'd all be all right. If the Queen Mother gathered the valley into her stronghold, nothing could harm them.

As they flew nearer the hold, Cimree saw armored angel sworn hovering in the air above the walls and parapets, holding spears. All of these warriors were women, and they were the most powerful in the land, remaining vigilant and observing the mountains in every direction. *What an honor to be among their ranks,* she thought.

Once they finally reached the huge walls, they flew over them before lowering gently to the courtyard below. As soon as they landed, the grafting magic left her.

"That was ... that was easy," Cimree said. "It felt so natural."

Trinati smirked. "That's because you shared *my* grafting, Cimree. I am an Eyriemaester."

Cimree's shoulders drooped. That was disappointing news. Oh, to have an affinity with birds. It must be a glorious thing. It made her feel so insignificant to know that the eagle that had bonded with her had done so only to please Trinati.

The surrounding walls rose so far above her she had to crane her neck to see the tops. Trinati led her to a wide set of stone stairs leading to a higher section while Cimree gaped in amazement around her. The imagination required to design such a masterpiece. The labor to build it on a mountaintop. It was all so impressive.

They reached an entrance door where more angel sworn were stationed as guardians, but they recognized Trinati and did nothing but nod in respect and pull open the door for them. As they walked, Cimree admired the huge windows that let in an abundance of light, and the wonderful food smells coming from inside. It was midmorning, and they'd come so far to reach this place.

At long last, they were brought to the Queen Mother's private residence within the keep. Cimree had a distant memory of meeting the Queen Mother before. Her hair had been white, which was so unusual. In fact, she was the only person with white hair throughout Clairvaux, one who wore that color willingly by not indulging frequently in the fruit of the Gallows Tree. But though her hair was white, her skin was smooth and unwrinkled, and a look of wisdom radiated from her eyes. She managed to look elegant even in her simple tunic and trews. Cimree noted the grafting wand tucked neatly into her belt, and she knew it was the one given to her from the Oldknow at the creation of the world, before the fallen angel Asmodeus tricked her husband into tasting fruit from a tree they'd been admonished not to. Being in her presence struck Cimree with awe and guilt for all her infractions.

"Trinati, this is a pleasant surprise," the Queen Mother said. They clasped each other by the forearm and touched foreheads together. "What brings you here this fine day?" She noticed Cimree and her smile faded. The joy turned to seriousness. Her look pierced to the innermost soul. "I see you brought Cimree with you."

The tone of her voice revealed she was expecting to be disappointed. It made Cimree want to squirm.

"Queen Mother," she managed to get out. The last time she'd met with her was when she was eight summers and assigned to work in tallow-making. However, Cimree didn't have an affinity for making candles, and hers were always malformed.

"There is an animal killing our people," Trinati said with an urgent tone. "We need to sound the horns to warn the people."

"Killing?" the Queen Mother said, her brow wrinkling in confusion.

"We've lost four hunters already. Deep claw marks were found. Because of the mist, we haven't seen it yet. Well, Cimree has. She saw it after Damion died."

"What was Cimree doing in the mountains?" the Queen Mother asked sternly.

"Looking for edelweiss. She was the last to see Damion alive and found his body just after the attack." She quickly related the story, and the Queen Mother listened attentively and with great concern.

"Captain Jodocus suggests going to Montheron and asking Azra about this. The behavior does not seem familiar to any of us. Even if a bear went savage, it wouldn't act this way, would it? And it leaves no prints in dirt or snow. The hunters haven't been able to track it."

"This is highly unusual," the Queen Mother said. "But I see no need to get Azra involved."

"He might have knowledge from his journeys."

The Queen Mother gave Trinati a calming look. "My knowledge of the animal kingdom surpasses his, Trinati. I was here, in Clairvaux, when the Oldknow gave us dominion over every beast of the earth. The Oldknow allows us to rule over the fish of the rivers, the birds in the air, and every creeping thing." She lifted her eyebrows slightly as if reminding Trinati of something she should have already known.

"But what sort of creature is this, then? One that can seem like a person yet also snuffles and wails. Others have heard its shrieks. It was not the sound of a snow lynx."

"Nor would a snow lynx attack an angel sworn," the Queen Mother said. She had seemed concerned before but less so as they talked. "Complacent" was the word Cimree thought of. "I know the nature of animals. Some can be territorial and try to establish dominance over a region. That seems to be the case here."

"These are no wolves," Trinati said.

"I didn't say it was. But animals all act according to their instincts. Their bounds are set. They are not as intelligent as we are. Their behaviors are predictable. I am convinced that within a few days, this creature will move on and rejoin its pack."

"But what if it is savage? Shouldn't we hunt it down and kill it? If another animal eats from its carcass—"

"Trinati. I know all this already. I appreciate you coming and expressing concerns. But there is no need to go to Montheron. This will resolve itself in a few days. When the mist clears, we will be able to see it better. There are some creatures that can appear to be manlike. They are very territorial and aggressive. It may have wandered too far from its familial pack. Give it a few more days. Everything will go back to normal. You'll see."

Trinati nodded, but Cimree could see the doubt and concern in the other woman's face. Was she feeling a little rebellious? That was surprising.

"And you brought Cimree here because she was out of bounds?" the Queen Mother said with a pleasant voice but condemnation in her eyes.

"No, I wanted to bring her to Montheron too. She's the only one who has seen it."

"Well, that won't be necessary, then. I don't think this cause deserves blowing the warning horn. Just advise the people to be aware of their surroundings, that a predator has wandered into the valley. If it comes to the valley floor, then we'll just have to dispose of it. That's all that needs to be done."

"Of course...but are you certain we should wait? Shouldn't we at least...find out what it is?" Trinati said hesitantly. To Cimree's surprise, she looked disconcerted.

The Queen Mother put her hand on Trinati's arm. "Animals will break into cottages if they are hungry and smell food. Have the villagers secure their doors at night, which is when most animals like this forage. I'm not worried, and neither should you be. Show your confident nature in this matter, Trinati. It will help calm the people."

"Thank you, Queen Mother." Trinati knelt and bowed her head before her.

The Queen Mother, her white hair glistening, reached down and laid her hand on Trinati's head. "This is a good opportunity for you to demonstrate your leadership."

Then her eyes fixed on Cimree. "And this is a good opportunity for *you* to demonstrate obedience. No more wandering the mountains, Cimree. Stay where you belong."

Cimree felt a shiver travel down her spine at the powerful look of command the Queen Mother gave her, and she quickly bobbed her head.

SEVEN

ANIMAL

As the grafting magic released, Cimree wished she could hold on to it forever. Gliding down the mountainside from the Queen Mother's palace had been an experience she never wanted to forget. Being able to see the entire valley of Clairvaux from end to end had been magnificent. Farther into the distance, she had seen Lake Beatriz where other villages and communities had been built on the threshold of Clairvaux. She'd even seen the miniscule fortress of Montheron on an island of rock in the lake, her eyesight enhanced by the bond. Trinati remained with her until they touched down on the road near the cottage Cimree and Milena shared.

"I'm going back to the village to speak with Captain Jodocus," Trinati said. "Remain in your home and tell no one what was discussed."

"I can't tell Milena?" Cimree asked in confusion.

"'No one' means *no one*. Consider yourself lucky the Queen Mother didn't rebuke you."

"I don't see the harm in what you asked for or the harm in telling my mentor, who already knows what happened."

"I'm so glad that a youngling such as yourself sees the situation so clearly. That with all your vast experience, you've concluded you know best."

The edge in her voice rankled Cimree. "That's not what I meant."

"Do you know how many lifespans the Queen Mother has lived? Seek not to counsel her but to accept her counsel."

Cimree felt a surge of heat in her cheeks. "You don't agree with her decision either," she said.

Trinati's nostrils flared. "If you think I'm disloyal to her, in any way—"

"I didn't say that," Cimree protested. "I observe people. You went there fully expecting her to trust your judgment, and it surprised you when she dismissed your concerns. I know you wouldn't defy her. But don't pretend you were happy about it."

Trinati seemed to be struggling with her emotional reactions, which led Cimree to conclude she'd struck the mark accurately. She waited for the other woman to speak.

"I was surprised," Trinati finally admitted. "But I cannot second-guess her reasons nor doubt her experience. She walked this valley with the Oldknow back in the beginning. None of us have her perspective or her experience."

"But what if she's wrong?" Cimree asked softly.

"I don't think she is," Trinati said. "Just do as I told you and go about your day. We will handle this the way the Queen Mother has instructed us."

Cimree nodded and turned toward the cabin. She paused, glancing back and watching as Trinati began to float toward the sky, holding her distaff in her hand so hard that the tendons blanched. Then she turned back, walked up to the front door, and pushed at the handle, but it was barred.

She knocked on the door. "Milena!" She knocked harder when no one replied. "Milena!"

After waiting for several moments and hearing no sounds from within, she left the porch and walked around to the back of the cottage. In the little garden they'd been tending that morning, she saw the tools still lying there. That was peculiar. Milena was very particular about putting things away.

When Cimree reached the back of the cottage, she gaped in shock. The back door wasn't just open, it had been broken off its hinges. Claw marks gashed the framing. Her stomach dropped with dread as fear ignited in her veins.

She wanted to cry out her mentor's name again, but her mouth was too dry. Fear twisted inside her, writhing like snakes. Warning her of what she'd find inside the quiet cottage.

No, no, no! her mind repeated. *Not Milena. Not Milena!*

She froze with indecision. Should she run back to the village and get help? Should she go inside and confirm her darkest fear? Had the creature come off the mountain at last? Was it among them in the valley? What should she do?

Cimree took a fearful step forward, creeping toward the gaping hole in the wall. Her skin prickled with dread. What was she doing? She should run. Flee. But what of Milena? What if she was alive, if barely? What if Cimree could stanch the bleeding? It made her want to vomit. She took another hesitant step. Then another. The darkness inside the cabin was impossible to see through. No creaks. No noises of any kind, except the susurration of the wind.

Cimree gripped her dirk and drew it, holding it tightly in her fist. Her arm trembled with worry. She reached the stairs leading up to the back porch. When she put her full weight on the first step, she heard a little scuff on the stone. Biting the inside of her cheek, she carefully crept up the steps. Her heart was thundering in her throat.

Carefully, as quietly as she could, she edged to the doorway, using the framing to block her from view of anyone or anything inside. At the doorway, she saw how deep the gashes were in the wood. And she saw the broken part of the crossbar on the floor just inside. The door had been secured.

Milena had been inside when it had come.

And it had broken down the door. What kind of animal would do that?

She'd learned, as a child, the story about the First Woman and First Man. About the garden and the two trees—the Gallows Tree, which bore fruit that allowed one to live forever. And the Serpent Tree, which held the Serpent who deceived the First Man and brought about his expulsion for disobedience. It was the First Woman's constancy and sense of duty that had earned her the right to rule. And the dominion over all animal life had been granted to the pair. The word "animal" had a deep significance too. The word *"animus"* meant *breath*. A creature with the breath of life. A creature that feeds on living things. One with a variety of senses and the ability to adapt and respond to surroundings.

Animals were subservient to the angel sworn. The Oldknow had willed it so.

Animals did not break down doors.

What was this thing? Cimree peeked inside again, trying to calm her galloping pulse. She turned and looked back at the garden and noticed tendrils of mist creeping through the herbs. When she'd come down from the mountain with Trinati, there had been some clouds wreathing the northern mountains, but the valley floor had been clear. The clouds were lowering again like they had the previous day. Memories quickened her fear.

Another kind of panic, one based on the safety of her mentor, spurred Cimree to step inside the cottage, dirk in hand. The shutters were all closed, darkening the space. The smells of dried herbs and medicines disguised another smell. One that was unfamiliar and grotesque. It was musky and horrid. It lingered in the air.

Carefully, she began to search the shadows. The table had been toppled. A shattered bowl was on the floor.

Cimree found Milena's body by the front door. There was no surviving those awful wounds. An expression of terror was trapped on Milena's face.

Just as it would be trapped in Cimree's mind forever.

"M-Milena's dead!" Cimree gasped, panting. She'd run all the way to the village, even ran past Wegner, who had tried to stop her from entering the high council chamber. Trinati was there with Captain Jodocus, and both had turned with startled looks when she'd burst inside with her news.

"Where?" Jodocus asked.

"The c-cottage. The back door was barred. But it was broken. Snapped! She's dead, Trinati! And it's *your* fault!"

Trinati rose from the chair she'd been sitting in. "She was dead when you got there?"

"Yes!" Cimree said, trying not to sob. "I went inside. Thought I could help save her. But she was clawed to death. Just like Damion and the others. This thing is not an animal. Animals can't do this!"

"Actually, they can," Jodocus said sternly. "A long time ago, a bear cub got trapped in one of our stone shelters deep in the woods. It couldn't get out, and its mother couldn't get in. It tried to claw through the door to get at her cub. We found the dead cub in the spring."

"Milena isn't a bear cub!" Cimree shouted at him. "She was my mentor. And she's *dead*."

"Calm down," Trinati said, her face mottled with emotion, though she held it in check.

"How can I be calm?" Cimree demanded. "Maybe it was coming for me? I don't know. But it killed *her*. She was my friend. My teacher. Oh, Trinati, she's dead!"

"I'll go to the cottage," Jodocus said.

"Don't go alone," Trinati said. "Take hunters with you. I'm going back to the Queen Mother."

"I can't face her again," Cimree said through her tears. "I might scream at her."

Trinati gave her a bemused look. "I wasn't planning on

bringing you. I'll get there faster on my own. I must persuade her to warn the valley."

"What if she refuses?" Jodocus asked, his voice deadly earnest. Cimree felt that he believed the Queen Mother might resist such an appeal as she had before.

"It's foolish to try and cross a river before getting to the bridge," Trinati said. "Go."

"You shouldn't," Cimree said. "It's not safe for any of us."

"My sword is forged from celestial iron," he said. "I'll use it. I'm not afraid."

Cimree was terrified.

Trinati put her hand on Cimree's shoulder. "Go to the Silberhorn. Get some food."

"I'm not hungry," Cimree said.

"Won't you just do as you're told?" Trinati snapped.

Cimree looked up at her defiantly. "Milena did. And she's dead."

"Well, you can't stay at your cottage anymore. Stay at the inn. I'll come find you when I return. Just ... do as I say."

"You were right about sounding the horn," Cimree said. "It should be done. The people need to be warned."

"They will be," Trinati said. "I think she will listen to me this time."

"I don't believe it," Cimree countered.

"That's not my problem," Trinati said. She nodded for Cimree to leave. "And tell no one."

She obeyed, begrudgingly, and walked down the street by herself. She adjusted her route whenever others came near. Talking to people when her heart was broken would be too much for her. Once she'd arrived at the Silberhorn, Milton gave her a small room to rest in, one that got her away from others. But sleep eluded her. She kept seeing in her mind Damion's dead face. Then Milena's. The horror of what she'd witnessed made her weep. Eventually, several hours later, the smells from the common room roused her hunger.

She trudged downstairs, feeling horrible about herself and worried about all the people who were enjoying their meals. Milton offered her the same little table she'd shared with Milena the previous day. He'd asked about her, but Cimree had just shaken her head and said nothing.

After she'd been sitting for a little while at the table, Milton came with a skewer of meat and a carving knife. Every person could eat what they wanted, but it was considered unseemly to indulge. The skewer was a nice shank of venison, and he carved out a serving for her, putting the tip of the skewer on her plate before carving it off. She used a little fork to seize the piece of meat. Milton went from table to table, using the skewer handle to carry the meat to each patron.

He came back a little while later. "Some fried cheese and honey might do the trick," he said with a genuine smile, offering her a little bit he'd cut from the segment of crisped white cheese. She smiled in gratitude, and he took a little container of honey and drizzled it on the cheese.

Cimree took little bites from it, savoring the blend of flavors and the sensations in her mouth. The soft interior of the cheese. The crispy exterior. The sweetness of the honey. The combination was comforting to her in her moment of anguish.

She was just about to take another bite when the dull moan of the warning horns began to wail across the valley.

Eight

The Mission

Unnerved by the noise of the horns, Cimree lingered in the common room after she was done eating. Her heart lay like a large river stone in her chest. She'd wept over Milena. But that was over, and she wanted answers. She waited for news to come from the high council. She waited for Trinati to come for her. Neither happened.

At long last, someone came to the Silberhorn. A hunter of Clairvaux who spoke hurriedly to Milton. Cimree wondered if she would be spoken to next, but the hunter left as soon as the brief communication was over. Then Milton lifted his voice and quieted the noise in the room.

"The horns have been sounded," Milton said, holding up his hands as he sought calm. "The high council will address us tomorrow morning. The hunters will enforce a curfew. No one is to be out at night without permission. That is all I know."

"Can I return to my lodging?" one of the patrons asked. "Is it safe?"

"Of course you may, or you may stay here as well, until the high council addresses us on the morrow."

"Is the valley under attack?" someone else asked.

"I don't know anything else," Milton said. "The Queen Mother will look after us. We'll be told what we need to know. That's all I have to say."

Cimree was disappointed. But then, as she thought on it, she realized that Trinati didn't owe her any answers. What had happened on the mountain and what was happening in the valley were of much greater importance than the life of an insignificant apprentice. Cimree finished off her drink and scooted her chair back. She returned to the small room with a single bed on the second floor that Milton had given her earlier. After climbing the steps, she walked down the corridor, the commotion from the common room dimming as she retreated from it. She went to the door of her room and twisted the handle. A cool breeze from inside surprised her. The room was frigid.

Trinati was standing at the balcony door, swathed in a cloak. Her quiet presence startled Cimree.

"W-What are you doing here?" Cimree asked.

"Shut the door," Trinati said.

Cimree went inside and closed it. It was dark, but the ambient light from outside showed enough to see. Trinati said nothing, and her face was hidden by shadow. New worries began to bloom in Cimree's chest. There were questions she wanted to ask but didn't feel brave enough to do so. So she waited for Trinati to speak.

"The Queen Mother has a mission for you, Cimree."

"What sort?"

Trinati came in from the balcony. She was holding something in her hand. An object that was unfamiliar.

"Do you know what this is?" Trinati asked.

"I can't see it in the dark."

"Come closer, then."

Cimree obeyed. It looked like a piece of fruit. Not just any fruit. This one had a peel on it, a peel in layers like a young pine cone. The fruit was dark. Her heart throbbed with dread. "Is that from the Gallows Tree?"

"Yes," Trinati said. "I was told to pluck it myself. And to give it to you."

"Me?" Cimree asked in confusion.

"Not to eat from it, Cimree. To offer it to Azra. We're leaving for Montheron tonight."

"You mean—?"

"The Queen Mother wants you to persuade Azra to help us. He hates the Queen Mother. He hates me. If he will return voluntarily to Clairvaux and help us destroy this beast, you can give him part of the fruit. It will reverse his age, make him young again. He's refused every offer thus far. You must persuade him, Cimree."

"I know nothing about him!"

"That doesn't matter. The danger to Clairvaux is real. A few years ago, a war band of Vikander attacked Montheron. Azra helped defend it, despite his old age. When lives are at risk, he does the right thing. He won't listen to the Queen Mother. He won't listen to me. You must make him listen to you."

"Why was I chosen for this? Why not someone else, someone from the high council?"

"The Queen Mother chose *you*. You are the only one who has seen this creature and survived. There's a chance it may have your scent. That it went to the cottage because it smelled you there. If that's true, getting you away from the valley is also prudent, as it might draw the creature away from here."

Trinati extended her hand with the fruit. "Take it."

Cimree held out her hand, and Trinati put the fruit on it. The skin was waxy, the layered points, sharp against her flesh. "Why are we going tonight? I thought the high council was to offer an explanation tomorrow morning."

"I've already spoken to the high council. They will take charge of the evacuation while we're gone."

"Evacuation? We're not abandoning the valley are we?"

"Of course not. It will take time to retreat to the fortress in the mountains. We'll have a few days to travel downriver to Lake Beatriz. And from there to Montheron. We've been assigned some hunters for protection. Wegner is also coming as he is very knowledgeable about such things. I will lead the mission."

"But what am I supposed to say to him?" Cimree pleaded.

"I can't tell you. It will be up to you to figure it out. Put the fruit in your pack. Safeguard it. We need to get going now."

"I don't have suitable clothes. Or things to travel with."

Trinati gave her a sigh and pointed to a rucksack leaning against the wall.

✦❧❀❧✦

CIMREE HADN'T EXPECTED the day to end like this. She was walking through the woods with Trinati and Wegner—both from the high council—along with four hunters as guardians, and a third companion who Cimree vaguely knew from the village. She wouldn't stop talking.

"My name is Darcia," the woman had said when she introduced herself to Cimree. "You're Milena's apprentice, I think, isn't that right? I don't think we've met before, but I suppose it's because I haven't been injured. I like your cloak, did you make that yourself?"

Being lambasted by all the questions and small talk left Cimree feeling too tongue-tied to answer, but that didn't stop Darcia from going on.

"I think it's lovely. The wool looks very comfortable. Are you cold? I imagine you're nice and warm with it."

One of the hunters had disappeared into the darkness ahead. They were swift and shadowlike in their movements, but one of the four always remained in the rear of their company, his bow in his fist, an arrow nocked, his head swiveling back and forth as he scanned their surroundings.

Wegner had a large pack strapped to his back with a bedroll tied underneath and a water bladder swinging on the side, and he kept an even pace, walking alongside Trinati as they followed the footpath in the moonlight. The Silver River was on their right, burbling and rushing, half-hidden by a row of trees. Its unyielding pace was headed in the same direction they were going, ultimately feeding the lake where Montheron awaited them.

"I came to Clairvaux when I was six," Darcia said. "My parents gave me as a tithe. They had six other daughters and had been wanting a son to help with the farm. I lived in several places during my learning periods, including Montheron, but I requested to come back and stay in Clairvaux, and the Queen Mother permitted it. I haven't been out of the valley since then, have you?"

Cimree shook her head no but didn't respond. The constant questions were wearing on her.

"Montheron is beautiful. It guards the entrance to the valley. Well, not exactly the entrance. The lake does that. I wonder if we'll go by boat or if we'll walk the whole way there. This is exciting. I don't think I could have slept tonight. I feel so honored that the Queen Mother chose me to be part of this mission. Don't you feel the same?"

Cimree still didn't answer, but Darcia didn't seem to take offense at all. She just kept on talking.

After they'd walked for several hours, Trinati announced they'd stop and camp for the rest of the night.

"Good, I was beginning to feel tired. A rest would be perfect," Darcia said. "We should reach Montheron within a day. It's your first time there. Wait until you can see it in the distance."

Cimree shrugged off her pack and began to clear a spot in the detritus of the trees.

Trinati squatted near her. "Check the fruit every day. It will not spoil. But make sure it is safe. You are its guardian. You must be diligent."

Cimree was exhausted by that point, ready to collapse on her bedroll and fall asleep. Wegner had removed his pack and was setting up camp himself. The hunters were invisible in the darkness, but Cimree felt like they were nearby, keeping watch over them. She checked her pack for the fruit. The edelweiss she'd found in the mountains was still there, its fragrant flower familiar and sweet.

"Why did you bring *her*?" Cimree asked in a whisper, nodding toward Darcia, who was already bedding down away from them, her back toward them.

Trinati rose, looming over Cimree's kneeling form. "Every person in this company serves a purpose. Some may be obvious, some are not. There are four temperaments of people, Cimree. Those who enjoy company and those who do not. Those who take charge and those who hold back. And then there are all the combinations these traits manifest together. When we reach Montheron, Darcia's talents for speaking freely and gaining information will be very useful. She cannot help but be what she is, just as you cannot help being what you are. You serve different purposes."

Cimree shook her head, too exhausted to think about what Trinati had said. Although, looking at the others, it did stand to reason they were all vastly different. Wegner had been very quiet during the walk, although he'd asked occasional questions. Darcia had hardly stopped talking. Trinati kept the pace and drove them to keep up. What value did Cimree bring? What was her temperament?

She unrolled her blanket and lay down on it, adjusting her cloak to cover herself and preserve warmth. She imagined she heard a whisper in the woods, probably two of the hunters conferring with each other.

As she lay there, trying to fall asleep, she thought about finding Milena. Grief shot through her again. As they'd walked, the march had helped distract her from her sorrows. But now that they were stopped the numbness had faded, replaced by the shards of memories that stabbed at her. Milena had lived several lifetimes. She'd partaken of the fruit of the Gallows Tree multiple times, reversing her age and starting life anew. To have it cut off so brutally was abhorrent. Cimree held back a cry as the images burned in her memory came forward: the wounds on Damion's chest, the blood on her hands, the roar that sent chills of fear down her spine and sent her racing down the mountain. Then when she had finally thought things would be taken care of, the dread she felt coming upon the broken back door, followed by the horror of seeing her mentor, her friend, damaged beyond anything she could have imagined, fear frozen on her familiar face.

Cimree's hand went to her rucksack, and for just a moment she thought of another effect of the fruit she was carrying. It could take away memories if you ate enough of it. The more potent the emotion, she'd been told, the deeper the impact it made on one's mind. Everyone was different and some could remember further into the past than others. Cimree's earliest memory was being lost and afraid. So there wasn't, to her knowledge, a precise amount of fruit that triggered the total lapse of a memory, though the angel sworn knew that becoming an infant would erase all memories completely. But maybe she could just have enough to forget her pain from the past couple of days? As she mindlessly reached into the pack, her hand closed around the hilt of her dirk, and it comforted her just a little. Enough to realize forgetting would help no one but herself in the moment.

The wind through the branches and the distant churn of the waterfalls helped her begin to doze off. One of the hunters approached and began to speak in a low voice to Trinati. Two of the hunters were men and two were women. They were experts at living off the land. They knew the plants and trees and animals.

But they didn't know the kind of creature that was stalking the valley of Clairvaux. Cimree began to be afflicted by her memories again: Damion sprawled on the mountainside, eyes vacant. Milena trapped inside the cottage, both doors secured before she'd died.

She was grateful they were doing something about it. Anything. But what if this creature could not be destroyed so easily? What if others would meet the same fate? She would do what she could to prevent it. Even if that meant confronting a stranger and trying to persuade him to help. Why had he chosen to forsake immortality? What had caused him to rebel against the Queen Mother?

And why did the Queen Mother believe that Cimree stood a chance to persuade him? Was it her own inclination for disobedience? Was that her special gift that would be used against him?

Now the asp viper was more cunning than any beast of the mountains made by the word of the Oldknow. And the serpent said to the woman, "Indeed, shall you not eat of every tree of the garden?" Then said the woman to the serpent, "The fruit of the trees of the garden and every bush thereof we may eat, but the fruit of the tree that thou hangest from the Oldknow hath commanded not to eat or touch, lest we die." And then said the serpent to the woman, "Not surely you will die."

— Origin, the Tale of the Queen Mother
of Clairvaux

NINE

Awakening

The slow shift of dawn began, and Cimree was awakened by the scrape of a metal pot against stone. It had taken her a long time to fall asleep, so she was still exhausted and didn't want to rouse yet, but she heard the noises of the others and decided to open her eyes. That's when she saw the snake coiled next to her chest.

Her immediate reaction wasn't fear but interest. Why had it come close to her; was it seeking warmth? The scales were dark gray with black wedged stripes down its entire body. Its triangular head was resting on its coils. It had bronze-colored eyes with two narrow pupil slits and seemed to be gazing at the others in the camp. The forked tongue came out and tested the air.

"Cimree, don't move!" Trinati said. "That's an asp viper."

"Oh, they're very dangerous!" Darcia said in a quavering voice. She hastily retreated.

"Don't ... move," Trinati repeated.

Cimree didn't feel any fear, although she heard it in their voices. Wegner rose from the ring of stones he'd gathered around his cooking pot and backed away nervously. "I'm surprised there are any serpents so close to Clairvaux," he said. "I thought most had been hunted down and killed."

Cimree watched in fascination as the forked tongue flicked out again. The color made her think of a snow lynx.

Trinati drew her long knife.

"Don't hurt it," Cimree said. "It will slither away when it's ready."

"It could bite you," Trinati said.

"I think it was cold and came near me for warmth."

"How can you lie there so calmly?" Darcia said. "I can't bear to look at it!"

"Just stay still," Trinati said. "I can cut off its head."

"Don't," Cimree said, feeling revulsion at the idea of killing it for no reason. From what Milena had taught her, snakes rarely bit people. Only those who attacked them on purpose or accidentally stepped on them. Most snake bites, even from asp vipers, were rarely deadly. There were so few bites that Cimree had never encountered one since she'd been an apprentice healer.

"Why isn't it going away?" Darcia asked worriedly.

"Let me start the fire," Wegner said. "Maybe the smoke will drive it off."

"If I can get close enough ..." Trinati said, cautiously stepping forward.

"Leave it alone," Cimree said. "It will leave on its own. I'm not frightened."

"Why not?" Darcia demanded. "Oh, look at its mouth! Ugh!"

The viper opened its mouth, revealing fleshy bulbs with its fangs. It looked like it was yawning, not threatening.

Trinati hoisted her long knife as if she were going to throw it.

"No!" Cimree shouted, holding out her hand over the snake. Her wrist and forearm were exposed. But the asp viper didn't strike.

"Cimree!" Trinati scolded, her eyes blazing with anger.

"Let it alone," Cimree said. She felt no danger at all. The snake would leave when it was ready.

Darcia peered out from behind a tree, gaping at the scene. Wegner had backed away again as well. Trinati brandished the long knife, giving Cimree a rebuking look.

"It's not going to hurt me," Cimree said.

"Oh? It could *bite* you," Darcia said.

"It won't." The black stripes looked so intriguing, especially combined with the gray scales. "Put down the dagger, Trinati."

Trinati lowered her dagger, but she looked at Cimree and the coiled serpent with revulsion.

The snake yawned again and then slithered away, which made Darcia squeal, even though it was going the opposite way.

Wegner let out a sigh of relief. "Asp vipers are very poisonous," he said. "You're lucky it didn't strike you when you thrust out your arm like that."

Cimree could see the fearful looks in everyone's eyes. There was a certain loathing for snakes. Cimree hadn't ever encountered one before, so she didn't have that natural response.

"Do you have ... affinity for snakes?" Darcia asked her with a grimace.

"I was just beginning to wonder," Trinati said, sheathing the long knife. "That was very reckless, Cimree."

"I don't know anyone in the valley who has an affinity for serpents," Wegner said, scratching the back of his neck. "They tend to hide from humans."

"So does Cimree," Trinati said, looking at her with annoyance. "If it had bitten you, it could have delayed our mission. You should have listened to me."

"I couldn't let you kill it," Cimree said.

"Why?" Darcia asked. "It's just a snake. You know the Origin story. Snakes are evil."

"Animals are not good or evil," Cimree said. "They just have instincts. It came near me for warmth, I think."

"And it chose you?" Trinati asked. "I think you're right, Darcia. Have you discovered any affinities so far, Cimree?"

"No," she answered. "But I've never seen a snake before." Suddenly, she was curious. She wanted to test the idea with her distaff. Could she bond with the asp viper? Would it even want to?

"Well, at least it's gone," Trinati said. "Let's get some food and break camp. We should reach Montheron by late afternoon if we hurry. What do we have to eat, Wegner?"

"The hunters found some eggs, which I was about to boil. And some huckleberries. We also have some bread and cheese for the journey."

"Excellent," Trinati said. "We'll head out right after we eat."

THE EGGS BURNED Cimree's fingers while she peeled them, but with a sprinkle of an aromatic blend, the yolk was gooey but delicious, and she fanned her mouth after eating it. She quickly ate a slice of bread and cheese and then rolled up her blanket. Before Trinati could harass her, she checked the Gallows Tree fruit to make sure it was still there. In the morning light, the purple skin with orange and yellow ends looked exotic. Then she cinched the pack closed and watched as Wegner began to tidy up their breakfast.

With the sun out, she was able to see the variety of stones and boulders that were nestled throughout the woods. The sound of the Silver River was prominent, the smells of the trees and vegetation pleasant. She squatted near a rock and drew her distaff. Was the asp viper even nearby anymore, or had it slithered far away? Animals had to be nearby in order to form a grafting with them. She gazed at the distaff in her hand, feeling a peculiar and giddy feeling of wanting to try. Her heart was heavy still at losing Milena, and the excitement that morning had been a needed distraction.

Cimree closed her eyes and invoked the magic, trying to sense if the serpent was near.

She found it immediately, hidden beneath a fallen log. It was watching her. She could sense its interest in her, not fear. Excitement began to bubble inside her. She invoked the grafting magic and bonded immediately to the asp viper. There was no coaxing or pleading, just an instantaneous connection. Suddenly she could smell things in a heightened way. She heard one of the hunters approaching from the woods. The sense of hearing was incredible! She also sensed the heat coming from Trinati, Wegner, Darcia, and even the coals that Wegner had snuffed out with the pot of water he'd used to cook the eggs. Heat showed as color in her vision. The feelings thrilled her and worried her. She was training to be a healer. But these instincts were raw and powerful. She also felt an incredibly profound maternal instinct as well. A desire to protect her companions and keep them safe.

"One of the hunters is coming," Cimree said, and the way she perceived her voice was strange. It was like she was hearing herself from inside her chest, not from her ... ears. Snakes did have ears, but they were connected to their jaws. Her hearing was enhanced but different from her human sense.

Trinati looked at her in confusion. A few moments later, the hunter strode into their camp. A woman. She walked up to Trinati and began to speak softly to her, out of earshot. But Cimree heard her perfectly.

"Parin is missing," the hunter said. "He didn't come back from the dawn patrol."

Trinati frowned. "Why would he have wandered off?"

"I don't know. I was going to send Abria to look for him but wanted to check with you first."

"We don't have time for a manhunt," Trinati said. "The Queen Mother wants us to fulfill the mission as quickly as possible."

"I know. But should we go on without him? Parin isn't reckless."

"Parin isn't a fool either. I'll have the eagles look for him. Let's keep going. We need to get to Montheron."

"As you wish," the hunter said. "We're ready to depart."

Trinati nodded, put her hand on the hunter's shoulder in a comforting gesture, and then raised her voice. "It's time to go. We'll walk the rest of the way to Montheron without stopping. It's a downward slope, so we won't need to graft with any animals unless you get too fatigued."

Wegner nodded and hastily gathered up the cooking supplies before hoisting the full pack on his back. Darcia was ready to go.

Cimree released her connection with the asp viper. She had the slightest of tingles at the ends of her toes. The enhanced senses she'd experienced dwindled and faded. It was disappointing. She slipped the distaff into its holster at her belt and slung her pack on her shoulder.

Trinati walked up to her.

Cimree spoke first. "I checked the fruit. It's there."

"I saw you earlier. But I noticed you had your distaff. Did you try a grafting on the viper?"

Cimree swallowed and nodded.

"Did it work?" Trinati looked both interested and disgusted.

Cimree nodded again. She saw the other two observing them, but Trinati was speaking in a low voice.

"Of all the creatures to have an affinity for, you chose a serpent."

"I didn't choose it, Trinati," Cimree said defensively.

"But it's curious, isn't it? It was a serpent who persuaded the First Man to eat of the fruit that cursed humankind, which was why he was driven from Clairvaux, never to return. A serpent, Cimree." She frowned and shook her head. "Well, hopefully you will be persuasive to this other man, this prisoner at Montheron. The Queen Mother *trusts* that you can be persuasive."

"I don't know anything about him," Cimree said. "You haven't told me anything."

"It's better if you don't know."

"Why?"

Trinati smirked. "You'll understand better when you meet him." She turned and looked at Wegner, Darcia, and the hunter. "Let's move."

TEN

ANGUISH FOR THE DEAD

They came down from the mountain valley of Clairvaux, following the churning rush of the Silver River. Clouds wreathed the alpine mountains around them. The wind teased the air with smells—pine, wildflowers, and rich earth. Cimree felt like she was awake at last. All around her, she sensed snakes—the small and harmless ones, water snakes that used the river to hunt, and a small variety of poisonous ones that hid from Trinati's group as they marched past. It stood to reason that she hadn't noticed an affinity for serpents because there were not many in the valley of Clairvaux at all.

Why snakes, though? Before the experience that morning bonding with one, she had never even considered it a possibility. And what did that mean for her as a healer? Snake bites were very rare, but she had to assume she would have some inherent ability there to heal them. That was interesting. Or would her path be better as one of the valley hunters?

She found herself preoccupied with these thoughts as they descended into the mountain valley of the interlake region. The pace was challenging, but she did not struggle to keep up. Wegner looked the most hard pressed with his enormous pack of supplies, but he was tall and fit, and he seemed to be well. Since the misadventure with the asp viper, Darcia had left Cimree alone the rest of the morning. Cimree changed her pace until she was striding alongside Wegner.

"Do you need help carrying anything?" she asked him. "I could take one of your pots."

"Thank you, but no. It seems like a lot, but I am fine. The weight is balanced."

"Going back up the mountain may prove more challenging. I'm happy to help."

"That's kind of you, Cimree, but going back up the mountain won't be difficult for me. My affinity is for fish. Many breeds swim upriver to spawn."

"Fish? I didn't know that was yours. How long have you known?"

"Since I was a lad. I've always loved to fish. And the power of water has been my specialty for many lifespans. Waterwheels—gristmills—are my favorites. It seems that *you've* discovered your affinity at long last. Milena was always curious what yours would be."

"She told you that?" Cimree asked, feeling a pulse of warmth and sadness.

"Mentors report to the high council regularly about their apprentices."

Cimree had not really thought about this. She wondered what Milena had shared over the years. "What did she say about me?"

"Such discussions are normally private, you know. But considering the circumstances, you should know that she had a lot of faith in you. Some people think you are shy, but you're not. You just prefer not being in crowds. Being a healer is a good path for you. But there are other paths too in which you'd excel."

She felt another throb of warmth. "I don't know what else I could do."

"There's no rush to discover it, Cimree. We all have gifts and talents. You are impetuous and prone to dodge the rules. But you are also very young. Milena thought highly of you, and so do I."

"Thank you," Cimree said, feeling self-conscious but also grateful.

"Just a bit of advice, though? If you are open to it?"

"Of course!"

"Even a Beesinger can get stung." He gave her a friendly but warning look.

CIMREE GAZED upon the beautiful jade waters of Lake Beatriz, which stretched as far as she could see. Wegner explained that the Silver River brought vast amounts of stone dust from the mountains, giving the lake its vibrant hue. There were villages all around the lake's borders, mostly small ones, full of people who preferred living under the protective shadow of the angel sworn. These villagers were not allowed to partake of the fruit of the Gallows Tree. That was a privilege reserved for those who had sworn the oaths and given up their past lives. Since the angel sworn were strictly celibate and did not marry, they lived in a way where all resources were shared equally. Every person worked and did their proper share. Occasionally, a family might tithe one of their children to the Queen Mother to be raised as an angel sworn. Orphans could also be sent. It made no difference. The Queen Mother accepted everyone who came voluntarily.

Once they'd reached the nearest village, the three remaining hunters had closed ranks and joined them in the walk. The fourth was still missing. As they passed through the neighboring villages, Cimree noticed the looks given them by the inhabitants. There were nods of respect given. Some villagers knelt as Trinati and her companions walked by. Obeisances were common and made Cimree feel peculiar, since such things were not the custom in Clairvaux itself. They stopped to drink at a stone trough of water, and some villagers presented gifts of food for them to eat. It felt like an offering of sorts, an expectation to feed travelers. The food was simple fare—little bowls of pottage with vegetables and sparse amounts of meat.

The dirt roads were well maintained, built by the angel sworn to connect the villages to each other along the rim of Lake Beatriz. Trees and mountain crags intercepted the shoreline in places, causing the trails to wind up and down as they passed.

And then, to Cimree's dismay, they reached a portion of the road where the low stone wall marking the path was disfigured.

Trinati paused to observe the chiseled marks that had cut out the beautiful edging along the stone. She turned to Wegner with a frown of disapproval.

"A new ritzen," Trinati said to him. "I've only seen this kind of damage farther away. None this close to Clairvaux."

Wegner nodded. "The youth make these scars in the stone. They take pleasure in defacing things."

"It's unacceptable," Trinati said. "The culprits should be caught and punished."

"That is for the curia regis to attend to," Wegner said. "It is one of her duties."

Trinati scowled. "What's been done is disrespectful."

"Clearly and deliberately," Wegner agreed.

Trinati signaled for them to move on, and they continued down the forest road. Twice more, Cimree noticed ritzen defacing the stone. Each time they passed one, Trinati sighed.

At last they reached the village of Iselt, which was the largest one they had encountered. This one had inns and fortifications, as well as a thriving harbor.

"Darcia, go ahead and secure a ferry to Montheron for us," Trinati said.

"With pleasure," Darcia said and quickened her pace to go ahead. One of the hunters fell in step next to her. In Iselt, their presence was not treated as unusual or a special circumstance. The villagers there just ignored them and went about their business, pushing carts stuffed with farm goods, or haggling among fish-mongers for the latest catch. The smell of the village was more rank and fetid. Cimree felt uncomfortable immediately. She did not sense a single serpent.

Trinati brought them to the wharves where small fishing boats and barges were gathered. Cimree noticed people handing over coins in exchange for items being purchased, and the greedy looks of the people made her stomach clench with unease. Would they have to pay for something in Iselt? Did Trinati have any coins? Cimree's stomach was starting to grumble, but no one offered them any food.

A man was causing a ruckus nearby, pointing at them and raising his voice, while several bystanders were trying to pull him away. "But where were the angel sworn when my boy was killed?" he pleaded. "I can speak my mind! And I shall! They promise protection, but people are dying, and they do nothing!"

Trinati turned and gave the fellow a reproachful look.

"Sorry, mistress! Beg your pardon, mistress!" said one older woman.

The man struggled against the fellows restraining him. "I'll speak! Where were you when my boy was ripped apart! I've no son now. No wife either. What of me? What am I to do? Where is my comfort?"

"Don't be a fool!" a man growled in his ear. They were trying to haul him away, but he struggled.

"Stop," Trinati said, holding up her hand.

"Mistress," said the older woman, wagging her head, "it's of no concern! It was a bear attack. That is all."

"No bear did *that*!" the man shouted.

"Bring him to me," Trinati said curtly. The bystanders who'd been holding the man back relented immediately. They suddenly looked at him as if he had the pox and didn't want to be seen touching him.

The older woman kept shaking her head, looking dismayed by the scene the man had caused. She was probably part of the village council and knew such behavior would reflect poorly on them and their curia regis.

Cimree was curious, though. Wegner looked pensive, and the two remaining hunters each had a hand on the hilt of their mirror blade. One word from Trinati and they'd attack. Common villagers were no match for angel sworn.

The man ambled forward, not looking the least bit chagrined. "My name is Beckom. And my boy was slaughtered by some savage animal. He'd been afraid to go into the woods. Didn't say why. Didn't come back that night. When I went to look for him, I found him scratched up to bits. I've seen a bear attack before. This was nothing like it."

"When did this happen?" Trinati asked.

"Fortnight ago. And no one here would do a thing about it!" he said condemningly. "What am I to do? My wife died of milk fever along with our second born. Raised my son the best I could all alone. And now what have I got? A sore back and a grieving heart." His eyes flashed with hostility. "And where were *you* when my boy died!"

A silence fell over the crowd. A whisper could have been heard. This man was defying not just any angel sworn, but the Queen Mother's archangel. Cimree could feel the man's anguish, and she felt pity for him. But he was acting beyond the order of things. Maybe he hoped Trinati would slay him for his defiance.

The story sounded too familiar to be coincidence. The creature she'd seen in the mountain had come this way. And maybe it had killed others. Cimree looked from the distraught man to Trinati.

"I am sorry for your loss," the archangel said imperiously. "But your blame is without justice. You want others to solve your problem. Grieve for your son. Then get back to work. If you do not, you do not deserve to remain."

Cimree caught her breath. The man would be expelled if he did not get in line and do his duty. Being sent away from the protection of a community was tantamount to a death sentence. Every person had to do their part. But alone, it was impossible to survive.

The man's jaw slackened. The realization of his actions seemed to have dawned on him finally. "I meant ... no disrespect," he said hastily.

"Oh, I think you did," Trinati said coldly. "Get out of my sight."

The man trembled and then fled the wharf. The bystanders shook their heads in disbelief, looking relieved that the man had been treated patiently when he'd acted so recklessly.

Darcia approached with the other hunter, her eyes wide with surprise. She'd undoubtedly witnessed the scene.

Wegner spoke softly to Trinati. "You were very patient."

"I doubt any woman will have him after that outburst," Trinati scoffed. "He's doomed himself."

Cimree felt that harshly said. The man's son had been savagely killed. Should he not be shown some compassion? Trinati's disdain rankled in Cimree's heart.

Darcia joined them. "There's a barge waiting for us," she said.

"Did you have any trouble persuading him?" Trinati asked with a look of discontent.

"Not at all," Darcia said. "He was only too willing to serve us. He asked if we were hungry, and I said yes."

Trinati chuckled softly. "We'll feast soon enough at Montheron. But at least he was considerate to ask."

"Do you think Captain Odeon knows of the attack on the man's son?" Wegner asked Trinati carefully.

"Captain Odeon? If I know the man at all, he's in the thick of it already. But we haven't come all this way to inquire after a dead villager." She turned her gaze on Cimree. "Have we?"

The pressure Cimree felt to succeed weighed heavily on her.

She would have handled the situation with the villager and his loss so differently. Would have tried to comfort him at the very least. But then, what did she know about the world and its strange ways?

And what did she know of the prisoner she was to persuade?

Nothing.

ELEVEN

ISLE OF MONTHERON

Water lapped against the hull of the barge. It was loaded with cargo bound for the fortress of Montheron near the other side of the lake. As a cargo ship, it had a small four-man crew who kept to themselves and broached no conversation with the angel sworn aboard. Cimree noticed their frequent surreptitious glances and sensed their mood was more one of fear than that of respect.

Darcia moved from her position on a cargo bench and sat next to Cimree. "Have you been to Montheron before?"

"I've never left Clairvaux," Cimree answered. "You? Didn't you say you've lived here before?"

"For several years," Darcia said. "Until the Vikander attacked. That was terrifying. I asked to go back to Clairvaux after that."

"Who are the Vikander?"

"They're a tribe of raiders who live in the north. They attacked during the solstice festival when there were few defenders. I don't even think they knew about the solstice. It was just blind luck on their part." She shook her head and shivered. "Everyone here had to defend the island. Many died. It would have fallen except for Azra, from what I heard."

Cimree wrinkled her brow. "So you've met him?"

"I've never spoken to him. But Captain Odeon, on occasion, would let him walk outside his cell. And I saw him during the battle against the Vikander. He's ... he's very skilled. For an old man." She laughed softly.

"He refuses the fruit of the Gallows Tree."

"Yes. I hear he's very stubborn. And angry. Even after defending Montheron, the Queen Mother didn't forgive him. He was sent back to his cell."

Cimree rubbed her legs. "I think I'd be angry too."

"He and the Queen Mother had a falling out ages ago."

"Do you know what from?"

Darcia shook her head. "No one does. I'm not even sure if Trinati knows." She kept her voice low at that part, glancing quickly at the other woman who was in conversation with Wegner near the prow of the barge. The hunters were seated together, speaking in low tones.

"Trinati knows more than she lets on," Cimree said.

Darcia grinned. "I like you. So, since you've never been there, let me tell you about Montheron. It was built six centuries ago on that rocky island at the edge of the lake. Captain Odeon studied under Wegner and is an expert craftsman as well as strategist. The lower part of the island has homes and shops for trade with the lower classes. They are not angel sworn but pay homage to us. The citadel built at the top of the island is for our kind. From its towers, you can see nearly the entire lake. It is a bastion of the angel sworn in this region. After it was built, Wegner diverted another river to feed the lake, which increased its depth enough to cover the land bridge, making the island fortress."

"That was very clever," Cimree said.

"Wegner is very clever. They dammed up the river with a system of sluices and locks to control the water flow into the lake. He comes to inspect it, now and then, to make sure it works properly. The mortals built villages around the lakeshore, and each one has a curia regis chosen to lead it. They are the ones who pay homage to the angel sworn and are the local rulers. For more urgent matters, they bring those to the attention of Captain Odeon."

"Is Captain Odeon fair?"

"Of course he is. They bring him certain cases for punishment as well. Those who will not respect the rules can be put in the dungeon for a time. Taking away a person's liberty can induce reflection on the harm they've caused."

"That doesn't seem to have worked on Azra," Cimree remarked.

"Indeed not. As I said, he's very stubborn. Oh, look, you can finally see it in the distance."

Cimree shifted her gaze and saw that Darcia was right. Lake Beatriz was beautiful amidst the high ridges surrounding it, which were thick with forest and growth and the occasional waterfall. But around a bend in the cliff, she saw the island fortress in the distance, the entire formation covered with homes of thatch and wood at the base and then a distinguished fortress cresting the island with a single spire aimed skyward. The walls of the fortress were incredibly tall and showed multiple levels climbing higher, built into the rocky face of the island. There was some greenery at the lower levels, including gardens and areas too steep to build on. Her breath caught in wonder to see such a graceful and well-balanced fortress in the middle of the vast jade lake.

"The Vikander tried to attack ... that?" Cimree asked in awe.

"They had some superstition about it being a lychgate. That some horrible undead creature was keeping the lake in its thrall. If they'd attacked when the garrison was full, they wouldn't have breached the outer wall."

"Where are the dungeons? Below the waterline?" Cimree asked, trying to take in the sight.

"Oh, no. They're part of the lower wall of the fortress." Darcia pointed. "Some of the prisoners can see outside and even smell the water and the meals being cooked below or hear the noise of laughter and song."

It made Cimree wonder what sort of man would have endured such privations for so long. She was becoming even more curious about this fallen angel sworn. She checked the opening of her pack again and saw the purple-skinned fruit right where she'd left it.

THE BARGE REACHED the wharf jutting from the lowest level of the island fortress. There were other barges there as well and stores were being unloaded. To feed an island of this size with no land to farm or raise herds must require considerable resources. No doubt they kept stores in the larder and fished the lake for other kinds of fresh meat.

They were met on the dock by a soldier with an emblem on his tunic of a heron in flight, his hand resting on the hilt of a mirror blade.

"My name is Andrin, and I serve Captain Odeon. He saw you coming, my lady." Andrin bowed his head respectfully.

"I recognize you," Trinati said.

"And I you. I fought for the angel sworn when the Vikander attacked."

"You had a wife and were expecting a child, if I recall."

"I'm pleased you remember someone so insignificant," Andrin said meekly, bowing again. "We have three little ones now. Two girls and a boy."

The fact he was married and had children meant he was not an angel sworn. But his deference and meekness did seem genuine. Cimree looked to Darcia to see if she recognized him, and she nodded that she did.

"We appreciate the greeting," Trinati said.

"Well, I would be honored to escort you to Captain Odeon.

We've been dealing with grave matters of late. He apologizes he wasn't able to come down in person."

"What sort of grave matters?" Trinati asked as the company fell in behind her, and they followed the young soldier up to the gatehouse and passed through.

"There have been savage animal attacks all through the lake country," Andrin said as they walked. Cimree increased her speed to hear better and Darcia's expression of concern mimicked her own.

"Oh? Say more if you please," Trinati said.

"Wolves, my lady. You can hear them howling at night all around the valley. There have always been wolves in the interlake region, but these are different. More aggressive. They've been attacking the edges of the villages. At first they'd only attack livestock. Now they're attacking villagers."

"That's unusual."

"Highly unusual and especially for these parts. People are hunkering down in their cabins at night, and the wolves are roaming freely, cutting into pastures and savaging flocks. We've lost count of the number of carcasses."

"Any incidents with bears attacking?" Wegner asked.

"Even the bears fear them," Andrin said. "We've found their carcasses too."

"How long has this been going on?" Trinati asked.

"A fortnight or so? We have new villagers coming to Montheron with every cargo shipment, trying to move here, but there just isn't room for them all. It was already crowded before the wolves started up."

"What are the hunters doing about the wolves?" asked one of the hunters who had come with them. "How are they thinning their ranks?"

"They've been hunting the packs. But more just keep coming. And these wolves aren't fighting each other for territory."

"Bizarre," said the hunter brusquely.

"Apparently so," Andrin said.

The roar Cimree had heard had sounded nothing like a wolf's howl. And these wolves were attacking bears? Usually bears were the dominant predator, weren't they? The street was very crowded as they pressed through and continued up the winding path leading to the citadel. Cimree could see the fear in people's faces as they did business in the small shops lining the road. The buildings stood so close together and were so numerous that there were few alleys and only an occasional stone trough for water. As she passed one structure, she sensed the strong presence of a serpent and turned her head, finding one inside a glass cage by the window. The serpent called to Cimree's mind, begging her to free it from captivity. She hadn't sensed any serpents since coming into the villages.

"So what brings you here, my lady?" Andrin asked. "Are you here because you heard of it?"

"You overstep your station," Trinati said with a tone of rebuke.

"I beg your pardon, my lady. I meant no offense."

As they climbed the next section of road, it became steeper. There was a little shrine built to the angel sworn on the left side of the road, and it was flocked with people who were murmuring prayers. Beyond that was another gatehouse, guarding the steps leading to the walled fortress higher up. There were many guards stationed there, holding back a crowd of people begging to be allowed inside.

"Clear the way," Andrin ordered the men, and they marched faster when the guards pushed aside enough of the mob to make a path for them. Cimree watched as the crowd began to recognize that the newcomers were going to be admitted, and they began to increase their moans and cries for help.

"Let us in too!"

"We can't go back, it's too dangerous!"

"Please! Please, have mercy on us!"

As Andrin and the guards cleared the path, Trinati passed the crowd saying nothing, but Wegner looked troubled, and Darcia stared at the people, her mouth frowning with pity. The hunters were all impassive, which made sense with their training, but Cimree's heart hurt for these refugees who had come seeking protection and were thwarted in receiving it.

Beyond the wall was a massive set of stairs leading up, and they climbed quickly. As they passed a shadowed alcove, Darcia pinched Cimree's arm and pointed. "The dungeons," she whispered.

Eventually, they reached another level. The inhabitants at these heights were angel sworn, as noted in the fine tunics and young faces. But there was fear here as well. They might live above the lives of the aging and infirm, but they were aware of the suffering below. Angel sworn stood along the wall with spears and shields, awaiting commands. As soon as the people recognized Trinati among them, there were murmurs of relief.

Captain Odeon strode forward and met her, dropping to one knee in reverence. "Trinati, I'm grateful you've come. Has the Queen Mother learned of our plight?"

Everyone was looking at her with hopeful expressions. Trinati gazed at the faces as they all began to gather near her. She had not come to save them. She'd come bearing grim news of her own. Cimree wondered how she would handle the situation.

"Of course I've come to help," Trinati said with a broad smile and a look of confidence. "Captain, we will discuss this privately. Darcia, would you take Cimree with you? You know where to go, I believe?"

And with that subtle order, Cimree realized she'd be offered no further help in preparing for her reckoning with the Queen Mother's enemy.

TWELVE
THE PRISONER

The dungeon beneath the fortress of Montheron was already teeming with people. It was not a dank or fetid place, but the cells were small with iron bars, and there was no privacy at all, though there was good drainage and the smell of burning pitch instead of human waste. Cimree's chest constricted with worry as she followed Darcia and the guard Andrin down the interior corridor to the last cell on the right. There were openings in the stone, windows they could be called, and the noises from the crowded town below wafted up along with the smells of chimney smoke and cooking meat.

The precisely carved stone and joists were assembled meticulously, as were all things crafted by the angel sworn. Even the dungeon had a certain elegance to it. As they neared the last cell, her stomach lurched, and then they were there. The prisoner was doing a handstand, balanced on his palms, cords of muscles tensed and quivering as he shifted position to maintain balance.

With the gracefulness of a trained warrior, he flipped down to his feet again and rose, white-and-gray hair damp with sweat. He rubbed his mouth, the surrounding wrinkles and crags evidence of his advancing age. His eyes were gray too. Instantly, unmistakably, she felt a keen revulsion on seeing him. Also, a feeling of danger—immediate and pronounced.

"Who's this?" the man, Azra, said to the guard, sizing up Cimree quickly, his face betraying his instant dislike.

"Trinati brought her," Andrin replied, stepping aside. "I don't know her name."

Azra snorted. He looked at Cimree without disguising his reaction. "What do you want?"

"I'm Darcia," said Cimree's companion with a cheerful smile. "This is Cimree."

"I don't care," Azra shot back angrily, and Darcia's smile wilted.

"We're from Clairvaux." Darcia tried again.

Azra was staring at Cimree with such intensity and disgust that it made her want to shrink.

"Say what you're going to say and then get out of here," Azra snarled.

Darcia's mouth hung open a moment before she looked to Cimree and nodded for her to start talking.

"Why do you hate me?" Cimree asked, feeling that rebellious part of her coil up inside at such unprovoked hostility.

"I don't know you well enough to hate you," Azra said. "But I do hate the Queen Mother, so maybe it's just that you're here doing her bidding that annoys me."

"I came seeking your help," Cimree said.

Azra walked to the bars, grabbed them, and shook them violently. Darcia flinched and took a step back. "I am so *anxious* to help you. Why don't you let me out?"

Cimree noticed that Andrin was gaping at the prisoner too, as if his conduct were totally unexpected and not normal.

Cimree stepped closer, against her instincts, while her insides squirmed with warning and danger. "I didn't ask to come here."

"And I didn't ask you to come. Yet here we are. Say what you will and go away."

It was pointless. Utterly pointless. The man's hostility was palpable. He didn't want to help. He wasn't going to help. He just wanted revenge.

"Several hunters have been killed," Cimree said. She'd drawn closer to him but remained out of reach in case he lunged at her through the bars.

"A pity."

"My mentor, my teacher, has also been killed."

"A murderer is loose in Clairvaux. How terrible for you."

"No man did this," Cimree said. Her emotions were churning. "They were clawed down. Ravaged by a beast. But not any beast we know of."

He paused his insults as he considered her words. "Why did she send *you*?"

"I'm the only one who's seen it. Well, a glimpse of it anyway."

"You're a hunter in training?"

"I'm a healer."

He frowned, looking perplexed. "Surely not."

What did that mean? Did he see another aptitude in her instead? "My mentor was Milena. And she is dead."

He gave her a quizzical look. "Where did this happen?"

"Well, the first hunter was killed at the northeastern cliffs. I'd seen him, alive—"

"No, where was Milena killed?"

"At our cottage. The doors were secured. It broke down one of them."

He frowned again. "A bear might be desperate after winter, but not this time of year."

"It wasn't a bear. It didn't sound like a bear."

"Bears can be quite hostile when provoked," he said condescendingly. "Or surprised. Believe me, I've experienced it."

"Azra, others have been killed too," Andrin said. "Here in the lake country." The beseeching way he addressed the prisoner revealed that the two knew each other quite well. That was interesting.

"And you're telling me this now?" Azra said with a tone of rebuke.

"The hunters believe a rogue pack of wolves has come."

"What I saw wasn't a wolf," Cimree said.

Azra shook his head and gave them both a look of frustration. "No wolf is better than a trained hunter. And wolves don't break down doors. They'll encircle prey and trap them inside and wait them out, but they won't go *in*."

"But these wolves are different," Andrin said. "Some are calling them gévaudan."

"How are they different?" Azra asked.

"What's a gévaudan?" Cimree interjected.

Azra looked at her. "When people are driven mad with hunger, sometimes they turn on other people for food. It's a sickness of the mind. Men who become like wolves. The gévaudan."

"What I heard is these wolves can't be grafted with," Andrin added pointedly.

"What?" Azra said with dismay.

"I overhead this. I didn't think that was possible."

"All animals are subject to scionwood," Azra said. He gave Cimree a mocking look. "Isn't that the way of things?"

Cimree nodded. "The hunter who was first killed, his distaff was still in his belt. He didn't even draw it or one of his swords."

"This is very strange. But still, a diligent hunter should have been aware of their surroundings. It would not be easy to get that close without being detected."

"There was a lot of mist that day," Cimree said.

The man's expression shifted instantly. A look of recognition.

"What?" she demanded.

"This attack happened in the mist?"

Cimree was baffled why that made any difference. "And?"

His entire countenance changed. The contempt left. The bravado left. It was replaced by ... fear.

"You know this creature?" she whispered.

"Did it keen? Not like a red deer, but a roar that—"

"Sent shivers down my back," Cimree said.

He grunted, looking away from her finally. His memory had been touched. This was familiar to him.

"What is it?" she asked again, coming closer. Would he try to grab her?

"I've heard of such a beast," he said solemnly. "There are mountains far away called the Tirich Mir. There's a legend there of a creature that walks like a man. That preys not for food but for fear. The local tribesmen call it ... the Fear Liath. They're terrified of it. And they do not lack for courage."

Cimree looked over at Darcia. She looked afraid just hearing about it.

"Can it be killed?" Cimree asked.

"There's only one way," Azra said in a whisper.

She leaned closer. And realized, too late, that she shouldn't have.

Azra lunged. He grabbed the shoulder strap of her pack and yanked her hard against the bars. The sudden pain and confusion startled her, and she tried to break free, but for being an old man, he was exceptionally strong. She was able to wriggle free of one of the straps.

"Azra, don't!" Andrin shouted. "This will only end badly for you!"

Cimree tugged herself free and backed away, staring as he opened the pack and withdrew the purple fruit. Then he backed away from them, deeper into the cell. Cimree felt outraged that he'd tricked her. Trinati would be furious too.

"Give that back," she demanded hotly, her voice quavering.

He peeled off some of the rind.

"Azra!" Andrin gasped. "They'll kill you!"

He sank his teeth into the fleshy part of the fruit. Then he tore away another part of the peel.

"Give it back!" Cimree shouted. "Please!"

He bit another large chunk from it, chewing it quickly, swallowing. He looked pleased with himself. She knew the risk he was taking. The fruit was intoxicating. It took the strongest of wills not to devour the whole thing. Most often, people were granted a single slice from it to reverse their aging and become young again. Eating the whole thing would turn you into a helpless infant.

"I'm getting Trinati," Darcia said and raced down the corridor.

"Azra," Andrin said in despair, shaking his head. He hadn't drawn his weapon. He probably knew he didn't stand a chance against someone from the Long Patrol.

Cimree grabbed the bars. "Please, you have to give it back. If you eat too much—"

"You think I don't already know this?" Azra said with an incredulous look, as if she were the one being foolish. He ripped off another part of the peel and sank his teeth into it ravenously.

"Open the lock!" Cimree said to Andrin.

"It's forbidden," he said. "And I don't have the key."

Cimree reached through the bars in desperation, but he was too far. "Please. Just stop. Don't do this. All your memories will be gone. We need you!"

He paused at those words, juice dribbling down his chin. "Maybe I don't want to remember anymore," he said huskily. Then he took another big bite.

Cimree winced, straining through the bars. She'd been tempted earlier to do what he was doing. But every angel sworn knew the risks of eating too much. She feared he'd do just that.

"What you know, what you've learned, cannot be replaced," Cimree said earnestly. "You are the only one who can help us. Please. Don't eat the rest."

He'd devoured at least half of it. The fruit had a stringy quality to it and was the color of an orange sunrise or a marigold flower.

He wiped his chin again with his knuckle, paused, then swallowed. The fruit of the Gallows Tree began to work immediately with the first bite, but the age transformation could take days or weeks, depending on how much fruit had been eaten.

He tore another part of the peel off and took one more big bite, and Cimree closed her eyes in despair. Whatever the intent of the punishment from the Queen Mother, the result was that it had driven him mad.

Then she felt something brush her hand. She opened her eyes. He was holding the rest of the fruit out to her.

She took it, and the juice dripped from her hand.

Their eyes met and she felt a connection to him. She suddenly realized he'd done everything deliberately. He'd deduced she had the fruit with her. He'd taken it by force instead of having to bargain for his youth.

"I didn't mean to hurt you ... well, not permanently." A flicker of a smile and a gloating look in his eyes triggered her to pull her arm back through the bars.

"You tricked me."

"Oh, but don't we always blame a serpent for our own folly?" he said mockingly.

Her insides shriveled at the mention of the story from Origin. Wasn't *she* supposed to be the cunning one?

"At least tell me how to kill this creature, this Fear Liath."

He shook his head no.

"You already took the fruit!"

"But I want my freedom," he said with blazing eyes.

THIRTEEN
RESTLESS ONE

The prisoner sat at the back of his cell, head hanging low, and waited in silence. Cimree tried to get him to speak, to reveal what he knew, but he would not. He was waiting for Trinati to come, and Cimree feared what would happen when she did arrive. The fruit had been a bargaining tool to get Azra's support. He'd eaten at least two-thirds of it and yet had made no promises. In other words, Cimree had failed dramatically.

"Will you not help us?" she said once again, her voice plaintive.

Azra didn't even look at her. He just sat there, hands crossed over his knees, waiting.

Andrin shook his head and muttered to himself. The steady noise in the dungeon disguised other sounds, but they could tell when Trinati arrived with Captain Odeon because there was an immediate clamor. Darcia led the way. What had she told Trinati already?

Cimree's stomach twisted uncomfortably. She wanted to be away from the dungeon, away from Montheron, away from *people*.

As Trinati reached them, her expression was serious but not angry. That was a surprise. She should be furious. Captain Odeon looked stern as well, his armor glinting in the rushlight. A few other guards were with them, wearing the armor of the angel sworn and bearing blades.

"It's my fault," Cimree said before Trinati could say anything. "I got too close to him."

"How much of the fruit did he eat?" she asked curtly.

Cimree had wrapped the remainder in a bag she kept in her pack. She produced it and held it up for Trinati to see. Captain Odeon eyed the remaining fruit with interest. She wondered how long it had been since he had partaken of it.

Trinati examined the remainder, put it back in its bag, and nodded for Cimree to return it to her pack.

"I'm sorry," Cimree said.

"You surprise me, Azra," Trinati said, ignoring Cimree's apology. "I thought you were above roughing up young healers."

Azra lifted his head and Cimree noticed a change in his countenance. Some of the wrinkles had faded. His liver spots had already vanished.

"I did what I had to do," Azra said brusquely.

"It didn't get you out of your cell," Trinati said, gazing at the bars and looking superior.

"I could have left a long time ago if I'd wanted to."

"Rather presumptuous, don't you think?" said Captain Odeon.

"I could have done it, Odeon. I just didn't fancy being hunted by the Long Patrol. Besides, this was between me and the Queen Mother. Until now."

"Now it's getting interesting," Trinati said mockingly. "What do you mean?"

"I don't find the situation interesting," Azra said. "It's catastrophic."

The way he said it caused a ripple of fear to wash through Cimree.

"How?" Trinati demanded.

"I won't tell you. But I will tell the Queen Mother."

"That won't do, Azra. Tell me what you know, and I'll decide whether you should see her."

"You don't have time to negotiate this, Trinati. Everyone on this island is about to die."

Captain Odeon frowned and stepped forward. "How can you know that?"

"You really want me to say it, here in the dungeon, where so many can hear?" He was raising his voice as he spoke.

Trinati looked incensed. "I warn you, Azra—"

"I'm the least of your problems right now, Trinati. Let's go up to the fortress to talk about this privately. Then you can make your choice."

"You are not leaving that cell without a Tanaquil amulet," Trinati said. "You can't be trusted."

"I expected no less from you," Azra shot back. "I'll wear it. Gladly. But I want *her* to control it."

He'd pointed at Cimree. She was confused, having never even heard about that kind of amulet before.

"Cimree? Why her?"

"I have my reasons."

"You are in no position to—"

"I am, actually, in a position to be of help to the angel sworn. I know about these creatures. I can see what's happening right now, and you don't. Let's discuss this privately. You don't want a panic. I've *seen* what happens when people panic."

"And I suppose you'll demand a distaff too?" Trinati said in disbelief.

He held up his hands and shook his head.

Trinati turned to Captain Odeon.

"He's never acted like this," Odeon said in a low voice. "Not since he was brought here. I'll admit, I'm unnerved."

"You should be," Azra growled.

Trinati was always so confident, so assured of herself, but

Cimree could see the indecision in her eyes. She was struggling, not wanting to make a mistake. Trinati turned to Cimree.

"I do have a Tanaquil amulet. The Queen Mother gave it to me so that we could bring Azra back to Clairvaux."

"I don't know what that is," Cimree said. She felt a throb of fear.

"It's part of the grafting magic. But instead of binding us to an animal, it allows us to bind person to person. One must be the dominant party in the bond. A female to male."

Cimree felt another shudder. "I don't think so. Have Darcia do it."

"Unacceptable," Azra said. "I won't agree to wear it."

"You do not get to decide who uses it," Trinati said, eyes flashing with rage.

"Do you think I'm that foolish, Trinati? I've known the Queen Mother longer than you. I know how she thinks and whom she uses. And I know the grafting of a Tanaquil must be voluntary for it to work. You can't force me to wear it."

"You can't force *me* either," Cimree said, glaring at Azra.

"Ah, but you'll do as you're told," Azra said mockingly.

Cimree felt a surge of heat in her cheeks. And rebelliousness. She folded her arms and looked away.

"Captain," Trinati said, "I want him bound in chains and dragged up to the citadel. We won't use the Tanaquil yet. If he tries to escape, kill him."

Cimree stared at her in shock. She was about to protest, but she saw the glare from Darcia accompanied by a subtle shake of her head.

"I'll come willingly in chains," Azra said. "Just get me out of here."

THE MARCH UP to the top of the fortress had lost all its awe and splendor. Cimree felt like she was drowning in the events of the past few days. The fruit from the Gallows Tree had been wrenched away from her by Azra, who had then demanded that *she* be bound to him. No, it was binding him to her, and would that give her some sort of control over him? She'd never heard of grafting magic being used that way before. Never human to human. The Oldknow had made all creatures and beasts to be subservient to the First Parents. And when the First Man had partaken of the fruit of the Serpent Tree, he had forfeited his position to jointly rule, and so authority had been given to the Queen Mother. That was the order of things.

Cimree kept to her own thoughts as Darcia walked alongside her, the garrulous woman quiet for once and looking pensive and troubled. Azra's chains rattled and clanged against the stone steps, but Cimree's trepidation was allayed by the angel sworn defenders who surrounded him with their celestial iron blades drawn. The weapons were blindingly beautiful but deadly dangerous. Andrin had been sent back down to the gates to handle the crush of people trying to come to Montheron, leaving Captain Odeon and Trinati to bring up the rear, talking in low voices.

When they reached the huge doors of the inner fortress, the guardians stationed there opened them and greeted the company. The smell of flowers filled the air as they walked across polished floors devoid of any stain. The huge vaulted ceilings showed master craftsmanship. In one of the grand hallways, they encountered Wegner, who frowned at seeing Azra in chains.

"We're going to Odeon's study," Trinati told him. "Join us there."

"As you wish," Wegner said, clasping his hands. He had several acolytes around him who immediately dispersed when they heard the order.

Cimree thought it might be nice to explore the fortress a bit and visit the grounds.

"Do you want to show me around?" she asked Darcia.

"You're coming with us," Trinati said, shaking her head. "Darcia, you can spend your time as you like."

Cimree's stomach squeezed again. They went through several passages, climbed up steps, and then reached another set of doors. Inside was a beautiful and cozy chamber with enough natural light from the fading sun coming in from the huge windows. The stone walls and arches were all scrubbed and clean. There were a reading couch and a window seat flanked by wooden shelves on which sat rows and rows of leatherbound books, and Wegner immediately approached them and began perusing the tomes. Odeon had the guards position Azra near the far wall and stationed them outside the door before closing it, and then he walked to the window seat and turned, folding his arms and gazing imperiously at the prisoner.

Cimree, not sure what to do with herself or even why she'd been invited, sat down at the edge of the couch and watched as Trinati gave Azra a wary look and began to pace.

Azra ignored them all and gazed around the room with a look of longing. It was a far cry from his normal cramped quarters.

"You wanted a private audience. This is all you will get." Trinati's brow furrowed. "Speak."

"We need to evacuate Montheron," Azra said solemnly.

"That seems entirely imprudent. And indefensible considering the circumstances. We're safer behind walls than strewn out over open country."

Azra sighed. "The wolves harassing the lake country, I've heard them howling at night. They're communicating with each other."

"That's what wolves do," Trinati said condescendingly.

"This is going to be more difficult if you keep thinking about it the way you're used to thinking. Let me put it another way. Wolves tend to harry their prey. They go after the young. The infirm. These are more like the gévaudan."

Trinati's voice was hard. "Those aren't wolves, but men who

act like beasts. I've been a hunter before, Azra. Quit lecturing me and get to the point."

"What happens when a rival pack encroaches on their territory?"

"They fight. Each pack has a leader. The leader is paramount in the animal kingdom. They don't share territory, they fight over it."

"Exactly!" Azra said with energy. "I've been listening to the howling. They aren't warning each other. Threatening each other. They are working in unison!"

Trinati frowned. "They can't."

"They are now!" Azra said acerbically. "You know the normal behavior. They herd animals into difficult terrain where the advantage of speed is compromised. Red deer are faster on open ground, so they herd them into forests. Wolves are canny predators and take advantage of the change in situation. I'm telling you that *we've* become their prey, and they are herding *us* into Montheron."

"But an animal cannot think like we can," Trinati objected. "They cannot just change their nature."

"They can't. You're right. But they can be controlled with a grafting wand."

Trinati looked over at Captain Odeon, her brow wrinkling.

Wegner coughed. "What you're suggesting is that they are being controlled by a higher intelligence."

"At least someone was listening," Azra replied.

"And what are the wolves going to do, Azra?" Trinati said dismissively. "*Swim* to Montheron? The people would be safer if they were here. Without suitable prey, the wolves will hunt somewhere else. Their hunger will drive them."

Azra rubbed his brow, looking frustrated. "Of course the wolf packs aren't going to cross the lake, Trinati. Their purpose is to consolidate us into one place. Here."

"We have enough stores of food to last for months," Captain Odeon said.

"Enough to feed the entire lake country, Odeon? I doubt it.

I've seen refugees after they've been driven from their villages. I've seen the consequences of ruthless kings and queens and vicious armies. But deprive a family of defenses against a threat. Take away their ability to gather food for their children. The worst instincts of human nature come out. The greatest of which is *fear*. What people do when they are afraid."

Cimree understood. She'd been listening to his words with eagerness, feeling everything he said was true and based on what he'd seen during his lifespans.

"The Fear Liath has already passed through this way. Maybe it will come back," she said.

He held up a finger and pointed it at her. "You should listen to her."

Fourteen

Decision

"Captain, take Azra to the kitchen and get him something to eat. I'd like to consult with Wegner before making any decisions." Trinati's voice was measured, cool, and commanding.

"Very well," Captain Odeon said. He gave Azra a stern look, and the prisoner gathered himself and began to walk to the door, but not without another look at Cimree, a look she found impossible to read. Was he warning her? Pleading with her? Wary of her?

Cimree wasn't sure whether to go or stay. She hesitated, not wanting to attract attention to herself but also feeling the awkwardness of the moment.

"Please stay," Trinati said, turning her head slightly.

Cimree felt relief that her presence hadn't been discounted.

Captain Odeon shut the door, but it opened a few moments later when Darcia entered. It was just the four of them again.

Trinati turned in a half circle to look at the new arrival. "What have you learned since we arrived?"

Darcia's expression was neutral. "There is fear throughout the citadel. Everyone is in a state of agitation. Too many people are trying to come to the island every day, and there are worries about food shortages. Worries that they'll be cast out. Those who are here don't want anyone else to be allowed in. I've never seen Montheron in such a tumult."

Trinati nodded. "Neither have I, not even when the Vikander attacked. This is different."

"It feels so," said Darcia. "The wolves have been killing the young and the infirm. Not animals. They're killing humans."

And that, to Cimree, seemed beyond what normal animals would do in the natural world. She continued to listen keenly without interjecting.

"They've been altered," Trinati said. "It's grafting magic. I'm sure of it. Wegner, what do you think is happening?"

"I've hardly had sufficient time to put together the evidence." Wegner demurred.

"I know, old friend. But we don't have the luxury of ample time. I need to make a decision *now*."

"Rushed decisions are usually terrible ones," Wegner said with a cautious smile.

"That is why I have all of you," she answered. "We represent the four temperaments. Do you think what Azra said was logical?"

"It was a combination of logic and emotion," Wegner said. "He was afraid. There can be no doubt about that. He's had more time to consider the devolving situation. Taking the fruit from Cimree was an attack of opportunity. He knew his advancing age would make him less likely to survive what's coming. I don't think he did it out of malice. More like ... desperation."

"The Queen Mother suspected he would," Trinati said. "That's why I gave Cimree the fruit."

Cimree blinked and startled. "You knew he'd attack me?"

"We suspected it, yes."

"You used me," Cimree said, feeling her cheeks heat.

"Do you not *use* herbs to treat wounds?" Darcia said.

"Herbs don't have feelings," Cimree countered.

Darcia shook her head and gave Trinati a knowing look.

"Feelings are important, Cimree," Trinati said. "But they tend to get in the way of good judgment. The Queen Mother thought your naivete and lack of guile would be disarming to Azra. But they weren't. He was provoked by you. Captain Odeon said Azra's reaction was visceral."

"It was," Cimree said vehemently. "And I don't like him either. But that doesn't mean I don't think he's right."

"See? Emotions do not have to rule our decisions. The Queen Mother anticipated the reaction. I thought she might be mistaken, but she was correct that bringing you would alter events. You have a way with people, Cimree. It's very peculiar."

It didn't sound like a compliment. She felt some disdain from Trinati and Darcia, though none from Wegner.

"So what are your choices?" Cimree asked Trinati.

"Do we bring Azra back with us to Clairvaux now, or do we stay and try to help the current situation here. There has been no word of these problems yet, so we must send word immediately. But before I make a decision, I should like to have input from each of you. Darcia?"

"I want to leave," Darcia said. "We came here to fulfill a task. Let's bind Azra with the amulet and bring him with us."

"Noted. He only agreed to be bound to Cimree. Interesting."

"I think he agreed because his aversion to her might help him fight the grafting magic," Wegner said. "I think Darcia or you would be a better person to control the bond."

"He won't submit to me," Trinati said.

"I'd do it," Darcia quickly offered, and Cimree felt she sounded too eager.

Trinati shook her head. "He won't accept either of us. But the Queen Mother knew he'd accept Cimree."

Cimree had no idea why. What was it about her that had informed the Queen Mother's decision?

"I don't understand this kind of grafting magic," Cimree said. "What is a Tanaquil amulet?"

"It's an amulet worn over the heart because it gives power over emotions," Trinati said. "We don't know its origin. The Queen Mother believes it came from one of the Oldknow's other worlds. A woman was wearing it, one who came searching for the Gallows Tree. The Long Patrol encountered her, and she used its magic against them. It could make someone afraid and helpless or enraged. Even lovesick. She had a magic that allowed her to speak in our language and called herself Tanaquil."

"I've not heard that part," Darcia said, pursing her lips. "All I know is the Long Patrol killed her."

"It happened long ago," Wegner said. "The Queen Mother feared that others like her might come in search of the tree."

"Yes," Trinati agreed. "Tanaquil had a mark on her shoulder. A brand burned into her flesh. And using the amulet causes a pattern, a disfigurement on the breast. A stain."

"Why would someone want to use that kind of magic, then?" Cimree said, aghast at the thought of magic that could torment someone's feelings.

"Because the stain can be reversed with the fruit of the Gallows Tree," Wegner said. "It has no long-term effects. It's how Azra was brought to Montheron in the first place. How he was subdued."

That made sense and explained how he knew about it. He'd already worn the amulet and felt its power.

Trinati reached into her pocket and removed a tarnished amulet made of brass or bronze. It was engraved with a whorl-like pattern and had a chain woven through the top. As soon as Cimree saw it, she felt curious. Trinati approached and held it out for her to handle.

Cimree took it and rubbed her thumb across the grooves. There was power contained within it. An ancient magic that whispered to her invitingly.

She tried to hand it back. "I don't want to." But Trinati did not accept the amulet from her.

"Yes, but I *need* you to wear it," Trinati said. "Azra must be controlled. He is too knowledgeable and powerful to be set free."

"But I refuse," Cimree said.

"Cimree," Darcia admonished, shaking her head.

"You refuse?" Trinati said archly. "You've lived among us this long and understand that the first law of heaven is obedience. If you want to become an angel sworn, you must be willing to obey your superiors."

Cimree opened her mouth to object, but she suddenly realized the terrible situation she found herself in. She knew about the dangers. About the Fear Liath and the wolves they had started calling gévaudan. About the panic starting in Montheron. If she was not willing to obey Trinati, she would be exiled from Clairvaux and have to rely wholly on herself.

"This is for the best, Cimree," Darcia said. "You were sent on this mission for a purpose. Now is the time to fulfill it."

Cimree turned to Wegner and saw compassion in his eyes. He did not judge or accuse her. But then again, he was a man and had to be subservient to the wishes of those in power. His empathy gave her a meager amount of comfort.

Had the Queen Mother anticipated all of this? Was this course of action all according to her wisdom and plan? She'd given Cimree so little information to help her persuade Azra. Maybe it hadn't been intended that she'd succeed. She must be an unwitting part in a grander strategy.

Cimree stared at the amulet in her hand. Her options were limited. She could deny them, be exiled from the angel sworn. Would they lock her up in a cage too? She imagined not, since she didn't have the knowledge that Azra had. But only those willing to follow the order of things were allowed to live near the angel sworn. Where else could she go?

"I'm sorry, Trinati," Cimree said meekly.

"What are you sorry for?"

"For doubting. I will do it."

"Good," Trinati said smugly. "Now, put the amulet on. We must bind it to your heart first."

Cimree slung the chain around her neck and let the amulet thump against her chest. It wasn't very dense, not by weight, but there was a peculiar heaviness about it. Like it was made up of more than just metal. Like it contained the weight of a thousand emotions. A thousand lifetimes. She blew out her breath slowly, trying to calm her racing nerves.

Trinati drew her distaff, and Wegner stepped closer, curiosity in his eyes, but Darcia looked a little jealous and held herself back.

Trinati used the tip of the scionwood to touch the middle of the amulet. It was strange for Cimree to think that she had a bit of metal that had been worn by a woman from another world, or at least one made by the angel sworn to resemble that one. It was part of the liturgy of the angel sworn that the Oldknow had created other planets in distant parts of the universe, though they were all connected and populated with people. What kind of world had made this amulet? And why had they wanted to control emotions so much?

She felt a buzz in her heart, an anticipatory excitement as the magic of the amulet fused to her soul. Her insights began to quicken. There were so many ranges of emotions, just like there were ranges in colors and tastes. Cimree had always been sensitive to her feelings, and that inclination fit wonderfully with the Tanaquil amulet's power. There was no resistance or confusion. It felt totally natural to be wearing it.

Trinati lowered the distaff and put it back in her belt. "There. Do you feel different?"

"Not really," Cimree said. "I feel quite the same."

"Well, that will change. When he dons the amulet, you will immediately begin to feel Azra's emotions as well as your own. His resentment. His anger. His unjustified feelings of betrayal. His hatred. You must remember that his emotions are not yours. But you will be able to temper his with the medallion. To soothe his rage. Or provoke it."

"Why would I want to provoke it?"

"Listen carefully. This creature in Clairvaux, this thing called the Fear Liath, impacts emotions too. You will be going with Azra to destroy it. You must take away his fear and drive his rage. That is what your duty is, what the Queen Mother expects of you now."

Cimree opened her mouth, realizing what she'd just committed to doing. This was all part of the Queen Mother's plan.

"It will all be all right," Darcia said. "I would have done it."

"But you are not comfortable in the wilderness," Trinati said. "Cimree likes to roam out of bounds. Consider this a consequence for that previous choice of yours as well. At least you have permission this time."

"So I'm to go with Azra to hunt the thing and destroy it?"

"Exactly. Well, he'll do the destroying. He's very good at that."

"So if the Fear Liath is coming to Montheron, as he thinks, then we'll face it here?"

"Better here than Clairvaux," Trinati said. "We may be staying for several weeks."

The door of the room was yanked open, and one of Captain Odeon's defenders came in, blood dribbling from his nose.

"He escaped," the angel sworn panted.

Trinati's eyes filled with wrath. "How is that possible?"

"He stole a dirk from someone. It all happened so quickly. He then wrenched a distaff away and began to graft in a frenzy, before leaping from the kitchen window. Captain Odeon is injured."

Cimree reached down to her sheath and discovered, to her horror, that her dirk was missing.

Azra had been planning his escape all along.

FIFTEEN
ROGUE HUNTER

"I want him captured before sunrise," Trinati said angrily. "He cannot escape. Take me to Odeon." They started for the door.

"I know the island," Darcia said as she started after them. "Let me help with the search." A nod from Trinati showed her acceptance of the offer.

Cimree felt conflicted about it all. She'd been used as part of his effort. He'd managed to swipe the fruit from her. He'd stolen her dirk as well. But surely he didn't think he could escape the island with every angel sworn searching for him? Angel sworn that could see in the dark, could hear the slightest noise. If he tried flying away from the island, he would be seen by the defenders. His best hope would be to hunker down and hide within the confines of the island.

"Trinati," Cimree called out as the other woman reached the door.

Trinati gave her an icy look. "Time is precious."

"I'm aware. One of the soldiers who was in the dungeon. His name was ... Andrin. There was a connection between him and Azra. If he is looking for a place to hide, he might go to Andrin's home."

Trinati paused, her brow furrowing. "That was useful, Cimree."

"I am trying to be," Cimree replied.

Then the others were gone, leaving her and Wegner alone in the room.

"What will happen to him?" she asked Wegner.

"Are you asking if he'll be slain?"

Cimree pursed her lips. "He knows too much. What he knows can help us."

"That's why killing him isn't the priority. But he is an expert at survival and getting out of difficult situations. The bites of fruit he had earlier will make him younger by the moment. He's never tried to escape before." He tapped his lips. "That implies he feels the risks of staying are too great."

"I'm feeling the same myself."

"Yes, but what about all the people here at Montheron who rely on the angel sworn for protection? We can't abandon them."

"Of course we can't. But wouldn't it be better to evacuate them?"

"I would advise against that, Cimree." He looked sympathetic, but he was a thoughtful man, one used to weighing the merits of all the facts.

"You can advise all you want, but it's Trinati's decision."

"As it should be."

"Well, at least she listens to you, Wegner."

Cimree rubbed her face tiredly and swayed slightly on her feet.

Wegner noticed and asked, "When was the last time you ate?"

Cimree shook her head, uncertain, as the mention of eating caused her stomach to grumble.

"Let me take you to the kitchens."

THE SIZE of the kitchen was well beyond what Cimree's imagination had predicted. The number of bread loaves produced in its plenteous ovens was staggering, and different kinds of meats sizzled on rotating spits, dripping fat into the flames. Huge rinds of cheeses of varying colors were stored alongside sacks of vegetables and bundles of fragrant herbs. Seeing some mint leaves made her think of the cottage, bringing Milena's death to the forefront of her mind. The fruit of the Gallows Tree could recover a sick person dying of tumor, but it could not bring someone back from the dead. But even knowing there was nothing she could have done to save her, Cimree felt the weight of responsibility.

She and Wegner ate at a table in the bustling kitchen busy with cooks and their apprentices weaving around in an intricate display of efficiency, and she enjoyed talking to him but even more so the companionable silence that they shared in the isolated table. He ate his portion slowly, savoring it. All angel sworn had conscientious lives. No one ate to excess. Or slept beyond the morning hymn. There was a mindfulness in all things except in talking. But then, the tongue was the hardest part of the body to tame, and Cimree knew she was overly sensitive to people's words or even their expressions.

The sun had fallen, and with no light coming through the windows, the rushlights were lit, causing shadows to play against the walls. They were brought a single slice of pumpkin bread to share, and they nibbled from it, enjoying its blend of spices. Inside the kitchen, there was no sense of the commotion happening in the citadel or the search underway for Azra. She worried about him, though. Worried he'd choose to die rather than be imprisoned again.

"I just noticed a change in your expression, Cimree. Is something troubling you?"

Wegner had been so easy to sit with and so undemanding of attention that she'd nearly forgotten he was sitting across from her. In fact, she felt so comfortable with his feelings—which she could sense while wearing the Tanaquil amulet—that it removed much of her normal anxiety of wondering what people were thinking or feeling about her. She perceived Wegner's kindness, and that he was a very patient man. So it made her feel easy around him.

"I was worrying about Azra," she said. "I don't want him to die."

"You care deeply about people."

"Isn't that proper for a healer?" she asked.

"Of course it is proper. But we all have many skills and interests. Why limit them?"

"I have many lifespans to discover mine," she said. "But I still can't help caring about people. I don't like the way Trinati treated that man in the village we passed."

"How do you mean?" he probed. Maybe he already knew and was trying to draw her out.

"There's a certain arrogance among the angel sworn. In how they treat mortals."

"That is your perception?"

"It is. It makes people resentful."

"I can see that," he agreed. "I suppose a certain ... callousness develops after being alive for so long. Seeing mortals making the same trivial mistakes over and over again."

"How so?" she asked.

"There are many examples I can think of, but let's start with a common one. Mortals like to ferment things into different kinds of drinks because of the stimulation they experience imbibing them. Yet many do it to excess. They compromise their internal organs. Even after being told or shown how harming it can be, they do it anyway. They will not listen to wisdom. Others eat to excess. Others choose to be indolent."

"Surely not all earthborn do this?"

"No. Of course not. The Queen Mother has shown a higher way of living. One that has many intrinsic benefits. We gain those benefits by adhering to the precepts. But we do tend to look down on those who refuse to do the same."

"Does that not mean we should adjust how we teach them?"

"Ah, but some people will not be taught."

"That doesn't really answer my question, Wegner."

He smiled at her. Trinati wouldn't have tolerated it. "There is a limit to someone's willingness to learn, Cimree. It's a matter of choice, of the teacher, how far to indulge, how patient to be with willfulness."

He was right. There were some who would always rebel. She felt that instinct as part of her own nature. She'd felt its urges many times. Oh, she had a lot to learn still.

Cimree looked over his shoulder as Darcia came rushing into the kitchen and quickly glanced from face to face until she spotted them.

When Wegner noticed her diverted attention, he turned and then waved to Darcia, who came hastily to them.

"They found him!"

"Thank goodness." Cimree sighed.

"I'm grateful he didn't escape. Where is he?" Wegner asked.

"In a tight place. Not easy to get to. He's agreed to submit to the Tanaquil amulet. Trinati wants you to come with me." She was looking intently at Cimree.

Cimree plopped the rest of her pumpkin bread slice into her mouth and rose from her seat. "Thank you for sitting with me," she said to Wegner.

"It was my pleasure."

Cimree and Darcia left the enormous kitchen and went outside into the upper courtyard. The wind had a chill to it, and there were hazy clouds blotting some of the stars. A sickle-shaped moon hung on the horizon, and though it was dark and very little could be seen of the lake, its smell was distinguishable even from the heights.

Darcia withdrew her distaff. "She wants us to fly down. Can you bond with birds?"

"I've done it twice," Cimree offered.

"There are some pigeons roosting nearby. Draw from them."

Cimree nodded and pulled out her distaff. She sensed the birds in a roost, making little coddling noises in their sleep, and invoked the grafting magic. Immediately she felt their resistance. The refusal to be roused.

Darcia finished her grafting, and the magic had her floating off the ground. She frowned at Cimree and swished her distaff again, using her own will to create the connection. It worked instantly, and together, they lifted over the wall and began to glide down on the air currents, heading toward the rooftops of the village below. The thrill in Cimree's stomach was giddy. She shivered and not just with the cold.

"Follow me," Darcia called out to her, angling to the left. Cimree saw, with her bird-enhanced vision, the steep ramp leading up the citadel from the lower portion. She'd heard once of a giant wooden wheel, powered by people, that dragged a chain and lifted deliveries up to the citadel fortress. She felt the tingling sensation of a lack of blood flow, but it wasn't painful yet.

They lit gently on one of the streets teeming with people. Some were huddling in blankets beneath the edges of rooftops. There was clearly not enough room for everyone who had come that day, and Cimree's heart panged at seeing how many were children.

Darcia took her past the building that had the snake in its glass box by the window. Cimree felt the serpent's presence instantly, felt it pleading for rescue once more. Her heart went out to it as well, but there was nothing she could do at the moment.

"This way," Darcia said. She released the grafting, and the tingles began to fade from Cimree's feet and fingers. The buildings were jammed closely together, many of them several stories high, with steep roofs and draining gutters and piping. As they approached an alley, Cimree noticed the angel sworn warriors guarding it, their celestial iron swords drawn and glowing in the darkness.

Darcia led them into that alley, and they had to walk single file because the walls were so close.

"How did they find him?" Cimree whispered.

"You were right. He'd gone to that soldier's home, hoping they'd hide him. But the man was loyal, and when he had the chance, he slipped away and reported it. There are defenders on the roof above us in case he tries to escape that way."

A mewling cat darted away from them as they got too near it. The alley sloped down before reaching a junction of other buildings and a sudden drop. There wasn't much light down below, only a thin amount of moonlight. No rushlights.

"It's dark down there," Cimree said.

"Trinati is with him."

She wondered what sort of boxlike pit would be in such a place. It had a metallic smell to it.

"Did you bring her?" Trinati's voice called from the dark.

"She's with me," Darcia said.

"Send her down. I told you she would come, Azra. And that she has the amulet."

Cimree felt nervous energy, but she went to the edge of the pit, where she saw some small stone steps leading down that she hadn't seen as they'd approached. Darcia waited above while she carefully managed them. Without the enhanced powers from the grafting, she felt weak and vulnerable.

"Stop there," Trinati said when Cimree was partway down. She obeyed.

"I see it." Azra's voice sounded slightly different. Less husky.

"I've honored the terms on my end," Trinati said. "Will you honor yours?"

"I will."

Cimree could sense the others' emotions too. Trinati was

feeling cautiously triumphant and pleased that she'd been able to hunt Azra down so quickly. Azra on the other hand was more difficult to comprehend. He was tired and hungry, defensive, but not cowed. There was a confidence in him that was surprising considering the circumstances. The emotions were nuanced of course, and she only caught a glimpse of them. Like a scent of something familiar.

"Cimree, take off the medallion and bring it to me," Trinati said.

Cimree pulled off the chain and stepped into the dark. When she reached the edge of blackness, she caught a change in the shadows as Trinati approached, holding out her hand. The amulet was handed over. Then Trinati edged deeper into the shadows.

"Now, Azra. Put it on."

He didn't refuse.

Cimree felt it the moment he slipped it around his own neck. She felt the grafting magic flare inside her chest. Felt it *bind* him to her. The feeling of intimacy was so intense and sudden that she gasped.

In the darkness, his eyes began to glow silver.

So said the Oldknow to the serpent, "Because you have done this, more cursed are you. A greater curse above all livestock and more than every beast of the field. On your belly you shall slither, and dust you shall eat in all your days. And enmity I will put between you and Woman and between your seed and the seed of her dominion. She shall bruise your head. And you shall bruise her heel."

— ORIGIN, THE TALE OF THE QUEEN MOTHER
OF CLAIRVAUX

Sixteen
Rioting

"I warn you, Azra," Trinati said in the shadows. "Do not try to take the amulet off. You are grafted to it now."

"I know what happens, Trinati. This is not the first time I've worn it."

"That you wear it at all is your fault. You have forsaken your oaths. It is a mercy that you were permitted to live. At least you will no longer wear chains and languish in a cell."

"The cell *I* languish in isn't made of stone or barred with iron. I've submitted. Is that not enough for you?"

"It is sufficient." Trinati turned and approached Cimree. "He will obey your orders and you will obey mine. Is that clear?"

"Will it hurt him?" Cimree asked. She didn't understand the warning Trinati had made, but she felt uneasy about causing someone else pain.

"Only if he tries to remove it himself," Trinati said. "But that's his choice. The two of you are bound together. You will always know where he is, no matter how far he wanders. And he will know where you are. You have dominion over him. Don't abuse it."

"I don't even want it," Cimree said. She felt a surge of resentment, but it didn't come from her own heart. She sensed it in Azra's. It was difficult enough to bear her own emotions. How would she handle sharing his as well? It troubled her deeply.

"Let's go back to the citadel," Trinati said. She stepped around Cimree and went up the steps.

Cimree couldn't see the strange glowing eyes in the dark. His eyes were shut as he endured a feeling of resignation. But even though he was in shadow, she knew exactly where he was. The connection was powerful, like having an extra sense that she'd previously lacked. The thought of doing harm to him was akin to hurting herself. Her whole being recoiled at the thought.

"Why did you go to Andrin?" she asked him as she heard the scrape of Trinati's boots moving up the steps.

"I tried to persuade him to leave," Azra said. "It's going to be terrible here when the angel sworn are overrun. I don't think he's going to heed me, though. He's too ... obedient." The way he said the word dripped with disdain.

"We should return to the citadel."

"I'm your slave."

"I will not treat you like one."

He chuffed. "We'll see."

Cimree turned and climbed up the narrow steps. She did not hear him follow, for he was as stealthy as a cat, but she felt him, just a little brush against her mind that he was behind her.

Trinati was wearing an impatient scowl when they emerged. "I'm going to fly back to the citadel. Bring him to the kitchen for some food while I confer with Captain Odeon. They'll find you both a place to sleep for the night. We'll discuss more tomorrow."

"Very well," Cimree said meekly. Trinati looked warily at Azra before removing her distaff to perform a grafting and then rose effortlessly into the sky. The defenders that Trinati had left to escort them were all giving Azra angry looks.

She felt Azra's smugness and lack of concern for their feelings about him.

"Let's be on our way," she said.

"Wait."

She turned to look at Azra and noticed more changes in the rushlight. There were streaks of color in his hair. More wrinkles had gone. He handed her the dirk.

After taking it from him, she slid it back into her belt sheath. "I'd prefer you not steal anything from me again," she said flatly.

"I won't be able to now without you knowing," he answered with a crafty smile.

Cimree tried not to scowl, but she imagined her expression wasn't innocuous. She started down the alley the way they'd come, led by the defenders who would escort them. The ones guarding the rooftops began to soar skyward, the glowing metal of their celestial iron swords revealing their ascension into the dark sky.

The main street was still thronged with people, even though it was dark. Someone cried out from an upper window to be quiet and they were answered by the furious shout of a figure hunkering on the curb.

"You want to trade places? Come down, then, and trade with me! I've a family and a dog. We'll stay in your quarters gladly!"

Other angry voices joined in agreement and Cimree heard the window abruptly close. The air was seething with unbridled emotions. The people who had come to Montheron were desperate. But on arriving, their desperation had only grown. How would all these people eat? As she passed, she saw the hungry looks of children. Saw the frustrated concern of parents trying to quiet them. And she felt guilty that her belly was satisfied. She'd seen the bread ovens and the sizzling meat. All while these refugees went hungry.

They passed the little shop that had the snake in the window and she felt it instantly, pleading with her to free it. Of all the creatures in the natural world, why was she drawn to serpents? She ignored its plaintive thoughts, increasing her speed.

"You have affinity for snakes?" Azra whispered in surprise.

"So what if I do?"

"An odd affinity for a *healer*," he said in an amused tone.

"I didn't choose it."

"Nor did I choose mine."

"And what is your affinity? Wasps?"

Azra chuckled but made no reply.

When they reached the lower gates leading to the citadel heights, they discovered a crowd had gathered there. The noise they were making was raucous as they demanded to be let inside. It was a bewildering scene. The entire island belonged to the angel sworn, as did its fortress. The earthborn who inhabited the island had all made promises and vows in order to live there. The demands were forceful and long-lasting.

"Won't get in that way," one of the defending escorts said as they joined him at the edge of the crowd.

A bystander noticed them. "Are you going inside? Can we go inside? There's no place to sleep. The shops are all closed. There's no food. There's room up there, I know it."

Another came up to Cimree, a mother holding a baby. "Please, my lady! Can you bring my child up there? At least she'll be safe with the angel sworn. Please!" One of the defenders crowded in front of her to give Cimree some space.

"We should fly up," murmured one of the other defenders. "I don't like this."

"Can you graft with birds?" the first asked Cimree.

Before she could respond, Azra said, "I can."

"Please, my lady! My lady! I beg you!"

More were gathering around them. Some began shouting demands.

Azra stepped in front of Cimree, his eyes latching onto hers. "Give me your distaff."

She felt so rattled she wasn't even sure she could graft with anything, so she slipped it to him. He took her arm at the elbow, squeezing firmly but not too hard. He quickly started weaving the magic, and the two of them rose above the courtyard. Her stomach thrilled with the flight. The other defenders joined them, causing cries of frustration from the crowd below.

"Let us inside!"

"We need food!"

The cool night air made her shiver. Tangible relief came as they soared above the walls and then the next barriers. She felt only a slight tingle in her toes as the magic carried them up before they alighted down behind the fortress walls. He released the magic and then handed the distaff back to her.

"You're inexperienced," he said. "You'll get better in time."

"Thank you for getting us out of there, Wasp," she said with a teasing tone.

"I wasn't talking about your grafting skills. With the Tanaquil amulet, you could have repulsed the entire crowd. You could have made them fear us."

"But why? They were already afraid. And besides, you're wearing the amulet now. How could I have used it on them?"

He shook his head, giving her an incredulous look. "You've much to learn, little one."

The other defenders hovered nearby but did not land. One of them spoke. "We have new orders from Captain Odeon. Farewell."

Cimree nodded and looked at Azra. "Hungry?"

"Very," he said.

She thought she knew where the kitchen was, but after two wrong turns, Azra grunted and pointed the right way. Even with the lateness of the hour, the kitchen staff were still working hard. Cimree assumed they were making food to share with the people, but she could not be certain.

They picked a small table at the edge of the kitchen, and Cimree felt the stirrings of hunger inside her as well. Azra ate some bread in quick, hasty bites, then agreed to some meat when a servant came by holding a skewer. He quickly devoured it, licked his fingers, and then drank an entire pewter mug of water.

"You'll make yourself sick eating that fast," she said.

"Have you even eaten from the fruit of the Gallows Tree?" he asked her.

"Of course not. I'm just a novice."

"Well, you'll find it stirs up a prodigious appetite. Every part of my body is being renewed, and that requires sufficient sustenance. This is not uncommon. I could eat that entire skewer and still be hungry."

"How long does it take? For the fruit to finish the transformation."

"About a fortnight. I feel younger already."

"I was afraid you were going to eat the whole fruit. That you wanted to forget."

"There are some things I would rather forget. But I can't pick and choose. And I don't want to forget what the Queen Mother did." His eyes began to smolder with hate. "Some things must be remembered."

"Do not speak evil of her in front of me," Cimree warned.

"I wanted to explain why I wasn't irrational." He waved the servant over and began accepting more slices of meat. "What vegetables do you have?" Azra asked. The servant answered with an impressive list. "Bring them all."

Cimree was sated after a short while and was amazed that Azra kept eating. It took a while, but he finally began to slow down. To chew the food more methodically. She'd never encountered someone so ravenous. Maybe he had affinity for hungry bears.

"I hope we leave for Clairvaux tomorrow," Azra said, elbows on the table. "We should go before the chaos starts."

"But if the Fear Liath will come here, would it not be wise to face it here instead? You'll need to teach me about the amulet so I can help you fight it."

He looked away, a musing expression on his face. "No, there will probably be a riot here first. They're going to storm the fortress and try to take control of it."

"Would they dare?" Cimree asked in surprise. "After all we've done for them?"

"Trust me, Cimree. Even in Clairvaux, they would turn on each other if they felt the true danger of what's about to happen. I fear that not even Clairvaux will be safe. We cannot expect them to behave rationally. They'll behave like animals. You'll see. There's a savage part in all of us."

The confidence in his voice made her stomach clench with dread.

SEVENTEEN
ANGEL OF DEATH

Cimree wiped the sweat and steam from her face. Bathing in outdoor streams or beneath a waterfall in Clairvaux was typically a shiver-inducing experience. But most cabins and dwellings had steaming huts, which were especially nice in the winter months. The étuves in the fortress were filled with hot rocks in a basin, and pulling a lever introduced water, causing steam. Every moist breath felt like it was cleaning her lungs. She sat on a towel on a small stone bench, her entire body warm and perspiring. There were twelve different cells on the women's side and twelve for the men, and she was grateful to have some privacy by getting up early.

Cimree rose and took the towel with her to the cooling pool at the end of the stone corridor. The steps went down directly to it and she set her towel on the railing. The water was cool but not as frigid as the Silver River. She swam several laps before coming out and drying off with the towel. Voices of newcomers echoed down the stone, which had its own peculiar scent. She scrubbed herself dry and then went back to the changing room near the entrance where she'd left her clothing and pack. More were coming to take advantage of the étuves, and she couldn't help overhearing conversation.

"Even more mortals arrived this morning," one of the women said dismissively to a companion while removing her tunic. "Why do they keep coming?"

"It's the gévaudan," said the companion. "Did you hear them last night?"

"How could you not hear them? They've been sounding off all around the lake all night long and now during the day."

"I heard an entire family was savaged and killed by them."

"Really? Not just the aged?"

"The entire family. The people need refuge. That's why they're coming."

Cimree hastily began to clothe herself, her concern growing again at the news she'd just heard. Wolves attacking families? There wasn't a shortage of game in the forest. There had been no drought or fires to disrupt things.

"I hope Trinati restores order," said one of the women.

Shhhh, scolded the other. They both looked at Cimree, and she realized that her presence made it difficult for them to speak freely. She had arrived with Trinati after all, so they would naturally expect her loyalty.

Cimree finished cinching her tunic belt and then pulled on and laced up her boots before folding up the towel and bringing it to a cart near the exit. She found Azra at the junction of the corridor between the women's and men's cells. Through the power of the amulet, she sensed his feelings—he was radiating frustration and anger.

"Is something wrong?" she asked him. His hair wasn't even wet. "Didn't you bathe?"

"Can we go?" he snarled and began to walk away. He wouldn't meet her eyes and had a slight red tint to his ears.

"Why are you so angry?"

"You wouldn't understand. I'm starving. Let's go."

There was something else in his feelings, but he was burying it in anger. It was an emotion she didn't understand or even have a name for. But it was insignificant next to the strength of his fury.

She struggled to catch up to him in the corridor. "Would you slow down, please?"

He did, but he would not look at her. His jaw muscles were clenched. When she'd seen him earlier that morning and told him her desire to bathe in the étuve, he'd appeared even younger than before. The rapid transformation was remarkable. Yes, he was hungry, but why was he so angry?

"You weren't this angry when we started. Did something happen?"

He chuffed. "If my feelings are bothering you, then dismiss them. I have every right to be angry."

"I'm sure you do, but I don't have the right to dismiss them. I don't even know how the amulet works."

"That's obvious," he said with an edge in his tone. "We're going to the kitchen, yes?"

"If that will help your mood."

"It will."

He wasn't willing to offer conversation during the rest of the walk, and when they arrived, the kitchen was crammed with people. She saw the anger in his eyes as he glared at the crowd. She even felt his desire to do violence.

"Let's get you some food," Cimree said. "Wait here." She went to one of the cooks and asked if they could have an entire skewer of meat, an entire loaf of bread, and some nuts and fruit. The cook looked wild-eyed at her until she explained whom it was for and that he'd eaten of the fruit of the Gallows Tree. That explanation satisfied the cook, and she was provided with everything she'd asked for in a wicker basket, which she carried back to the entrance.

"I've got some food for us, but I don't know where we can go to eat it."

"Follow me," he said, more patiently this time.

There were angel sworn coming down from the sky and rising up from the town below. The guardians were all wearing armor and carrying celestial iron blades. It seemed an army of them had arrived.

Azra took her around the base of the fortress to an open gate that revealed stone steps leading down to a garden. It was on the back side of the island, so there were no structures down below, just some cliffs abutting a forested area before the waters of the lake. Stone benches in the garden had sculpted areas that held blooming flowers, and their smell permeated the area. The walled section of the fortress ended high above them where she could see angel sworn sentries patrolling the battlements.

"How did you know about this little garden?" she asked as they reached the bottom of the steps and went to a stone bench.

"When the Vikander attacked several years ago, I defended this ground. The gate, actually."

She opened the basket, and before she could offer him anything, he reached inside, tore off a hunk of bread, and began eating it like a starving man. Cimree pulled out her dirk and began slicing strips of meat. Cattle by the smell. She watched in fascination as he gorged himself, but she cut some for herself as well and ate it quietly while he wolfed his down.

The nuts were salty and the pears were sweet. She wished she'd asked for some cheese, but she'd been in a hurry and fearful that he'd turn violent. She was satisfied long before he was and just sat there, watching him surreptitiously as he devoured the remainder of the food. There was nothing left when he was done.

"Are you still hungry?" she asked in a teasing voice.

"You could say that," he said, not looking at her but gazing off the cliff's edge into the distance.

"I can get more."

"I've had enough for now."

The anger was ebbing in him, but he was upset still. At what, she had no idea. It was uncomfortable being tethered to his emotions like this.

She sighed. "I know this is difficult for you. I didn't want it either."

"Yet here we are." He turned and gave her a withering look. "For now, worry about your own feelings. Not mine."

"I can't even feel my own feelings with yours so ... uncontrolled."

"Then stop them. You have that power. Suppress them. That's what the amulet is for. To make me more tractable."

"I don't want to do that, Azra."

"You may not have a choice."

She frowned. "Why do you say that?"

He shook his head like she was being irrational. "Do you know who I was when I served the Queen Mother? Had you ... heard of me?"

"Not really. That was a long time ago. Before I was even born."

He grunted and she felt another surge of rage inside him. "Let me inform you, then. I was Azrael. The destroying angel."

She blinked in surprise. "You?"

"I was the arbiter of the Queen Mother's justice. Killing is what I am very good at. You don't understand what's going on. Why I'm not at ease."

"You're worried about fighting the Fear Liath."

"Oh, that is not *all* I'm worried about. You're being a simpleton."

She opened her mouth, feeling a surge of resentment and offense. "And you're being nasty. And intemperate."

"And yet here we are," he repeated, as his fists clenched and his nostrils flared. "With you holding my leash."

"What happens if you try to take off the amulet?" she asked. "Trinati warned you about it."

"Ask her yourself. If you dare another scolding."

Cimree rose from the bench, angry and flustered and realizing too late that someone was coming down the steps. It was Darcia. She arrived out of breath.

"Trinati sent me to get you both. I thought you'd be in the kitchen, but I had to search and ask to find you. We need to hurry."

Azra gave Darcia a spiteful look. Cimree wasn't sure if she'd have to compel Azra to follow, but she joined Darcia and she could feel that Azra followed them, though more slowly than the previous evening. A hound on a leash.

They reached the citadel in short order, and Darcia took them to the great hall where they found Trinati, Captain Odeon, and Wegner consulting with other angel sworn. There was a debate happening, voices raised and looks of concern all around when they entered. Upon seeing them, Trinati nodded to Darcia.

Cimree approached, Azra at her side.

"Food did not appease them," Trinati said, after holding up her hand for silence. "There are too many crowded into the lower city. They will bring disease if they keep coming."

"What does the Queen Mother wish?" asked someone else in the crowd.

"I am here on her behalf," Trinati said. "We will give a warning. An ultimatum."

Cimree felt a surge of hate coming from Azra. Glancing at him, she saw his eyes fixed with malice on Trinati.

Murmurs of assent came from those gathered. The angel sworn were nodding in agreement.

Cimree was not sure of the significance. An ultimatum to do what?

Trinati raised her voice. "This island belongs to the angel sworn. We've allowed some mortals to share it with us by their strict adherence to our ways. These newcomers have defied us. I've spoken with the curia regis, and she wants the rabble ousted as well."

"What of the gévaudan?" a woman shouted.

"We destroy them. But we must preserve our authority here on Montheron. That is what the Queen Mother would wish."

Feelings of folly and bemusement came from Azra, and Cimree saw him shake his head.

"What would you do?" she whispered to him.

"We should abandon the fortress," he whispered back. "Let them pillage the food and the stores. You can't eat stone when all the bread is gone. They'll leave of their own accord if we just withdraw and come back later. But she won't. She will never abandon it. She cannot."

"Why don't you suggest it?" Cimree asked.

"I already know what's going to happen. They wouldn't listen to me yesterday. She won't heed me today. Some things can only be learned through suffering."

"Then I'll suggest it," Cimree said, feeling her heart sizzle with heat.

"You have hardly more standing than I do," he said mockingly.

"But someone should say it. Someone should plant the idea."

"A seed only grows if you don't crush it."

"Captain Odeon. Deliver the orders." Trinati folded her arms.

Captain Odeon straightened. "I've gathered the angel sworn from throughout the interlake region. We have a full garrison. If they rush the gates, we will attack and defend ourselves. I will deliver the warning personally. Be on the ready. More may be on their way."

She heard Azra snort.

"Wisdom and patience and temperance," Captain Odeon said. "Secure the fortress."

There were murmurs of assent. When the others began to disperse, Trinati approached Cimree and Azra, looking Azra in the eye.

"Go to the armory."

"You're really going to kill them *all*, Trinati?" he asked in a low voice.

She looked unmoved. "If they do not obey, they will perish. The decision is theirs."

And that's when Cimree realized what was about to happen. And why Trinati was sending Azra to the armory.

He was the angel of death.

EIGHTEEN

IN THE SHADOWS

"Wegner, may I speak with you?" Cimree asked in a low voice. Azra had left for the armory to fulfill Trinati's command, and Cimree could feel him walking, could sense his presence even at a distance, as well as the dark emotions he grappled with. He didn't want to be Trinati's tool of vengeance. He resented it.

"I have a few moments to spare," Wegner said, giving her a worried look. She saw the situation was weighing heavily on him as well. "Then I need to meet with Captain Odeon to discuss different ways of fortifying the gates. Let's talk in that alcove." He directed her to one of them while the murmur of voices echoed through the great hall.

Once they achieved some privacy in the nook, Cimree looked him in the eye. "Why don't we just leave Montheron?"

His brow wrinkled. "The Queen Mother would want us to try and help and not leave Odeon to handle this alone."

"No, that's not what I meant. What if all the angel sworn left? What if we abandoned the fortress completely? Let them have it."

His brow furrowed even more. "They would ransack it,

Cimree. Down in the town, some are defacing effigies already. They could do much damage. I don't see any good from leaving."

"They're afraid. They're hungry. But once they've eaten all the food, there is nothing left but shelter. They'll leave. Wouldn't that be a more peaceful way to resolve the situation?"

"Is this your idea, or did it come from Azra?"

"Does it matter where the idea came from if it is a sensible one?"

"That's a valid point, Cimree. But Montheron has never been abandoned. We built this fortress to protect the entrance to the valley of Clairvaux. It is a symbol of our people. We've permitted the earthborn to dwell among us if they abide by our ways. They are in rebellion. I think we've been patient so far, but there are limits."

"But what is happening out in the interlake region? Isn't this different? They're terrified of monsters."

"There are no monsters, Cimree. It is natural to fear what we don't understand. Now, I think it best if I meet with the captain and discuss defenses."

"Wegner," she said, catching him by the sleeve as he turned. "I'm bound to Azra by the Tanaquil amulet. I can feel what he feels. If he slaughters these people, I ... I don't think I can continue to do so. I'm a healer."

He gave her an understanding smile. "That amulet is more powerful than you comprehend, Cimree. It can banish *any* emotion. Trinati is not acting rashly in this case."

"Who says I'm acting rashly?" Trinati said, suddenly appearing next to them. "Did Azra say so?"

Cimree had wanted to avoid a confrontation with the archangel. She'd hoped to have persuaded Wegner, but he was equally determined not to abandon the fortress he had helped design.

"No," Cimree replied. "I was just discussing something that—"

"What did that rogue have to say?" Trinati demanded.

Cimree didn't want to tell her. It wouldn't do any good, and Trinati looked aggravated enough. "It's nothing."

Trinati scowled with displeasure.

"He suggested abandoning Montheron to the mortals," Wegner said.

Trinati grunted. "Of course his natural instinct would be to abandon something. Cimree, be cautious. You do not know the full facts of the situation. He has his own motives. That hasn't changed. I learned from Captain Odeon this morning that one of his lieutenants, Andrin, left Montheron last night with his family."

Cimree's eyes widened with shock.

"So you didn't know. Azra persuaded one of Odeon's trusted men to abandon his post during a serious conflict. I will not take counsel from a traitor. And neither should you. He will do as I command. You will see to it. Is that clear?"

"Yes, Trinati," Cimree said, her emotions buzzing with confusion. Azra had been with her the entire time. Hadn't Andrin turned Azra in when he'd gone to his home? But what if they'd made an agreement? She felt angry thinking she'd been duped or deceived by him.

Trinati put her hand on Wegner's shoulder. "There's more news as well. Some strange creature was seen in the town last night. Several witnesses saw it, but none were angel sworn."

"What kind of creature?" Wegner asked.

"Let's talk privately," Trinati said, giving Cimree a dismissing look. "It has no skin and climbed the walls like a spider."

The image Cimree's mind tried to conjure made her intensely curious, but she'd been sent away, so she left the great hall and its enormous stained-glass windows. She was about to ask someone for directions to the armory, but she sensed Azra's presence some distance away and followed her instincts to where he was.

The armory was a hive of activity with hammers clanging on metal and angel sworn coming in and out to retrieve gear, and the bustle, mixed with the heat of the forge, had Cimree quickly starting to perspire. She found Azra immediately, talking to a huge man who had the biggest arm muscles she'd ever seen. He was a giant compared to her.

Azra wasn't wearing armor, not in the traditional sense. He had added a cloak, but it didn't cover the shoulder guards made of thick leather and decorated with intricate designs. He had two swords strapped to his back and a long dagger at his waist, along with a small hunting bow and a quiver. Leather bracers were strapped to his forearms, and scabbard straps crisscrossed his chest over his dove-colored shirt. He looked younger still, his previously gray-and-white hair darkening by the hour. As soon as she walked in and noticed him, he turned and glanced at her, his expression stern.

She approached the two men, feeling emboldened.

"I thought you were supposed to get armor," Cimree told him, squinting at his new attire. He looked better suited to the woods than the stronghold.

"He was the captain of the Long Patrol," the bigger man said with a smirk. "They don't wear heavy armor. But he doesn't need to. He's faster than an asp viper. My name is Uorsin. You're the healer who came with Trinati's mission?"

Cimree nodded. The clanging noise was rattling her nerves. "Do you have all you need?" she asked Azra.

"I need a distaff. But I imagine Trinati is holding that privilege until later."

"Can we go?" she said, although her tone implied a command.

Azra looked back at Uorsin. "Good to see you, old friend."

Uorsin gave a lopsided smile. "I've heard that amulet is heavy to bear."

Azra gave him a knowing look. "You've no idea." Then he turned his gaze to Cimree and nodded that he was ready to leave.

Anxious to be gone, Cimree walked out of the armory and was

grateful for the cool breeze. She certainly did not have an affinity for blacksmithing. The constant noise had rattled her.

When they'd gone a little way, she stopped alongside the fortress wall and turned to face Azra. "Did you help Andrin leave Montheron?"

"Not exactly."

"Explain."

"Cimree, I broke free in *order* to warn him. I demanded that he turn me in and then gather his family. And I told him where to find shelter."

"But that is dishonorable."

"I did so because I didn't want him or his family to die. When the riots start, they're going to go after those loyal to the angel sworn first, starting with those who live below the walls. Everyone should leave Montheron."

"Wegner said we shouldn't abandon what is ours."

"And Trinati told you to stop listening to me," he said.

She wrinkled her brow. "How did y—?"

"I know her, Cimree. I've known her since she was a little girl and was gifted to Clairvaux by her parents. I've watched her and studied her and know her temperament. Her perseverance. Her drive. Her unwillingness to be deterred. It is, you may have guessed, similar to *mine*. But she can only think like the Queen Mother. She's determined to *be* like her, to *think* like her, so much so that it makes her every decision as transparent as glass."

"And you think she's wrong."

"I know she is. I don't think anyone who stays here is going to survive."

"Except the angel sworn. Is that what you mean?"

He shook his head no. "You've already brought proof that we're equally vulnerable. I just wonder how many people will have to die before the Queen Mother begins to believe in her own fallibility."

Cimree glanced up as an angel sworn swooped overhead, then

watched as he quickly plummeted down near them. He was a quick, lithe fellow with a hawk nose. "Trinati needs to see you both at once."

Cimree nodded and began to walk back up the road toward the steps leading to the great hall. Azra fell in beside her, saying nothing.

It bothered her that, though his words made so much sense, she was powerless to change anyone's mind about it. Was that one of the feelings in the mixture she sensed from him? Impotence. He recognized the danger that others rejected. And because he had forsaken his oaths, no one would believe him ever again.

It made her wonder whether the oaths were even in her best interest.

They hadn't made it to the great hall before Captain Odeon blocked their path. He looked furious. His eyes raked Azra's face and then settled on Cimree's.

"Both of you are needed."

Cimree bit her lip. Had the command been given? Was Azra to begin killing the people at the gates? She nodded.

Captain Odeon withdrew a distaff and handed it to Azra with a look of great reluctance. "Come with me. We're going to fly down into the town."

"Where are we going?"

"The curia regis's home." He continued to look at Cimree. "I hear your grafting is questionable with fowl."

"It's rather pathetic actually," Azra said, which made Cimree glare at him.

The captain grimaced. "Come with me."

Cimree shot another fiery glance at Azra, but he just looked at her stone-faced. His expression seemed to be saying, *But it's true.*

The captain took them far from the main gate and along the battlement walls, heading on a path downward. They passed sentinels on high alert, holding exquisite longbows, with baskets of arrows at the ready. The sentinels were fixed on watching the rooftops lower down. Captain Odeon led the way, walking instead of flying. The walls curved around the slope of the massive rock island. Eventually, it led to a small porter door embedded into the stone and guarded by three angel sworn.

As the captain arrived, they saluted him and then unlocked the door.

Captain Odeon peered outside into a small alley before motioning for them to follow him. The stench of human waste reached Cimree's nose, making her frown. She hadn't known about another door leading into the town and imagined the townsfolk didn't know of it either. The door was thick and bulky but much smaller than the main gate.

Before they reached the street, Odeon paused at the wall. There was an iron ring and a dead torch there. He twisted the torch slightly then pulled on the ring, and she heard a snicking noise. The wall opened inward. Odeon motioned for them to go in first, and once they did, he joined them, then pushed the wall back into place. They were smothered in darkness until the captain removed a glowing vial, which illuminated their faces.

"Where are we?" Cimree asked.

"This is the curia regis's home," Odeon said softly. "Her name was Maren. She was found dead several hours ago, and it took a long time before word could reach me because of the conflict at the gate."

Azra sighed and shook his head.

"How did she die?" Cimree asked.

"I hoped you could tell us," Captain Odeon said to her.

NINETEEN
FOUL CREATURES

A shiver went down Cimree's back as they cautiously entered the curia regis's dwelling. It was a modest home built of timbers and plaster. The plaster was ravaged with claw marks, while broken crockery and overturned pots debased the kitchen. Blood stained the floor in small puddles and smears, and the smell of urine and blood was oppressive.

"This way," Captain Odeon said. They'd entered from the back door of the dwelling, and he led them to the front door, where lay the woman's corpse.

Azra crouched by it, examining the body briefly before turning his gaze on the door. He began to search the scene.

The mewling of a cat sounded from the stairs, snatching Cimree's attention. It was a little one, and it poked its head through the rails as it looked at them and gave a pathetic cry. It was probably the lone witness of what had happened.

Summoning her courage, Cimree crouched by the curia regis's body and began to examine the injuries. Images of Milena came to mind, but this attack was different. There were lacerations—plenty of them—but not as deep. It did not look like a bear attack—the wounds were from a smaller creature. One with claws.

Azra stalked back and forth across the room.

"Is this similar to the attacks in Clairvaux?" Captain Odeon asked.

"No," Cimree answered. "It's a different creature entirely."

"A wolf?"

"Wolves go for the throat," Azra said. "Or attack the legs."

"Most of the wounds are on her arms, chest, and face," Cimree said, and she agreed with Azra's assessment. "She wasn't killed instantly. It was ... prolonged." The thought of the curia regis trapped in her own home during the attack was terrifying.

Azra went back to the kitchen. "This is where it started. It looked like she was making food. Dinner perhaps? When was the last time you heard from her?"

"She'd sent a report about the newest refugees and the lack of space for them. That was early in the evening. I imagine she was very busy."

"So it's likely she was gone for most of the day," Azra said.

"But how did it get inside?" Captain Odeon demanded. "The front door was locked. The back door wasn't, but it was closed when she was found. It almost looks like a grimalkin savaged her."

"What's that?" Cimree asked.

"That's what we call the feral cats who feed on the dead. But judging by the size of the wounds, it doesn't seem like a cat from Montheron did this. Plus, it would have no way to get inside."

"When Milena was killed, the door was smashed open," Cimree said.

"This wasn't the Fear Liath," Azra said.

"I know," Cimree agreed.

"She was trying to escape." Azra continued. "There's blood on the door handle. She'd dragged herself there. You can see the trail plainly. Then she was attacked again right there. She used her arms to try and protect herself, hence the ripped tunic and marks. It didn't go for the kill right away. It was ... playing. Like a cat."

"That's horrible," Cimree whispered.

"So I repeat. How did it get in?"

"I'll check upstairs," Azra said.

"You think it came from an upper window? How?" Odeon said with frustration in his voice.

"I don't know," Azra replied, shrugging. "The attack started there," he pointed to the kitchen. "There are bloodstains on the furniture over here. See the toppled vase? Then the curia regis dragged herself to the door and was killed."

"Surely she would have shrieked," Odeon said.

"We're closer to the front gates, and you can hear the mob outside," Azra said. "But she may not have screamed. Sometimes, when terror hits, it robs the victim of speech. She might have been too scared to cry out." He started for the stairs.

Cimree's stomach had shriveled with fear. She examined the wounds again and noticed a new detail. The bloodstained tunic revealed hidden damage. The monster had begun to devour internal organs first. What animal left its prey only partially devoured?

"Wait," she called out. Azra paused halfway up the stairs.

Captain Odeon looked at her with curiosity.

"What if it's still here?" Cimree asked.

As she gazed up at Azra, she noticed the glowing eyes of the cat. Only, it was no longer the size of a cat. It had transformed into a larger animal with sleek gray fur and savage fangs. Its tail swished with menace. The feline face had also changed, showing an almost human quality. It leaped at Azra with a hiss.

The grimalkin landed on him, ripping into him with its front and rear claws, which looked more like a hawk's talons than the needlelike claws of a cat.

"By the Mother!" Odeon roared in shock. Azra tumbled down the stairs backward, the beast ravaging him along the way.

Odeon ripped his celestial iron blade from his sheath, and the glow of the metal reflected in the predator's baleful eyes as they widened and locked on to the weapon. The beast vaulted away from Azra and launched itself at Odeon, yowling and hissing and slashing at him. He tried to swing at it, but the creature was fast and came up his arm. One swipe at Odeon's face sent ribbons of blood spraying. He roared in pain and tried grabbing the grimalkin to pull it away.

Azra was on his feet, blade in one hand and a distaff in the other. Cimree saw the wounds weeping blood onto his tunic, but his grimace was one of rage that she could feel burning. Odeon grasped some fur with his free hand and tried to yank it away, but the talons had pierced his chain-mail tunic, and it clung to him, impervious to his efforts to dislodge it. He dropped his sword as it was useless in such close range and tried using both hands, but the grimalkin quickly went around him, clinging to his back as it bit against his scalp.

Cimree drew her dirk and watched as Azra feinted at it with his sword. With it clinging so closely to Odeon, there was a risk of hitting the captain as well.

"Get it off!" Odeon roared, twisting one way and then another. He protected his head with a hand and yelled when sharp fangs bit through it.

Azra grunted and thrust out with the sword, hitting the creature with the point, nearly skewering it. Azra yanked the blade back, and the yowl of pain that followed was a sound that would haunt Cimree's dreams. The claws retracted and the creature fell to the floor. Then its moon-glowing eyes turned on Azra, and it launched at him next. What should have been a mortal wound hadn't stopped it.

Azra dodged as the beast flew at him, and it landed a few feet away, only to turn and vault at him again, hissing with malice. The warrior had imbued himself with grafting magic, and his reflexes were even faster than his above-average normal state. He landed another hacking blow against it with his blade, but it didn't seem to do much damage.

Captain Odeon bent down and retrieved his sword. His lips moved in a murmur as he held his distaff in his other hand.

The beast feinted and managed to snag Azra's cloak with its claws, clinging on and swiping at his ribs with another paw. Azra grunted in pain, twirled, and loosed the clasp at his neck, causing the creature to fall to the ground, the cloak shrouding its figure.

Both Azra and Odeon stabbed at it with their blades, piercing the cloak with the tips of their swords. The creature struggled and writhed beneath the fabric, but it wasn't dying. There was an unnatural vitality to it.

It finally freed itself from the cloak and launched at Odeon again, but he was faster this time and dodged it. Seeing Cimree, it hissed and charged her next. In the panic of the moment, she hadn't even thought to use her distaff.

Reflex took over. She'd never trained in the arts of war, but she had her dirk in her hand and she used it, her instincts suddenly flooding inside her. Like a snake's fang, she plunged the dirk into the grimalkin's neck. The claws ripped through her tunic, scoring her flesh as it yowled in pain, the sound and pitch different than before. A stinging pain bloomed in her.

Then Azra plunged his own dirk into the creature's spine and it went instantly still. The talons retracted, and it slumped to the ground, wheezing twice before stilling.

Odeon was panting and was about to plunge his sword into the creature, but Azra shoved the captain back.

"No!" Azra warned. "Celestial iron doesn't hurt it."

"How can that be?" Odeon said, breathing hard. He winced with pain.

"I don't know," Azra said. "It should have died multiple times. But the dirk caused it pain."

The creature began to shrink, to convulse, to transform back into its previous form. It lay still. What sort of magic had caused this transformation to happen? It had swelled to several times its natural size before reverting back. That was not grafting magic. It was something else entirely.

"What was that thing?" Cimree said, feeling the stings from her wounds growing sharper with the danger of the fight gone.

"It's not a creature from the natural world," Azra said. "I've never seen or heard of such a thing."

"The wildness of it," Odeon said, nodding in agreement. "It cannot be from this world, can it? It's like a grimalkin that is crazed."

"We don't know," Azra said. "But it killed the curia regis. I've no doubt on that score. And she would have been quite helpless against such ferocity."

"And it was already inside," Odeon said. "But surely it wasn't always this way."

Cimree agreed with his observation, as her heart finally began to settle down. She was relieved that she'd been able to injure it. A regular weapon. Not celestial iron.

"Something changed it," she said, looking at the captain and then at Azra.

"She's right," Azra said. "It's also not an accident that it started here at the curia regis's home. It's possible it is random, but I don't think so. Killing the curia regis will cause all sorts of harm. She was targeted."

"That means someone is behind these attacks," Odeon said thoughtfully. "Someone is causing these mutations."

"It took three of us to kill it," Azra said. "If Cimree hadn't wounded it first, it might have killed us all."

She hadn't even thought of that, and his acknowledgment of her help, even if it was unwittingly done, caused a little ripple of warmth inside her.

"As soon as it saw my weapon, it attacked me," Odeon said. "Was it drawn to the iron?"

"A moth to the flame," Azra said. "But in this case, it kills."

"The Queen Mother needs to know about this," the captain said. "There isn't just one creature. There are many."

"You've sent your defenders to hunt down the gévaudan," Azra said. "They might not be so easy to kill."

Odeon massaged his brow and winced. His cheek was still bleeding.

"Let me help," Cimree offered. "I can clean the wounds."

He shook his head. "We need to go back to the citadel. Trinati needs to know. We could gather some normal arrows instead of the ones with celestial iron tips. There are far fewer of those, however."

"This was no accident," Azra insisted. "The curia regis was targeted. I'm sure of it. The fear and swelling number of refugees are part of something bigger."

"I worry you're right," Odeon said. "We need to determine who is behind it. Who is causing these mutations? It is like grafting magic ... but twisted."

"Captain, we should evacuate Montheron," Azra said forcefully. "We should get everyone out."

"We can't bring them all to Clairvaux, Azra. And I won't abandon my post."

"But what if abandoning it is how you save everyone, Odeon? This may not be a game we can win."

"Who do you think is doing this? Surely you must suspect someone."

"I don't. And that terrifies me. I've been locked in that cell far too long."

Cimree gazed at him and she felt his heart. He was worried. He was afraid. But most importantly, he cared about the people who had fled to Montheron for protection. And he knew he couldn't protect them.

Cimree heard a purring sound. They all did and gazed down in surprise at the kitten. Its tail twitched.

TWENTY
CONFUSION

"Did you just *leave* the mewling cat there?" Trinati asked in dismay.

Captain Odeon sat on a chair while Cimree knelt nearby and worked to scrub clean his wounds. She felt the sting of her own still, but hers were not as grievous as the captain of Montheron's.

"Would you rather we brought it with us?" Azra asked mockingly.

"Did you leave it or no. Just answer the question!"

Odeon's voice was layered with fatigue. "We found a chest and locked it inside. Whether it will hold, I don't know. But our weapons seemed unable to kill it."

They were in the infirmary within the fortress, and several others were being treated for injuries—most caused by scuffles with the crowds.

"Looking at the damage done to all of you, I would never have supposed a cat capable of such violence." Trinati was pacing, her eyes feverish with the news they'd brought her. Wegner was there as well and looked equally disturbed. Trinati turned to him. "What do you make of all this?"

"I've never heard of such magic before," Wegner said. "It

caused a transformation into another form and then back again. It is a grafting of form. Fascinating."

"But who is behind it?" Trinati asked. "I agree with Azra that the focus of these attacks cannot be random. Nature did not make these creatures."

Wegner nodded in agreement. "There was also the report of seeing a different sort of creature climbing the walls. This feline threat you faced ... that seemed of a smaller order."

Odeon chuffed. "None of our angel sworn saw it. Imagination and fear can distort what is reality."

"But they cannot overturn truth," Trinati said. "There is an answer to these questions. And we must persist until we discover it. What we face here in Montheron is but a shadow of what will happen in Clairvaux."

"Now you begin to understand," Azra said.

Captain Odeon winced and twisted his back, then he gave Cimree a grateful look and a nod. "Thank you. I must resume my duties." One of the other healers had already brought him a clean tunic, without the claw marks and blood. As he put it on, she saw him grimace again.

"Are you in much pain?" Cimree asked. "I have some edelweiss. That could help."

"I will be fine," he said. "But thank you for offering." He rose from the chair, twisting again.

"You look awful," Trinati said to him.

"It was unpleasant to say the least," Odeon said. "Not injuries to boast of at any rate. The people have cause to fear. My soldiers are keeping alert for other grimalkin, but I don't think we should add to their terror by issuing ultimatums."

"I'll consider your advice," Trinati said, which Cimree took to mean she was still determined to keep them away from the fortress.

The captain gave her a nod and left the infirmary, pausing to thank the healers hard at work there. Cimree saw that he was a kind-hearted person, even if he was a stern one.

Trinati turned to Azra. "Your injuries aren't bothering you?"

"I've had worse," he said with a shrug.

"Still. Have Cimree tend to them." Trinati turned to Wegner. "Go find Darcia. I want a report on what she's learned from the rabble. I need to make a decision before nightfall."

"Of course," Wegner said and left.

Trinati eyed the two of them for a moment and then abandoned the infirmary as well.

"She's wrong," Azra said to Cimree.

"About defending the fortress?"

"She's wrong as to how much time she thinks she has to make a decision. They'll riot long before nightfall."

"How can you be sure?" Cimree demanded.

"Animals do not argue or reason when a threat appears. They flee from it. It is that instinct that preserves the herd or the pack. Every part of me is screaming that we need to fly from Montheron. Now."

"You could have fled earlier," Cimree said. "Why didn't you?"

"Because I care about the herd," he said. "It is also my instinct to protect them."

❧❦❧

Several hours passed. Azra ate twice more, and Cimree watched as the gray in his hair continued to melt away, replaced by dark locks. His injuries closed on their own because the magic of the Gallows Tree working to reverse his age also accelerated his healing. He showed her the various parts of the fortress, the giant wheel that was used to haul supplies up to the battlements, powered by humans walking inside its rim. He described the attack by the Vikander and how they had almost overrun the island's defenders because the Queen Mother had called for a solstice celebration, which had coincided with the attack. She also saw a number of gray herons flying by, which were the original denizens of the island rock for which the fortress was named and provided to many of the defenders the power to fly long distances. She asked Azra if his affinity was for the birds, but he said it was not and refused to speak more on it.

From the heights, they could see the rooftops of the dwellings farther down, speckled with bird droppings. The harbor was clogged with boats and rafts as more people continued to arrive. They were swarming the island, and the ruckus they made caused feelings of vulnerability within her. How many were sick or injured? She wanted to help and use her skills to alleviate the suffering, but she also knew that the people were half mad with worry and fear.

As they walked back toward the entrance of the fortress, Cimree noticed Darcia hurrying their way, and once she'd drawn near, she saw that her expression was pale with concern.

"Captain Odeon is very sick," she said. "He collapsed and was brought back to the infirmary. Trinati is there and wants you to come at once."

Surely there were more proficient healers among the angel sworn of Montheron. "Of course," she replied, feeling more than a little inadequate. Her concern for Captain Odeon made worry and dread blossom within her.

"He looked very bad when I saw him," Darcia said. "Didn't you treat his wounds earlier?"

"I did. I didn't think they were that serious."

"Well, you are inexperienced." Darcia sighed.

Cimree bristled at the condescending tone.

"What have you learned from your visits to the town?" Azra asked Darcia.

She gave him a wary look. "The streets are clogged with people. It smells awful. Some shops tried to close, but the people broke open the doors. They're nearly out of food despite the kitchens up here working day and night. Some people are saying that there's plenty of food up here and they should just smash the gates."

Azra sighed.

"We're not going to surrender the fortress," Darcia said. "I know that's what *you* want."

"You have no idea what I want." Azra seethed at her.

"Let's not argue," Cimree said, feeling even more uneasy. She quickened her pace toward the infirmary. She was still getting used to having access to Azra's cynical emotions, and they were beginning to blur with her own. She knew there was a way to tamp them down or contain them, but she felt uneasy about compelling anyone else's feelings.

"You're so sensitive," Darcia said to Cimree with a look of disdain before hurrying off ahead.

Cimree felt a surge of animosity, and knowing it would lead to another of Azra's outbursts, she gave him a warning look not to speak.

He saw the look. And he didn't speak after Darcia was gone.

When they reached the infirmary, it was even busier than before. Instead of a chair, Captain Odeon was laid out on a treatment table, beneath a pile of blankets. His skin was mottled and she saw blisters near the scratch marks on his bare arms and chest. His breathing was troubled, and he wasn't lucid. Three other healers were there, each looking confused at the symptoms. He looked gravely ill. No—he was dying.

Trinati was standing there, her lips firm and bent in a frown.

The chief healer looked young, but that was no determination of her experience. She looked at Cimree as she paused at the table. "He's been poisoned. We've tried several antidotes, and none have worked."

Cimree knew immediately that it was wrong. She felt it with confidence. "This isn't poison. It's venom."

"Cats don't have venom," the healer said dismissively.

Cimree looked at Trinati. "That was no ordinary cat. These injuries look like he's had a dozen snake bites. The swelling, the blisters near the scratches. Are there any asp vipers on the island?"

"There are none," the healer said, looking offended.

There was a serpent in the cage down in the town, but Cimree thought it imprudent to contradict the master healer.

"If it's venom, what do we do?" Trinati asked.

"He's going to die," Cimree said. "There is too much toxin in him. We need to give him some of the fruit. It will reverse the damage."

"Weren't you and the traitor also attacked?" the healer said forcefully. "You all had claw marks."

"I have immunity to snake venom," Azra said bluntly.

The healer looked incredulous and then shot an accusing look at Cimree.

"I may have it too," she said cautiously. "I've felt a little nauseous, but my injuries were not as severe as Odeon's."

The healer looked at Trinati. "The fruit is the only way. Do we still have the remnant of it?"

Trinati nodded. "Cimree does."

The master healer threw up her hands. "If my experience means anything, there is a chance he will recover on his own."

"He's going to stop breathing soon," Cimree replied forcefully.

"Give him the fruit," Azra said with an edge in his tone.

"And we should listen to you?" the master healer said. Her two underlings looked afraid, but neither were brave enough to speak up against their master. Cimree was grateful that Milena had never acted in such an overbearing way.

"I've heard enough," Trinati said. "There's no time to debate this."

"But she's a novice," the master healer said with scorn.

Trinati gave the master healer a look of disgust. "And she's been right so far. Go help others instead. This is outside your ken."

The master healer stormed away with her two underlings, one of which gave an apologetic look as she left. Trinati nodded at Cimree, who tugged open her pack and pulled out the bag holding the remainder of the purplish fruit. After tugging on the strings, she opened it and revealed the remainder of the purplish fruit. The fragrance from it was strong. It was beginning to rot. Once the peel had been tampered with, the decay began immediately.

"Will it be enough?" Trinati asked.

"I think so," Cimree answered. She was grateful that Azra had not eaten the entire fruit and rendered himself an infant. Cimree examined it and smelled it.

"Is it still good?" Trinati whispered.

"I'll cut part of it away," Cimree said. She withdrew her dirk and used the tip to peel the fruit. She cut away the parts that had touched Azra's lips. The core seed within it was stringy and dense, so Cimree shaved away the fruit.

"Hand me the seed," Trinati said. There was a rite required to destroy the seeds of the Gallows Tree. Cimree had a feeling from Azra and saw his eyes fixed on the seed. His emotion was difficult to identify but it felt like ... hope.

Trinati took the peel and seed and stuffed them back into the bag, which she secured to her belt. Her eyes flickered to Azra's and something unspoken passed between them.

Cimree took the wedge of fruit and pressed on Odeon's cheeks to open his jaw. She slid the fruit into his mouth and he reacted, his involuntary chewing reflexes triggered. His eyelids fluttered a moment and then remained closed. Cimree watched his throat for the swallow reflex that followed.

Cimree was satisfied that the fruit was inside him. As his body digested it, the fruit would begin to reverse his aging. She smoothed the hair from Odeon's brow and felt a little surge of feeling from Azra, which confused her again. The annoying tangling of their feelings was frustrating.

"I think he'll recover now," Cimree said.

"Trinati!"

The yell came from an armored angel sworn who was pushing

her way through the crowd toward them. She arrived moments later, her eyes intense.

"Yes, Luzia?" Trinati said.

"They're rioting at the gate," she snarled with fury. "A group of *men* are trying to break it down! Do we have orders to shoot them?"

A surge of despair exuded from Cimree and Azra's connection. Just as he had predicted, the riot had started before nightfall. Long before. That meant Trinati would have to make a decision. And he knew he'd be the sword of her vengeance.

"Pull the angel sworn to the upper gates," Trinati said. "Abandon the lower one."

"What!" Luzia shouted in outrage.

"You heard my command," Trinati said. She locked gazes with first Azra and then Cimree and raised her chin as acceptance, or was it resignation, shone in her eyes. She gave a sharp nod. "We need time to prepare to evacuate."

Hearken and know wisdom. The earth, after it was formed, was empty and desolate, because the Oldknow had not formed anything but the earth. Darkness reigned upon the face of the deep, and the compassion of the Oldknow brooded upon the face of the waters. The Oldknow took clay from the hand of the chief of the angel sworn and made the First Woman according to the patterned image and likeness, and the Oldknow left her lying for forty days and forty nights without putting breath into her. And the Oldknow heaved sighs over her daily, saying, "If I put breath into her, she must suffer many pains." And the archangel said unto the Oldknow, "Put breath into her; I will be an advocate for her." And the Oldknow said, "If I put breath into her, cherished one, thou wilt be obliged to go down into the world and to suffer many pains for her before thou shalt have redeemed her and made her to come back to her primal state." And the archangel said unto the Oldknow, "Put breath into her; I will be her advocate, and I will go down into the world, and I will fulfill Thy command." And the Oldknow said, "I will make for thee a Gallows Tree to conquer death, to provide time to perform this redemption."

— ORIGIN, THE TALE OF THE QUEEN MOTHER
OF CLAIRVAUX

Twenty-One

Fallen Angels

"Since you knew this would happen, what do you think will happen next?" Cimree asked Azra as they remained at Odeon's sickbed. Trinati had left to issue commands and prepare the evacuation of Montheron. Cimree's orders had been to remain with the injured captain and see to his care and revival. There was little she could do. The fruit of the Gallows Tree would perform this miracle.

Azra had refused the proffered chair and was pacing restlessly. He didn't answer her.

"Tell me," she urged. The master healer kept scowling at her, so she repositioned her chair to avoid her contemptuous looks.

"I'm surprised Trinati is even considering abandoning Montheron," Azra said brusquely. "But will she also abandon Clairvaux? I don't think so."

"But the mountains will protect us surely!"

He gave her an incredulous look. "They didn't protect against the Fear Liath."

"But it can be destroyed."

"You're certain of that?"

"I'm certain we'll discover a way."

"And I'm equally certain that there won't be enough time before Clairvaux falls. Look how quickly the situation changed here. Look how quickly the people went from being docile and subservient to charging the gates. How much time do you think we have?"

"I can hear in your voice that it's not enough."

"Do you think I'm toying with you?" he said angrily. "Our survival depends on dispersing. I'm grateful Trinati realizes the danger she's facing here. But it only postpones the reckoning. Do you actually think the Queen Mother will leave Clairvaux? She won't!"

"Maybe she can't," Cimree objected. "She has never ventured into the fallen world."

"Oh, she can," Azra insisted.

"How do you know?"

"She's told me. She was given a choice. To become mortal. Or to remain in Clairvaux. Her obstinacy and her choice prevent her from leaving. Nothing else. There is no ancient law binding her to the valley."

"Why would she tell you this?"

"She told me this and more. She confided in me. Long ago. I was one of her chief lieutenants. I was equal to Trinati in affection and trust."

"But you turned against her."

"It wasn't like that," Azra said with a growl.

"But you did revolt. You forsook your oath."

"I did."

Cimree shook her head. "Why?"

"You wouldn't understand."

"How do you know I won't?"

He stepped closer to her, his chin lifting defiantly. "Because you're innocent. And I'm tethered to you like a dog."

"I never wanted this, Azra."

"But you chose it."

"You chose it as well. You refused to be bound to anyone else."

He held out his hands. "I was surrounded by angel sworn who have been trained to hate me. I was cornered. And I thought you would be less inclined to torture me than any of the others because of your innocence. But I'm still a slave. And you hold the key to my cage." He tapped his chest where the amulet was resting beneath his tunic.

"What would you do if I let you go right now," Cimree asked him.

"I would fly away and get as far from these mountains as I could as quickly as I could."

She leaned forward. "Where would you go?"

He shook his head.

"Tell me!"

"To what purpose? I know a place where I could be safe. Far, far away. And I would ride out the storm and let these creatures destroy themselves." She felt something stir within him. His anger was a shock against her emotions, but this feeling ... it was a mixture of grief and longing and hope. This was a place he cared about more than anything.

"Where is this place?"

"It doesn't matter. We cannot go there."

"Why can't we go there?"

"Because the Queen Mother destroyed it," he said, his eyes flashing with rage. "She destroyed the people who lived there. Everyone. They were wiped out." His emotions burned so hot they were like flames in her mind. "But it's still there. And it could shelter us against these creatures. But the Queen Mother will not forsake the valley. She'd die first. And she will. And all of us will suffer the same fate. That's what's coming next, Cimree. We are *all* going to die."

"Then you must persuade her."

It was Captain Odeon who said the words. Cimree started

with surprise, seeing him lying there, color finally starting to appear in his ashen cheeks. His serious gaze was fixed on Azra.

Azra snorted. "You know as well as I that she's incapable of admitting when she's wrong."

"How are you feeling?" Cimree asked, brushing the back of her hand against Captain Odeon's forehead.

"Much improved," he said. "I'm very hungry. That means I've had some of the fruit?"

Cimree nodded. "We gave you the rest of it."

She heard the gurgle in his stomach and suppressed an involuntary smile.

"What happened to me? I passed out. The pain was terrible."

"That grimalkin creature had venom," Azra said. "The healers were doing it all wrong until Cimree came."

Odeon tried to sit up but only managed a groan.

"Let me bring you some food," Cimree suggested.

"I need to return to my post," he said. "But I do need to eat. It's a rather desperate feeling at the moment."

"I understand your pangs," Azra said with a smile.

Odeon tried again to rise and with help from both of them was able to sit up and swing his legs over the edge of the bed. He glanced at the nearby window. "How long have I been unconscious?"

"Several hours," Cimree said. "The venom was about to stop your heart."

He looked at her seriously and then nodded. "Thank you, Cimree."

Azra folded his arms. "That's not even the best part, Odeon. Trinati is preparing to evacuate Montheron."

His eyes widened. "I need to talk to her."

"The efforts are underway. You won't be able to persuade her. They started rioting at the gate. She called a retreat to the upper level."

"I need to get up there," Odeon said. He touched his feet to the floor and tried to support his weight but only began to shake before he slumped back onto the table.

"You need time to recover," Cimree said.

"This fortress and those who live here are my responsibility," he said with a grunt of pain.

"Ah, but you're just a man," Azra scoffed. "You only have delegated authority."

"Delegated or not, the people are afraid and need help."

"At the moment, they don't see it in the same light," Azra said. "How much of what we talked about did you overhear?"

"I know most of it already, Azra. And you are right. The Queen Mother will not be easily persuaded. But I believe she will prevail in this conflict. She *can* be persuaded. I've seen it."

"You've only seen what she wants you to see, Captain. I've seen her in public with her generous manners and wisdom. But I've also seen her in other places where she is her normal self. She won't leave Clairvaux. And she won't allow anyone else to either. Prove me wrong."

"I intend to," Odeon said. He sighed and looked at Cimree. "I need food. And I need to see Trinati. Can you help me?"

"Azra will get you the food," Cimree said, looking at the man bonded to her.

He arched his eyebrows. "Is that your order?"

"Stop being difficult," she scolded. "You remember what it's like being that hungry. Now get him some food." She turned back to Odeon and said gently, "I'll go find Trinati and tell her that you're awakened but are still too weak." She gripped his shoulder and gave him an understanding look.

"I don't like feeling this helpless," Odeon said, "but thank you."

Cimree gave Azra a sharp look. "Get going."

"Yes, master," he answered tightly. And he began to walk briskly away. He collided with the master healer who had her back to him, and Cimree felt a flush of gratification when the woman was knocked off balance. He'd done it deliberately.

"I've seen Azra eat because of the hunger. He'll bring plenty of food."

"I fear I could eat an entire round of cheese by myself," Odeon grunted.

"I'll find Trinati," Cimree said. She gazed at the wounds on his cheeks. They'd already shrunk and retained no unhealthy warning signs. "The scratches are fading already."

"Thank you again, Cimree. Milena trained you well."

Cimree felt pleasure at the praise, but also the pain of poking a too-recent wound. "I'll hurry." She started to leave and then paused and turned. "Do you know where Azra went? The location he mentioned that was so far away?"

Odeon nodded. "I don't know where it is exactly. I know the Queen Mother's vengeance was justified. The people of that region murdered angel sworn. Azra was sent to observe them. Learn their weaknesses. Their traditions. He was captured by them. They tortured him."

"They didn't kill him? Why?"

The captain chuckled. "He became one of them. Mastered their language. The nuances of their beliefs. He earned their trust."

"And the Queen Mother destroyed them?"

Odeon nodded. "She did. They were our enemies."

"How did Azra gain their trust? How is that even possible?"

"He did what no other angel sworn would have done. He became part of their tribe."

"How?"

"He married one of them."

Cimree's jaw fell open. "So he *is* a fallen angel."

"That's not how *he* sees it," Odeon said. "But yes. He is."

"I've never heard of such a thing," Cimree whispered.

"It happens. Rarely. Celibacy is an ideal, but it is not for every person. Few can adhere to all the oaths we make unless they are trained that way from youth as you have been. The lures of mortal flesh are potent. I don't know why he chose what he did. He's never told me. I think the only one he ever told was the Queen Mother."

Cimree's heart sank. "Thank you for telling me," she said.

"Trinati should have told you before you agreed to wear the amulet. But I suppose she had her reasons for not doing so."

His words, coupled with the look he gave Cimree, made her feel the decision had been deliberate and not an oversight.

TWENTY-TWO
CONFLICTING MOTIVES

Cimree seethed as she climbed the steps to the upper portion of the fortress. Her own emotions roiled with what she'd learned from Captain Odeon. She had been deliberately kept in the dark and thrust into a situation that was deeper and more confusing than she'd imagined. Azra's help was needed, but the Queen Mother was using Cimree as the tool to get what she wanted.

She was so focused on her inner turmoil that she nearly collided with an angel sworn heading down and muttered an apology after earning a curt rebuke from the woman.

What if Azra's fury was valid? What if the Queen Mother was at fault? But that was suspect itself. The Queen Mother was a paragon of the virtues she proclaimed. She had not succumbed to the lures of the flesh despite temptation from a fallen angel who had entreated her in the guise of a serpent. It was Azra who had broken his promises. He'd forsaken immortality to marry. To choose his own wife. There was nothing inherently evil about marriage and children, but the angel sworn lived a higher order. It was not compulsory but a privilege to do so. And with the requirements came the promised rewards of immortality. An angel sworn could live hundreds of lives and learn countless things. In Cimree's mind, the rewards far outweighed the sacrifices.

Yet Azra had chosen it voluntarily. Had he been seduced by evil? Why hadn't they told her? What more weren't they telling her?

She reached the upper hallway and strode down the corridor. She could sense Azra's presence in the kitchens below. His brooding feelings were also lingering in her own heart. But it was a separate part of her. She felt sorry for him. And confused. And she wanted to know more before making up her mind about him.

When she reached Odeon's private study, where they'd held their earlier meeting, she found Trinati conversing with Wegner and Darcia. Trinati's brow wrinkled on seeing Cimree.

"I didn't send for you."

"Captain Odeon is awake," Cimree said, panting, feeling that she'd intruded on a delicate conversation. Wegner looked conflicted, his mouth in a tight frown. Darcia looked frightened.

Trinati nodded. "Is he hale?"

"He's weak, but the fruit has countered the effects of the venom."

Wegner sighed and shook his head.

"What?" Cimree asked.

"Come in and shut the door," Trinati said.

Cimree obeyed, feeling the tension in the room ripple in her stomach. She pressed her hand against her abdomen to try to soothe it.

Trinati looked worried as she spoke. "We opened the gates and the people are flooding through in a panic," Trinati said. "They've already taken over the lower bulwarks and now are trying to force their way into the citadel. The dungeon is overrun."

"They're breaking things, looting things," Wegner said with dissatisfaction. "People are already defacing the stone."

Cimree knew how much he prized the citadel. The damage was causing him grief and anger.

"There aren't enough birds on the island to move us all at once," Trinati said. "We need to stagger the withdrawal. The mortals are in a frenzy. They won't listen to reason."

"Azra said that would happen," Cimree observed.

"How like him to gloat," Trinati snarled. "I may have no choice but to use him to hold back the rabble."

"They're frightened," Cimree objected.

"And they've invaded our sacred precincts," Trinati shot back. "Clearly they weren't frightened *enough* of us. We need more time. Every pigeon, every heron, every creature that can fly is being grafted into service to evacuate Montheron. We'll return to Clairvaux after we've gotten everyone out."

"But what about the mortals here?" Cimree asked.

"There are no good options left," Trinati said gravely. "We cannot bring them to Clairvaux and risk introducing sin to the valley. Will the married renounce their marriages? Entire families have never joined the angel sworn. It's always been just one. Getting them off the island puts them in danger to the gévaudan. And the grimalkin threaten them here. At least they'll be protected behind stone walls."

Trinati was right. There weren't other good options.

"Will you go see Captain Odeon?"

Trinati sighed. "I suppose I must."

"This will not be easy for him to bear," Cimree said.

"You think this is easy for any of us? We've abandoned outposts before when the people were unwilling to heed our ways. But this fortress is unique. It is ours. It is the last bastion before the entrance to the valley. And I'm choosing to surrender it."

Darcia sniffled and wiped a tear. Cimree had forgotten that Darcia used to live on the island. In another lifespan. For an angel sworn, a lifespan was a way of reckoning with the years of the mortal world.

"You've made the right decision," Cimree said as she turned back to Trinati.

"Have I?" It was a rhetorical question. "Tell Captain Odeon that I'll come down to the infirmary as soon as I can. Wegner, see that the doors are locked and keys collected. We'll take them with us. I don't want to make it easy for them to defile this place further."

"What do you want me to do?" Darcia asked in a teary voice.

"Make sure the word has spread. The angel sworn need to gather in the upper courtyard by the chapel."

Wegner nodded obediently and departed the room with Darcia at his heels. Cimree hesitated, seeing how preoccupied Trinati was in her thoughts.

She turned and gave Cimree a disapproving frown. "I gave you your orders."

Cimree stepped forward. "Is it true that Azra forsook the angel sworn for a mortal woman?"

"Yes." Trinati's eyes revealed nothing. Her reply was short and secretive.

"Do you know why?"

Trinati nodded but remained silent.

"I'm bound to him. Should I not be told more?"

"I was commanded not to tell you," Trinati said. "And if I'd foreseen this, I would have commanded Odeon to tell you nothing as well."

"But why?" Cimree objected.

"That is one of your weaknesses, Cimree. It's easy to ask why. It's more important to ask what. What does the Queen Mother want you to do? And then do it. Without hesitation. Without inquiry. The first law of heaven is obedience."

"Well, this is Montheron, not heaven. And I'm a mortal, not a full angel sworn. I don't understand why the Queen Mother wants to keep me ignorant."

"You may ask her when we return. But consider, Cimree. She has been on this world since the Oldknow formed her out of clay. She is more wise and more caring than you can understand. I will not betray her confidence or dodge her orders in order to satisfy your curiosity."

"You sound like you're trying to convince yourself," Cimree said, and she saw that her barb had struck home.

Trinati's frown deepened. "Have a care, little one," she said threateningly.

"I do care," Cimree said. "Maybe I care too much. I don't want to see these people injured or killed. Neither do I want any angel sworn to suffer. But Azra is convinced that fleeing to Clairvaux will end in disaster. That we must abandon these mountains. And he knows of a place far away where we might find shelter."

Trinati's lips wrinkled into a sneer. "If you're trying to persuade me, you're—"

"I'm not!" Cimree shouted. It was improper of her to interrupt someone who was decidedly her superior in every way. Trinati's eyes widened with surprise. And offense.

Cimree tried to calm herself down. Her knees were starting to tremble. "I'm sorry for yelling. I'm trying to be helpful. To provide information so that you can make the best decisions possible. You trusted me in the infirmary, please trust—"

"Because I knew, in that moment, your affinity for serpents gave you insights Master Healer Katarova didn't have. And because I knew Odeon's life was at risk." She stepped forward, her voice dropping lower. "What you are suggesting, what Azra is suggesting, is abandoning Clairvaux and the very tree that grants us immortality. We would *all* become mortal."

"But you have a seed," Cimree said, matching the whisper. "We could plant another tree."

"All seeds must be destroyed," Trinati said.

"But you haven't destroyed it yet."

Trinati gave her a fierce look. "I have not."

"You've already thought of it," Cimree said. "Haven't you?"

Trinati pursed her lips and said nothing. She gave Cimree a dismissive wave.

WAS IT POSSIBLE? Was Trinati considering defying the Queen Mother? All her talk of the Queen Mother's virtues and wisdom. Were they disguising another intention? One that she dared not reveal to anyone else?

Cimree thought on the conversation, the implications of it, while she watched Captain Odeon eat another entire skewer of meat, which Azra had brought from the kitchen. Though the infirmary was no longer as crowded, with the angel sworn readying to leave the island, some of the island's defenders had sustained injuries from the mob, so the healers were hard at work. When Cimree had offered to help, Katarova dismissed her with annoyance, showing she still begrudged Cimree showing her up earlier. That hadn't been Cimree's intention, of course. Even the heavenly host could feel slighted.

The afternoon was fading and Cimree was exhausted. She'd brought some fried cheese and honey from the kitchen, and that had helped revive her, but the threat and danger weighed on her heart. Azra was restless, pacing around the infirmary, always watching and observing the others who came and went.

Trinati arrived, several hours after Cimree had brought her news. She smiled at Captain Odeon and cupped his cheek in a tender gesture.

"Your life is spared," Trinati said.

"And I am grateful," replied the captain. "I was hoping to be able to talk to you."

"Of course. The evacuation is going well. The bulkier doors have stymied the masses for now. They're milling about, trying to figure out who among them they will listen to."

"I would like to remain in Montheron," Captain Odeon said firmly.

Trinati shook her head. "Out of the question."

"Please listen."

Cimree felt a surge of pride that he hadn't just submitted to her.

Trinati's eyes flashed but adopted a patient air, and she inclined her head to invite him to speak.

"This has been my post for centuries. If we all leave, they will believe that the Queen Mother has abandoned them. That we do not fulfill our oaths."

"They are the ones who have forsaken their oaths, Captain."

"I know. But they are mortal. And these dangers are ones that *we* have not faced before. I'll frankly admit I'm unsettled. But in my heart, I do not wish to abandon them to their doom. They will need leadership and guidance. With the curia regis dead, there is no leadership if we go. Permit me to remain and try to calm them."

It was a fair request, and Cimree felt it an honorable one as well. But he had to submit to Trinati's authority. He was bound to her decision.

"Captain, you are too valuable to us to lose."

He gave her a wry look. "I'm not intending to lay my life down, Trinati. After the angel sworn are gone, there will be a void. I will try to persuade them to abandon the fortress and disperse."

"They won't," Azra said.

Trinati shot him an angry look but said nothing.

"But I will try," Odeon said. "Allow me that. I can always rejoin you later."

"I admire your courage, Captain," Trinati said. "But I also value your advice and so will the Queen Mother. I think you should return with us. This will not be the last time you see Montheron."

Azra chuckled under his breath.

"You think the future is hopeless?" Trinati said to him with fire in her eyes.

"What I think does not matter to you," he replied.

"They're over there," Katarova said in a raised voice, pointing a finger at them.

An angel sworn rushed up to them, blood trickling from scratch wounds on his handsome face. Familiar wounds. He looked to be in pain.

"You were attacked," Trinati said, sizing him up.

"We all were," he said, panting. "My lady, the cats are all transforming into monsters. Into beasts. They're killing the townsfolk. You can hear the screams outside!"

TWENTY-THREE
THE RAVAGING OF MONTHERON

"Trinati, we must protect them!" Captain Odeon said forcefully. He tried to rise as if he'd take up a sword himself, even though one of the beasts had nearly killed him.

Trinati gripped his shoulder and pushed him back down. "We'll bring them into the fortress. The gates cannot protect us against these creatures. But stone walls will."

Odeon looked relieved. "We must not abandon them."

"We aren't." Then she turned to Azra. "Earlier I was intending to use you against the rioters. Now I must use you to save them. Your immunity to venom makes you the perfect choice. Go to the armory and take whatever you need. But get down there and start killing these things. Cimree will go down with you."

"She won't be able to help me," Azra said, his tone void of feeling. Cimree knew he was right, but it still stung.

"I'm not sending her with you to fight," Trinati said. "She's there to pull you out if things get too dangerous."

Azra's nostrils flared. "I can judge that for myself."

"But I trust her judgment. I'm not risking your life to save everyone else's."

Cimree felt his resentment, but he nodded to Trinati and

began to stalk away toward the armory. Cimree's feelings were still smarting as she strode after him and caught up. She could hear the screams as they neared the entrance, the shrieks of terror and pain. It made her feel awful.

"I didn't appreciate you saying that," she told him.

"I wasn't trying to wound your feelings. Just stating the obvious. Your training as a healer is valuable. But it's not what we need right now. The people are going to be slaughtered, and you won't be able to cure them."

He was right, but she still resented him putting it so bluntly.

When they reached the armory, Azra went to Uorsin directly. "I need mundane weapons. No celestial iron."

"But they dull easier," Uorsin said, wrinkling his brow.

"Even so. Celestial iron does not injure the creatures down there the same way."

"Over here," Uorsin said, bringing him to a rack of weapons on the wall. "These are made for ordinary defenders. I have some pikes, a few swords."

"Those will do," Azra said, grabbing two long swords from the rack. He hefted both, adjusted his grip, and twirled them. Then he handed over the celestial iron blades he still carried and sheathed the replacements instead. He also grabbed some daggers, sliding them into his belt.

"Any iron-tipped arrows?" he asked.

"None, I'm afraid. All I have are celestial iron."

"I wish you had time to make some," Azra muttered. He looked at Cimree and shook his head. "These will have to do."

"What would you have me do?" Cimree asked.

"I want you to stay on the roofline. You'll be watching for them and alerting me before I get surrounded. I can feel what you feel. I'll react to it. You don't need to shout. Actually, that would be dangerous. Cats are excellent jumpers and they can get on the rooftops. You need to watch yourself. Stay out of sight."

"I will," she promised.

He took her to the overlook part of the walls. The sunlight was fading fast and the screams were growing louder. The doors of the fortress had been opened already, and a flood of refugees were surging up the steps to get inside. Angel sworn patrolled in the skies, holding bows and quivers of arrows—which were useless.

The look of fear in the children's faces squeezed Cimree's heart. They did not deserve this. But they were victims just as much as their parents.

Azra withdrew his distaff and began to make graftings. He gave her flight first, adding that to himself as well.

"I'm giving you an owl's abilities. It will help you see in the dark as well. Does it hurt?"

She felt the tingles in her arms and legs, but it was not painful. She shook her head no.

Azra continued to weave more graftings on himself. Several more actually and she felt his pain through the medallion.

"Stop," she said, holding up her hand.

He looked at her and grunted. "I've hardly gotten started."

"You're in pain."

"Pain is an old ally," he responded and continued to graft powers onto himself. She could almost feel the throbbing tingles inside his entire body. The kind caused when a limb fell asleep and ached with restored circulation. She'd underestimated his capacity for enduring pain. He was strapping all these abilities to himself, adding quickness and resilience, strength and vision. Hearing, smell—he was enhancing all his senses. She'd never seen someone graft so many things at once yet maintain them with a fixed determination, and he did this even as his body was screaming in agony. She saw it in his eyes, saw the suffering, but also a willingness to endure it.

"I'm sorry," she whispered to him.

"This is what I trained for," he said simply. "We must hurry." He unsheathed both long swords and gave her a look of pure determination. She felt his resolve. Implacable. Fierce. He was preparing himself to destroy.

He began to float, and she invoked her grafting too and followed him down from the wall. People were running in the streets, trying to flee or seek shelter, any shelter, while others thronged at the ramps leading up to the fortress.

Where would Azra attack? She saw bodies littering the streets, some wounded and dying, but most had already perished.

Azra glided down into the main street, away from the crowd. There was one of the grimalkin creatures savaging a dead body. Cimree landed gracefully on the rooftop above and dropped to a crouch. She drew her dirk and gripped it hard, gazing down at the shadowy street. Several of the grimalkin were slinking toward Azra. One of them hissed at him and then leaped, claws extending as it tried to swipe at him.

Azra wasn't wearing a cloak this time. He'd given that up in the last fight. He dodged the attack and swiped at the beast with his blades, scoring it twice. But the injury didn't deter it and it immediately vaulted at him again, joined by another.

Azra caught one in the gut with the sword, then pivoted and slashed the other. She saw a third slinking in the shadows and pushed a surge of warning from her chest.

He responded to that and began to fly again, farther down the street, away from the crowds jammed together as they trampled each other trying to escape. He was trying to draw the creatures away from them.

Cimree worried she might slip on the rooftop, so she began to float and follow him, using the grafting magic to keep her aloft. More of the grimalkin were coming, making mewling noises as they stalked their birdlike prey. Oh, they were interested in catching him. The lithe and sleek creatures were larger than cats, and one jumped at him suddenly as he hovered above the street, but Azra rose out of its reach.

She didn't see the other one come from an adjacent rooftop. It was a blur of smoky fur as it collided with Azra, raking him with its claws and knocking him from the air. She cried out involuntarily, then clamped her hand over her mouth as she drifted to the nearest rooftop.

Azra dropped one of his swords onto the street, the metal clanging loudly. He drew a knife and plunged it into the enemy clinging to his back. The others came at him, yowling and hissing, and Cimree saw he was surrounded. There were four of them attacking him. She felt the shards of pain as his skin was pierced and ripped by the attacks. He managed somehow to get the one off his back and then threw the dagger into another before using the long sword with both hands, whirling the blade in a deadly spinning spiral. The cats hissed and jumped at him anyway, getting carved up by the sword in the process.

Another set of cats were coming up on him from behind.

He must have sensed her warning because he took flight and went farther back. Cimree heard a scrape on the roof and, glancing to the side, saw a cat appear over the edge, its eyes slitted with malice as it hunted her.

Cimree began to fly again and went over to the next rooftop, but the cat easily jumped the gap. Its whiskers twitched as it padded across the shingles after her. Birds had natural advantages over cats, but they were still the prey.

Azra plunged suddenly into the midst of the cats, striking in a series of blows as he raced through them. He cut them and skewered them, heading back the way he'd come. He landed and picked up his discarded weapon so he had two blades again. The cats charged at him, and more came from behind. He lowered himself into a defensive crouch, the blades at the ready.

Get up into the air! She thought in desperation. It was foolhardy remaining in the street for them to attack on the ground. Cimree counted at least eight mewling at him, charging at him, anxious to slice him to ribbons with their claws.

The cat beneath Cimree leaped at her, but she was out of its reach and it landed back on the roof.

Azra took flight just before they reached him and began floating back down the street toward the main gate of Montheron. He was luring them away. He toyed with them, sometimes lowering himself just to where they could leap at him, before jerking higher again. Another cat came from the rooftop opposite, but she saw it in time, and her mental warning prepared him to move. He landed on the street once more, taking a defensive stance, drawing them to him. More and more were coming. Twenty beasts, and all had swishing tails, like a cat enjoying its game with a mouse. The one stalking her hadn't given up yet. It followed her as she followed Azra. There was a thrill to this that unnerved her. She kept looking around for signs of threats and danger. The plan was working. He was drawing them away, bit by bit.

When he next landed on the street, he attacked a rogue cat who was separated from the rest. It hurtled at him, hissing and screaming.

Suddenly the grafting magic was severed. It didn't happen gradually, like when she couldn't hold on to it, but abruptly, as if the tether was cut. Cimree fell and slammed down onto the roof. Fear choked her.

The same thing had happened to Azra. He was in the middle of the street several buildings back, no longer joined with the powers of his affinities.

"Azra!" she shrieked in terror. The grimalkin that had been stalking her suddenly bounded at her, hissing and pawing. She used her dirk to fight back, but she felt the claws dig into her legs. Cimree could feel the sudden surge of terror inside Azra as well. He was trapped in the street. She was on the roof. There was no way to get back to the fortress. They'd be slaughtered.

"Jump!" Azra shouted to her.

She couldn't jump, not with the grimalkin swiping at her as

she parried with her dirk. The creature sank its front claws into her shoulders, and she watched its muzzle coming to bite her face.

Cimree hugged the creature to her chest and began to roll sideways. It tried to break free of her grasp as they picked up speed. Then they rolled off the edge of the roof. It happened so fast. Her stomach lurched as she realized she was two stories up.

The pavement came rushing at her as they fell.

Twenty-Four

A New Monster

Azra caught her. How he had gotten there in time, Cimree didn't know, but she landed in his arms before he buckled and spilled her into the street. The jarring impact stunned her, but the claws digging into her skin reminded her of the grimalkin attached to her. She stabbed at it with her dirk and Azra joined with one of his daggers, slicing down its spine until it shrieked with pain.

Azra grasped her by the wrist and pulled her back to her feet. Another creature launched at him, landing on his back. He went down again, deliberately or not, and thrashed until it was loose. Terror ravaged her insides as she realized the danger of the situation. Azra was down to two daggers for defense, and Cimree thought he must have had to abandon his long swords when he ran to catch her, plus, their graftings had been severed. They hadn't worn off—they'd been snipped. Though she could still sense the snake in the cage near the window. It pleaded with her yet again to free it.

Azra kicked the grimalkin away from him as several more came slinking into view.

"Run!" he shouted and sprinted to the window where the snake was. He smashed the glass with the pommel of his dagger, quickly clearing the frame while she dashed to him. Azra grabbed her by the waist and threw her inside before being attacked savagely by more of the creatures. She heard his grunts of pain—but she also felt the agony. He fought back, using two knives to strike the grimalkin.

Cimree panted with fear and emotion, but she responded to the serpent's pleading and pulled off the lid of the cage. Without any hesitation, she reached in and drew the serpent out, setting it on the floor, where it slithered under a cupboard. But she sensed it still, sensed its willingness to help her.

Cimree drew her distaff and invoked a grafting, connecting it to herself. It bonded instantly, fusing her with its speed and senses. A thrill went through her as the magic joined them together.

Then Azra vaulted through the window, getting away from the street and the death that hunted him. Blood trickled from cuts on his face. Hisses of fury came from the grimalkin as they attempted to jump through the window, but Azra blocked the way, using his daggers to ward them off, his breath coming in quick gasps.

"Back door!" he shouted to her.

Cimree had the ability to sense heat, and Azra had a red aura around him, as did the grimalkin he fought. Her sense of smell was heightened and allowed her to pick up the scents of death and rot, making her realize that the owner of the home had perished and that some of the food was already spoiling. In addition to her enhanced vision and sense of smell, she felt her reflexes were also quickened. She maneuvered around some furniture and found a rear door, and she pulled the latch.

"Open!" she called to him.

Azra darted from the window and followed her out. The cats mewled as they gave chase, eager to hunt, but Azra slammed the door shut before they could reach them. He continued to pant heavily, and she sensed his immense pain.

"Did you … graft with the … snake?" he managed to get out.

"It worked," she said.

"You're my eyes now. It's getting too dark and they'll have the advantage. We need to get to the curia regis's home. That door … by her house … will get us past the walls. Only … chance."

"How hurt are you?" she asked, as she intercepted another wave of intense pain.

"Doesn't matter," he gasped. He looked her in the face and grabbed her shoulder. "You need to use the medallion. My mind is going blind with fear."

"How do I use it?"

He released her and pressed his palm against his forehead. "You did it before. Just … invoke it. It responds to your thoughts."

The look on his face showed his pain, his fear, and his desperation. Cimree heard the hurried scratching noises of the cats on the door. They'd swarmed inside the room but didn't know how to get their prey. There was time.

Cimree lowered her chin and tried to activate the medallion. Its power began to rush through her, responding to her thoughts effortlessly. It amplified her feelings but it could also quench them. The medallion had power over all emotion. She reached into Azra's heart and began to siphon his frantic feelings away. Immediately his eyes began to glow silver and his breathing grew fainter.

"Thank you," he whispered. He straightened, loosening his arms, stretching his neck.

Cimree saw a heat residue coming from the entrance of the alley. A grimalkin had found them, and it let out a hiss. Azra rushed it, attacking savagely with his daggers until he'd left it twitching in the street.

She hurried to him and looked both ways. There were more cats farther up the street, heading their way. The yowls from the open window were fierce and frustrated. She could sense the serpent hiding still beneath the cupboard. Her own fear had vanished with Azra's, drawn into the Tanaquil medallion. Storing the feelings like a trough. How strange! How powerful!

"That way," Azra whispered to her, pointing away from the oncoming cats. "Run as fast as you can! On the third street, turn right into the alley. That's where we came from yesterday. Understand?"

"Yes," she agreed.

"Go!"

Cimree ran and immediately the grimalkin gave chase. She pumped her arms as she raced down the road. There were dead bodies everywhere, no sign of heat remaining in them. Azra kept pace with her, though he could have outrun her. The first of the grimalkin caught up to them, and he stopped to fight it. Another joined it, then another. He broke through them and started running after her. She could hear his boots thumping in pursuit.

She passed the first street and saw a single cat prowling. It hissed when it saw her and came charging, but she dodged it faster than she imagined possible. There were so many of them!

Cimree passed the second street, risking a look backward, and saw that Azra had stopped again and was stabbing another one. Would it remain dead? The one they'd killed earlier had shrunk, but it had started twitching again. Was there any way to kill these things?

The third street was coming up. Azra broke off the fight and again charged after her. She sensed his agony from all the claw wounds and bites, but he was no longer afraid. His emotions were all contained and he fought like a senseless beast himself.

"Next street!" he shouted to her.

Cimree glanced that way and saw something huge vault over from roof to roof. It was enormous, multilimbed, and had a maze of veins pulsating across its sinewy body. She saw it just before she turned into the alley. It straddled both roofs, like a massive spider. In the darkness, all she could really see was its bulk and the hot fluids rushing through its veins, giving off the peculiar heat aura. She wasn't afraid of it. Her own fear had been conquered. But some deep part of her knew she should be terrified of it. That this thing could kill her easily. She heard a strange guttural clicking noise come from it.

And then her grafting to the serpent was snipped, and all she saw was a smudge of darkness in the already shadowed alley. She sensed no presence, could see nothing, but she knew it was there, blocking their escape.

Cimree reacted. She took the well of fear the medallion had stored and sent it gushing at the creature. Every bit of fear, every bit of terror, every sense of disgust and loathing she poured at it.

For a moment, she connected with it, and she was startled to find that even this thing felt emotion. No sooner had she made the realization than it fled from her. A sudden wind gusted behind her back as the magic of the medallion swirled inside her. In the dimness, she caught a glimpse of the bulky creature continuing to retreat over the roofline and out of her sight. The way was clear.

Where was Azra?

Cimree turned and saw that the cats had caught up with him. They were ripping into him on all sides as he fought against them, but he was overmatched and unable to run. She pointed her palm at the beasts and unleashed the magic again. She could sense their frenzy, their wildness, and she snatched it from them, replacing the emotion with fear. The cats fled from her, caught in a flood of primal instincts that they could not resist.

She raced to Azra and tried to pull him to his feet. Dizziness clouded her mind. He gazed at her with a look of awe and grunted as he stood. She helped hold him up as they went into the alley, his arm draped around her shoulders. She felt sweat running down her ribs. But in her core, she felt power. The medallion made her truly impervious to emotion, and that was a heady feeling, especially for a woman who was afraid of people and their unpredictable moods.

There was no sight of the spiderlike creature again, but without the serpent's power, she wouldn't have been able to see it anyway. Mewling sounds were starting to come again from the mouth of the alley behind them. The creatures she'd unleashed the magic on had fled, but there were others coming. Drawn to the conflict. Drawn to the sounds and smells of prey.

They reached the secret door leading to the heights. Cimree banged on it with her palm. Azra slumped against the wall, readying his weapons. He gazed coolly at the approaching cats.

The door unlocked and swung open, revealing a blast of torchlight.

The cats hissed and charged as hands reached out and pulled them to safety. Angel sworn surrounded them. Some leaped to the wall and began shooting arrows down into the alley.

"What happened to your graftings?" one of the angel sworn said, a woman that Cimree barely recognized. "We saw you fall!"

Azra looked at her without emotion, his eyes still glowing silver. "Something cut the magic."

"But that's not ... possible," the angel sworn said with a look of fear.

Cimree could feel the woman's disgust as she stared at the two of them, at the glowing eyes and bloodstained clothes.

"Where's Trinati?" Cimree asked.

"Up at the fortress. I'd just sent her word that you'd fallen."

"We should go," Azra said.

"You can barely stand," Cimree told him.

"I'm well enough. Let's try the grafting again." He sheathed his knives and drew his distaff. She did the same. Once more, they began to conjure the grafting magic, and it flowed smoothly. Cimree wished the serpent were nearby, but it was too far away to graft with. Azra began to rise, and when he saw Cimree still struggling, he joined her to the magic effortlessly.

They flew up to the heights of Montheron. She kept looking down at the rooftops, trying to get a glimpse of the huge creature she'd seen traversing the rooftops. But there was no sign of it anywhere. Before they reached the top, they were met by other angel sworn defenders coming down. Cimree felt fatigued from continuing to hold on to the magic of the medallion, so she released her grip on it. Her own emotions began to flood back inside her. Fearfulness, rebellion, timidity, persistence. Having been stripped devoid of them with the medallion, she recognized the familiarity of their continual presence within her bosom. And it dawned on her that many of them made her weak.

The other angel sworn joined them and led the way back to the pinnacle of the fortress. As Cimree passed the masses of people trying to get inside the safety of its walls, she heard shrieks begging for help and protection. She and Azra had halted the attacks for a time, but they would resume again. And there was nothing to be done about it.

At the top, they found Trinati leading the evacuation, sending the angel sworn off the island. When she saw them, a look of pure relief came over her until they got closer and she saw their wounds.

"They did that ... to *you*?" she said, gaping at Azra. In the torchlight, Cimree could see rivulets of blood and his shredded clothing. He stood firm, erect, his lips pursed and defiant.

"Something severed the grafting magic," Cimree told Trinati in a low voice, for there were many around them.

"What?" Trinati demanded.

"We don't know," Cimree said. "But I saw something down there. Something huge. It moved from rooftop to rooftop. It's living, full of heat. But I don't know what it is."

"Others have seen it as well," Trinati said.

Cimree put her hand on her bosom. "I frightened it away."

"So maybe we have a chance," Trinati whispered. "If this thing can sever grafting magic, we need to get the angel sworn off the island before we're trapped here with the mortals. We must all leave. Right now."

"Leave now, or we *all* die," Azra said.

"I agree. We abandon Montheron now. There's nothing more we can do."

Cimree felt a twinge of regret. Of sadness for the people who would perish. But the amulet she wore suddenly flicked those feelings away.

And she hadn't thought to do it.

TWENTY-FIVE
THE DESOLATION

"But we can't just abandon them!" Darcia said wretchedly, tears streaming from her eyes.

Trinati had brought the group from Clairvaux together for a final meeting before announcing her decision to the rest of the angel sworn. Wegner's mouth was tight with grief as he considered all he'd just learned from Cimree's and Azra's perspectives.

Trinati shot Darcia a reproving look. "Get control of yourself!"

"I'm ... I'm sorry," Darcia said, wiping her eyes. "I cannot believe it's come to this. So many have died already."

"And if we don't leave," Trinati said forcefully, "then we all will die. I don't see any other way. Do any of you?" She cast her gaze at the rest, but it lingered on Azra. The claw wounds on his face had scabbed over.

With pursed lips, he shook his head no.

Trinati breathed slowly. "And you feel Clairvaux is equally threatened?"

"I do. We won't find shelter there. In fact, the mountains will trap us inside. If we try to escape later, we'll be no match for these creatures that are more naturally equipped."

"We can fly," Trinati countered.

"If they can't fly yet, we'll face ones that can." Azra looked resolved.

Cimree believed him. "These are no natural animals. They were created to destroy. To destroy *us*. We need to run from them."

"The Queen Mother won't," Wegner said with a frown. "She won't leave the valley."

"I will try to persuade her," Trinati said. "I must succeed." She sighed again. "In light of all we have seen and experienced in the last several hours, I see we have no other choice. Please tell me if I'm wrong."

Wegner shook his head. "If we had more time, we might be able to discover the nature of this enemy. But where things stand, it is kill or be killed. And we will not prevail if it comes to that."

"Agreed," Trinati said definitively. "I'll tell Captain Odeon. I do this to save lives. Many of the angel sworn have been poisoned by grimalkin. We need to get them back to Clairvaux to the Gallows Tree. Time is urgent." She looked at Cimree. "As you say the medallion can thwart that creature, you will remain until the end in case it comes up here."

"I will stay with her," Azra said.

Trinati shook her head. "You've done enough, and you're half-dead yourself."

"I'm staying," he said curtly.

Trinati frowned and then nodded. She gave them all a final look and strode out of the room. Darcia started to weep once more, and Cimree went up to her and hugged her. Wegner gazed around the room, at the stone walls and intricate structures that he had helped design. She sensed his turmoil, but he was determined and agreeable to the course of action.

Darcia looked into Cimree's eyes. "Can you take away this pain?" she asked softly. "My heart is breaking."

Cimree nodded and invoked the power of the Tanaquil amulet. Darcia's feelings were subsumed by the magic, draining from her like water from a broken vessel and stored within the amulet.

Darcia's expression became peaceful. She looked resigned but no longer tormented. She patted Cimree's arm. "Thank you. Sometimes it is better to feel nothing at all." She left the room and Wegner followed her out.

"Emotions are powerful things," Cimree said, more to herself than Azra.

"They leave scars," Azra said softly. "Scars that cannot be healed."

He was talking about his past. She felt a throb of resentment inside him from a past wrong. The desire for vengeance was still very potent.

"You speak from experience," she said.

He nodded but offered nothing further.

"Can I tend to your wounds?" she asked him, knowing he was still in pain.

"The fruit is still healing me," he said. "The scratches will be gone by morning. If we survive that long."

"You think our survival is still in question?"

"I must think that way," he answered. "To prepare for every contingency. We are vulnerable. I still think it's possible the Fear Liath is coming. We have to go. And that thing you saw, that new monster, it's aware of you. It's going to come back because you're a threat to it."

"Me?"

"Because of the amulet. Because of your power."

"I have no power," she said dismissively.

"You have more than you realize." Was it a compliment? It felt like one. And that made her self-conscious and pleased at the same time.

"Thank you," she said.

"Time to go back into the nightmare," he said, his eyes flashing with dread.

It was the darkest part of the night, not even the blush of dawn on the horizon. Screams echoed through the stone corridors, coming from all directions. The angel sworn were flying away, one by one, forsaking Montheron and the mortals who remained. The cat things continued to attack and destroy, but they were ignoring the mortals and going straight for the angel sworn in the upper heights of the fortress. Each time they pressed in on all sides, Cimree invoked the medallion and scattered them, driving them away through their instinctual response to fear. But that fear only lasted a few minutes before they were back again, hissing and clawing and trying to kill once more. Using the magic was draining her strength.

Azra had two long swords again and was using them to hold back their foes. He'd grafted more powers to himself, and so far, they had stuck. She sensed the prickling pain ravaging his body from the grafting magic, along with the wounds he'd sustained earlier and the fresh ones inflicted since. But his mind was impervious to it, and he kept fighting despite the lack of hope. Trinati and Montheron's strongest defenders were at their sides, trying to hold the bastion until the last angel sworn had gone. Even Captain Odeon was there, sword in hand, fighting for their lives.

As Trinati had planned, the angel sworn had been fleeing in small groups due to the shortage of birds, and once clear, they released the magic so the birds could graft with new people. Darcia and Wegner were already gone.

A new defender flew down to Captain Odeon. He had blood and grime splattered on his armor. "The last of the mortals is inside the fortress. We're ready to bar the doors!"

"How many of you are left there?" Odeon asked.

"Four of us left," the defender said.

Another surge of grimalkin came charging at them, streaking from the shadows, eyes gleaming in the night.

Azra's eyes were glowing silver as Cimree continued to feed him with magic to numb his emotions. She was getting more and more weary with each attack and each repulsion. The amulet was affecting her as well, draining her strength and alertness. She countered the fresh attack with another wave of terror, which drove off the grimalkin, back to the shadows, where they hissed impotently.

"I'll give the order, then," Odeon said. "You leave with the next group led by Uorsin. Without him, we wouldn't have lasted this long."

The defender shook his head. "I'm leaving with you, Captain."

Odeon frowned. "I'm not leaving, Banniger. I'm staying behind."

"No!" Trinati shot at him, her voice full of anger.

Captain Odeon looked at her. "I cannot abandon these people. I will join in their fate."

"You will obey me, Odeon," Trinati said, and Cimree felt her inner turmoil. She respected Odeon. She trusted Odeon. She was depending on him for something.

"My conscience forbids me to leave," he said implacably.

"We're staying with you," said another defender. "To the last."

Odeon turned back to Trinati. "Just go. We're all that's left against this madness."

Trinati's heart clenched with pain. Cimree felt it strongly and began to siphon that pain away with the medallion.

Trinati shot her a furious look. "Stop that!" she snarled. Cimree stopped at once.

"Go," Odeon said. "Uorsin will obey you. He's loyal. And you'll need him."

"You must come with us. I need *you*, Odeon!"

"I'm needed here even more," he said. Cimree saw that all the defenders who were remaining behind were men. Not a single one was a woman. She'd assumed they were the strongest and the toughest of the defenders. And she'd seen many women had perished during the raids. But these remaining few defenders were more loyal to Odeon than to the Queen Mother. In the end, that loyalty forged of respect proved stronger than mere obedience.

"With me!" the captain said to his cohort, and they all began to fly away, hastening to the last door, which they'd thrown closed in the face of their enemies.

"Odeon!" Trinati wailed. Yes, feelings were powerful. Cimree felt tears sting her eyes at the sacrifice being made. The cost was dear.

And so Cimree, Trinati, and Azra were alone in the courtyard. The grimalkin were slinking toward them again, mewling with hate.

"We can't stay here," Azra said.

Indecision momentarily washed over Trinati's face as she reeled from what had happened. She'd fought well against the grimalkin, for her skills with the blade rivaled Azra's. But she had some minor wounds, and Cimree worried about how much venom she had been inflicted with.

The grimalkin were coming from all sides.

"Fly!" Trinati yelled, rising into the sky.

Azra drew his distaff and summoned the grafting magic for Cimree. She felt the prickles in her feet instantly as she started to rise above the courtyard. The cats charged at them, and some even leaped to try to catch them as they made their escape. Cimree kept rising, heading away from the central spire of the fortress that seemed to pierce the sky. As she rose, she saw the stains of light from torches down below. She saw Odeon and his last defenders enter the fortress and shut the massive door. Walls of stone would help them against the cats. But they had trapped themselves inside with limited food and no support from the rest of the world. Would they survive somehow? She hoped so.

"I see it!" Trinati yelled, her voice throbbing with fear. She was higher than them.

Cimree gazed down, but in the darkness, she saw nothing but the swarm of cats in the courtyard below. "Where?"

"It's on the spire!" Trinati shouted.

Cimree gaped when she saw the smudge of darkness clinging to the spire, its misshapen head turned toward them as they flew away. Had it been on the rooftop the whole time? Or had it clambered up there after they'd left? It seemed to be extending a limb of sorts, but in the dark, it was difficult to tell.

A feeling of dread opened inside her just as the grafting magic within her failed. Severed yet again. Ripped from her.

Then they were all falling, plummeting from the sky like stones. Cimree bridled her fear with the amulet. She snatched it from all three of them and clamped her hands against her sides with her legs together. They were falling straight into the lake.

When she struck the water, the shock of cold and the speed with which she plunged into the depths made her ears scream in pain. Down, down, down she went. The brutal impact had jarred every bone in her body. She tried thrashing against the waters, her breath coming out in tangled bubbles. Where was the surface? Which way to swim?

She felt Azra grab her ankle and stopped kicking and struggling.

Her lungs needed air, and she hiccuped and sucked in water.

In seconds, everything went black as she fainted.

Twenty-Six

Thwarted Hope

Cimree vomited water once more, but at last she could breathe. She had no memory of getting to shore, but the feeling of firm hands against her back, pushing hard and deep to expel water fixed in her mind. She started choking and coughing.

"Thank the Oldknow, she's breathing!" It was Trinati's voice, garbled by the water in Cimree's ears.

Cimree felt pressure on her lower back again. Her limbs were weak and listless. It took some moments to open her fluttering eyelids.

Another push, another expelling of water, and she felt the delicious air fill her lungs, but the coughing still hadn't abated. She felt her teeth start rattling and her body shaking. With the convulsions of her body came a popping in her ears, and suddenly she could hear the distant howling of the gévaudan.

"We need to get her warm," Azra said.

"We can't risk a fire," Trinati answered.

"There's a hunting lodge nearby. For the Long Patrol. That would give us shelter and food and a fire."

"Agreed," Trinati said. "Cimree, can you sit up?"

"I think so," Cimree answered with another hacking cough,

weary to her bones. She pushed herself up and realized her backpack was gone. She touched her back.

"It's right here," Azra said. "I'll carry it. We need to get going."

Cimree looked around in the moonlight, and she only saw Azra and Trinati. When she looked past them in the moonlight, she wondered whether those who had departed before them had suffered a similar fate. Or had they arrived safely at Clairvaux? Captain Odeon and his stalwart defenders had remained behind. She didn't believe she'd see any of them again. It curdled her stomach.

Azra and Trinati helped prop Cimree up as they walked through the woods at the edge of the lake. The cold was becoming unbearable, and Cimree knew she was in danger if she remained wet in the frigid air for too long. Such circumstances caused many to become confused and incoherent. At least she was able to think. That was a good sign. But she would have been grateful to have an étuve nearby to warm herself in.

Before long Cimree had grown strong enough to manage on her own, and the walking had increased her body heat. The lake's edge was disrupted by boulders and bluffs so their route was often circuitous. They had walked for nearly an hour when they passed an abandoned farm that had no signs of life whatsoever. And then, after that first hour, they began to hear the gévaudan again, much closer this time.

"They've found our trail," Azra grunted.

"How far to the lodge?" Trinati asked.

"Not far. The walls are stone, so we should be safe once we get inside."

The howling came closer and closer and the group increased their pace. Even the night birds fell silent. The howls came from their right and left and from behind. Cimree looked into the gloom, trying to catch sight of them.

"There," Azra said. The lodge sat in a small cove along the lakeshore amidst heavy boulders. A small dock had been built leading to it, but there were no roads or trails approaching it from the woodside. Cimree smelled smoke.

Trinati sniffed. "Somone is already here," she said.

Azra approached the stone hut. The roof was slanted steeply on two sides, steep enough that snow wouldn't be able to accumulate much. The understructure all fit well beneath the curb of the roofline and was angled, built on layers of carved boulders as a foundation. The windows were all shuttered and blocked.

Cimree glanced around nervously, listening to the sound of the approaching gévaudan. Azra walked up the front steps to the porch and jiggled the handle. The latch was blocking it. He pulled out one of his daggers, slid it into the seam, and released it.

When he pushed open the door, the glow of a dying fire illuminated his face.

"It's Azra," he announced as he entered.

Trinati shot Cimree a confused look. She gripped her sword hilt and marched after him, Cimree trailing behind.

A family was sleeping by the remains of the fire, a woman and three young children. The father had a sword and stood in a defensive posture. The children were waking, rubbing their eyes.

Cimree recognized the father. It was the soldier, Andrin. The one who had turned in Azra. The two men embraced.

"What has happened to Montheron?" Andrin asked. He was unshaven, with a harrowed look in his eyes.

"It's fallen," Azra said. "We abandoned it." He turned and gestured for Cimree to get closer. "Come get warm."

"I recognize you," Trinati said, coming closer, scrutinizing the husband and wife. "You fought for us when the Vikander attacked."

"I did, my lady," Andrin said.

"You abandoned your post?"

"I saved my family," Andrin said, bristling.

"We're all tired and fearful," Azra interrupted. "Let's talk in the morning."

"I hear the gévaudan," said one of the little girls worriedly.

"They can't get inside," Andrin said reassuringly. "Go back to sleep."

"There are some extra clothes," the wife said.

"There are," Andrin agreed. "We haven't been here long."

Trinati nodded, and Azra increased the light by adding more wood to the fire. In the storage chests, they found new tunics, and the three newcomers hastily stripped and changed into new ones, then set their wet things near the fire. Cimree unpacked her backpack as well so that it would dry out too and not begin to smell. A little boy offered her a blanket, which she accepted and stretched out on the floor near the family. Azra inspected the door, secured it again, then went and checked every window. Then he spoke in soft tones to Andrin for a few minutes before climbing up into the loft. Cimree heard some hinges creak and realized there was a trap door heading up to the roof. She determined to wait for Azra to come down so she could talk to him, but she fell asleep, enjoying the warmth of the fire on her face.

✦⊱♦⊰✦

CIMREE AWOKE to bustling noises in the room. Light from the dawn came in through the upper windows near the roofline. With the extra light, she could see the latticework of timbers holding up the roof. It was not a large dwelling, but there was a cooking fire and chimney, some tables pushed to the side, and a few leather chairs for seating. Cimree pushed herself up on her elbow, feeling the tangles in her hair with her free hand. One of the children, the littlest, was sitting nearby, staring at her.

"What's that on your skin?" the little one asked, pointing to Cimree's chest.

Cimree looked down at the yawning bodice and saw a whorl of black runes just above her breastbone. It startled her to see the markings had grown so big. She sat up.

Trinati was talking to Azra in low tones by the front door.

"I d-don't know," Cimree confessed. "What's your name, little one?"

"Blanka," said the girl. "Is it paint?"

"I'm not sure," Cimree said, feeling self-conscious. She rose and brushed off her legs. She found her trews had dried and hastily put them on, then cinched her belt around her waist. Barefoot, she walked over to Trinati. "Is this normal?" she hissed, tugging down her bodice to reveal the runes.

She felt a jolt of emotion from Azra. He shook his head, his mouth twisting with disgust, and walked away.

"I don't know," Trinati said without concern. "It's a consequence of using the amulet."

"Wegner said as much. He said it was a stain. A disfigurement."

"And so it is. What is your concern?"

"I don't want it," Cimree complained.

"The fruit of the Gallows Tree reverses it," Trinati said. "It will go away. No one ever showed permanent harm."

"But it will harm me?" Her stomach dropped. "You might have mentioned that!"

"All magic has a cost."

"Tell me!"

Trinati pursed her lips, her eyes flashing with anger. "Later, Cimree. There are more urgent things to decide. More pressing concerns."

"You've told me little already, and now I see you're hiding something." Cimree's voice began to tremble with anger.

"Don't be impertinent," Trinati warned. "Others have worn the Tanaquil amulet."

"Have you?"

"Yes," Trinati shot back. She tugged down her own bodice and revealed no marks whatsoever. "No lasting harm. It is useful magic. But there is a danger in using it too frequently. I won't let that happen to you."

"And what will happen?" Cimree asked with growing concern.

"I see you won't be satisfied until I give an answer. Let me be plain, then. That amulet captures emotions. Yours. Others. It cages them to be used later. Sometimes they begin to ... to leach out. You will feel emotions that aren't yours. But as I said, it is used for short durations. The effects are reversible. It is a sign of *trust* that you wear it at all."

"How do I know if the feelings are mine or not?" Cimree asked.

"That's the thing about emotions. We don't really know where they come from anyway. Guard your thoughts and you will guard your feelings. Is that enough?"

Cimree nodded. "Thank you."

"You should be content with what you are given, Cimree. Stop demanding more. It is a sign of willfulness, and it displeases me."

The rebuke stung. Cimree looked down, nodded, and walked back to her things so she could put on her socks and boots. She felt it unjust that Trinati scolded her for demanding answers to a strange magic she'd been forced to take on. Had it made a similar mark on Azra's chest, or was Cimree the only one affected? Sometimes, it was so infuriating that—

She felt a throb in her chest and the feelings were snatched away. Had she invoked the magic unwittingly? Or had the amulet acted on its own? That was a frightening thought.

After tugging on her boots, she rearranged her things and stuffed them back into her pack. She noticed Azra had just finished talking to Trinati again and was starting for the door. She hurried to him.

"Where are you going?" she asked him.

"Trinati asked me to inspect the area. Make sure there aren't any threats when we leave."

"Can I go with you?" she asked.

He frowned. "I don't care. But you'd better bring your dirk just in case."

She'd forgotten to strap that on, so she went back to her things and grabbed it, along with her distaff and sheath. Azra unlatched the door and pulled it open, dagger in hand. He paused at the threshold, gazing outside, the sunlight highlighting his face. There were no scars or marks anymore. Once again he looked younger than he had the day before. She didn't know how young his final age would be since he had eaten so much of the fruit but the rejuvenation from the fruit tended to be very quick in the beginning before slowing down as the body reached the settled age. And once again, his injuries had been healed. He had on a new tunic and trews. His eyes looked gray in the sunlight as she approached him, piercing and cold like the alpine mountains. He turned and beckoned her with a hand gesture to leave first, which she interpreted from his feelings not as deference to a superior but as a show of respect.

As they walked around the hut, he kept gazing at the ground.

"Are you looking for wolf tracks?" she asked.

He crouched down and pointed to the soft earth. She could see the tracks clearly.

"They came close without howling," he said. "Very odd."

"What do you make of the signs?"

After shaking his head, he rose and began walking some more, checking the ground for signs she didn't really understand. But it was interesting to watch him move. She wondered what kind of affinity for animals he had.

"If you wanted Andrin and his family to be safe here, why did you lead Trinati and me here to find them?"

He paused in his inspection and looked at her warily. "When I told them to come here, I hadn't expected our graftings to be severed, us falling into a lake, or being hunted by monsters. This was the nearest shelter I knew of."

There was no dishonesty in his explanation. He hadn't just saved the lives of Andrin's family but he'd saved hers too. A surge of gratitude ignited within her.

He frowned and nodded.

She walked closer to him. "You know so much more than I do. The amulet, I have its stain now. Do you also have it?"

He tugged down his collar and exposed the upper part of his chest to her. She saw the thatch of chest hair, the crease of muscle. But no stain.

"It's the Gallows Tree," he explained. "Only you will bear the mark for now. Soon, it will be a burden we both share."

"Why do you call it a burden?"

He smiled, but it was a mocking one. "You will see soon enough."

And the Oldknow also said to the archangel, "It is not agreeable for Woman to be alone. Separation will not foster growth. A limb severed from a tree. An arm from the body. I will cause to be done for her a suitable companion." So the Oldknow caused Woman to fall into an inveterate state, a dream, a wish, a longing. The Oldknow took one of Woman's ribs and closed up the area with flesh. And from the crude member taken from Woman, the Oldknow made Man and brought him to her. "Do you take him, Woman? To be your companion and a helpmeet for you?" And the First Woman said, "Surely this is bone of my bones and flesh of my flesh. I will take him."

— ORIGIN, THE TALE OF THE QUEEN MOTHER
OF CLAIRVAUX

TWENTY-SEVEN
SUCCUMBING

Azra finished searching the area, and Cimree was impressed with his knowledge of tracking and reading clues from the ground. She was about to ask him a question about his past when three angel sworn came floating down through the trees, wearing gleaming armor and holding swords.

Cimree recognized the leader, though she couldn't remember her name. All three had injuries and signs of venom inside them. As they got closer, Cimree noticed spatters and dents in their armor.

"We've been scouring the woods all night," the leader said to Cimree after landing. She'd given Azra a derisive look. "Where is Trinati? Did she escape Montheron?"

"She's here," Cimree said.

Another defender spoke up. "Someone said you fell into the lake. Is that true?"

"Yes. Our graftings were severed. So we made our way here."

The door from the hut opened and Trinati came striding out. All three angel sworn knelt in reverence before her.

"My lady," the leader said.

"Rise, Luzia. You all look sick and weary."

"Many of us are injured," said Luzia, coming to her feet with the other two. "Thank the Oldknow you were spared." She lowered her voice. "Where is Captain Odeon?"

Trinati shook her head. "He chose to remain behind."

"He sacrificed himself?"

"He did, for all the good it will do them. There is a creature at the island. Unlike anything we've seen. It has power over graftings. We need to warn the Queen Mother of this new threat. Where are the others?"

Luzia pursed her lips and nodded with eagerness. "The majority of the angel sworn are hastening to Clairvaux as you directed. Away from the island, there are more opportunities to fly. Depending on the nature of the affinity. Some are fleeing like stags."

"What of the wolves?" Trinati asked.

"We outrun them," Luzia replied.

"Very good. Get back to Clairvaux. You will need fruit from the Gallows Tree in order to reverse the sickness within you. Do not delay. We will leave shortly and meet you there."

"As you command," Luzia said, bowing again. She turned to her two companions and then all three rose above the dense woods and were quickly out of sight.

Andrin and his wife and three children had gathered at the doorway.

"What of us?" the wife asked. "Can we also go to Clairvaux for protection?"

Cimree felt a flash of hostility coming from Azra and glanced at him, seeing his eyes fixed on Trinati's face.

"You are not angel sworn," Trinati said. "It is forbidden for you to enter the valley."

Andrin scowled. "Then what is to become of us?"

"You will have to go somewhere else," Trinati said.

Anger seethed inside Cimree. She felt the urge to take the anger away from Azra, but she resisted it.

"We can't go back to Iselt," Andrin said, shaking his head. "Most of the town came to Montheron. We have nowhere else to go!"

The look of fear in the children's eyes caused pangs inside Cimree. Their mother shook her head. "Please, my lady! My children. We cannot flee from the gévaudan. We need help! At least take the children with you!"

Trinati's brow furrowed.

"Would it be acceptable if only one of us went?" Andrin asked desperately.

Trinati gave a curt nod.

"I've done everything the angel sworn have asked of me," Andrin said with anxiety in his voice. He looked at his wife. "Take the children with you. Go there together."

"I'm not leaving you!"

Andrin looked helpless. The clot of emotions coming from Azra's heart made Cimree's insides wrench with grief.

"You must," Andrin said. He cupped her cheek. "Renounce our marriage and you can go to Clairvaux. You can all go. It seems the Queen Mother does not approve of men who have been husbands."

"Papa!" the littlest girl said in despair and began to sob.

Andrin dropped to one knee and embraced her. The other boy and girl hugged him. Andrin had tears in his eyes as he looked up at his wife. "Please, Perreta. You must!"

"But what will happen to you?" Perreta said, choking on her tears.

He grimaced. "I'll go back to the pass I used to protect. If the garrison is still there, I'll ... I'll join it."

"Husband, no!" Perreta said, sobbing.

"I cannot promise the Queen Mother will accept this sacrifice," Trinati said. "She would not want to divide this family."

Cimree felt a hot spear of rage from Azra's heart, and when she looked at him, she saw the anger blazing in his eyes. The fury of injustice and revenge boiled inside him. He said nothing, though. Whatever had happened to him felt dangerously close to this situation. What had he suffered?

Andrin wiped his eyes and rose. "It's the only way. If this purchases your lives, I will pay the cost. You can do it, Perreta. Renounce me. Renounce our marriage."

Trinati held up her hand. "No. Why don't we see if the Queen Mother will accept this first? Do not renounce him."

Perreta hugged Andrin fiercely, burying her face against his chest. The children clung to his legs. The misery in the moment stung Cimree to her core.

"We cannot linger," Trinati said. "Remain here, Andrin. Protect yourself. If there is another way, we will send word. If the Queen Mother accepts your wife and children and permits them to become angel sworn, I will send someone to tell you. That is all I can promise right now."

Andrin nodded in agreement. He stroked Perreta's hair and whispered soothingly to her. Then he broke away from her and crouched down to hug each one of his children.

"Cyrill," he said to the boy, "you must protect your mother and sisters. As the First Man did. You must be brave."

"But I'm afraid, Papa," the boy said, his lip quivering.

"I know, my son. You must be brave."

"I will be brave, like you," Cyrill agreed.

"Edwina," Andrin said, then kissed his oldest daughter on the cheek, "I'll miss you. You are always so helpful. Please be helpful now. Do what they tell you."

"I will, Papa. I promise!"

Andrin nodded and stroked her hair. He swallowed, trying to steel himself against his grief. Cimree felt tears trickling down her own cheeks. But she would not banish her feelings. She *wanted* to remember this moment.

"Papa, I'll stay with you," said little Blanka.

Andrin chuckled, wiping his eyes again, and stifled a groan. "I adore you, little one. I'm proud to be your papa." She hugged him and kissed the tip of his nose. Then Andrin, barely composed, rose and kissed his wife. She sobbed and hugged him back, and Cimree thought her own heart would break.

Andrin stepped back, hand on his sword hilt. He looked at Trinati. "Keep them safe, archangel. I beg you."

"I can offer no more than what I already have," Trinati said. "We must return to Clairvaux."

Andrin nodded. He looked at Azra and then the two men embraced. Cimree heard a whisper pass between them, and then Azra gripped the other man's shoulder and gave him a look of pride and determination.

Trinati looked over at Cimree. "Gather some food for the journey. We need to get back before nightfall if we can. The little ones will slow us down."

Andrin shot an angry look at Trinati for saying it, but he would not speak against her. Cimree went back into the hut and foraged for supplies to take along, then found a sack to put them in. They'd be following the Silver River back to Clairvaux, so at least there would be plenty of water. Cimree's heart panged at what the family was enduring. Marriage was not permitted in Clairvaux. What they practiced was a higher way of life, an act of self-denial that was even more important than conjugal relations. So few had that depth of commitment, and she could understand better why that was. The painfulness of the separation the family was enduring was almost too much.

Cimree left the hut with the bag of food.

Trinati gave her an approving look. "I must return to Clairvaux at once. I have a solemn duty to warn the Queen Mother and counsel her on what happened to Montheron. Cimree, you bring Azra and these with you. I put you in charge. I will also send defenders to find you and help bear this burden."

"Yes, Trinati," Cimree said. Of course Azra couldn't be in charge, even though he was the more experienced person. Because he had forsaken his oaths, he just could not be trusted in the same way again.

Trinati looked at the family and then drew her scionwood wand. She performed her grafting, flew up, and disappeared through the trees.

"Tell your father goodbye again," Cimree said to Edwina, Cyrill, and Blanka. They obeyed and then went to stand by their distraught mother. Perreta hugged Andrin once more before he walked back to the door of the hut, where he stood to watch them leave.

"Come, children," Cimree said coaxingly. "We must hurry before the gévaudan come back." Then she looked at Azra. "Would you lead the way?"

Azra nodded and gave Andrin a final inscrutable look. He started off into the woods. Cimree waved Perreta to follow, and they all started after the hunter. Blanka walked up to Cimree and grasped her hand. Cyrill and Edwina were holding their mother's hands.

Azra kept a steady pace, taking them deeper into the woods. She had no idea how close they were to the trail leading back into Clairvaux, but she knew that Azra was familiar with it. She hastened her speed and was surprised that Blanka was able to keep up.

"Azra!" she called to him, and he stopped, looking back at her, waiting for her to catch up.

"We need to keep moving," he cautioned.

"I know, but you said something to Andrin. What did you whisper to him?"

He started walking again, and she scooped Blanka into her arms and carried her so she could keep up. Perreta and the other two children were trudging hard to keep pace.

"I'd rather not tell you," Azra answered in a low voice.

"Please tell me."

"Do you command it?"

"It doesn't have to be like that between us," Cimree said. "I'm not trying to force you. I just want to know."

"Why?"

"Why are you being stubborn about it?"

"I have good reasons to be."

"And I have good reasons for asking. You never do anything by accident. You are always thinking ahead. You told Andrin to do something. I just want to know what you said."

A little smile quirked on his mouth. "If I did, will you countermand it?"

"You've been right about everything so far. I wouldn't dare."

She felt a little pulse of warmth in the connection between them. One that guttered out almost as quickly.

He turned his attention back to the forest ahead. "I told him how to follow us."

TWENTY-EIGHT
REFUGE

Howling sounded from the woods on the right, and Cimree's dread intensified. She carried Blanka in her arms, though they were sore from the effort. Azra carried the boy on his back, and Perreta worked with the last, holding her daughter's hand tightly. No angel sworn had come to relieve them that day, and the sun had set beyond the ridge of mountains, blanketing the vale in shadows. The churning rush of the Silver River separated them from a pack of gévaudan loping like gray phantoms in the growing dark on the other bank. Crossing the river would have been treacherous without grafting magic, and with the gévaudan keeping pace with them and ready to snatch them, it would have been deadly. Wolves had been howling behind them for some time, but another pack was approaching on the right.

"Why hasn't help come?" Perreta gasped, winded from the struggle. They had reached the outer part of the valley of Clairvaux, but they were still a distance from the nearest protection. The perimeter defenders were not in place, and they'd seen no one flying overhead throughout the day.

"Who can say," Cimree answered bleakly, trying to maintain

her courage. Even the birds had quieted. Along the mountain ridge, she saw a few familiar waterfalls in the distance, the ones nearer her home.

Azra jogged ahead, searching the ground. The forests were thinning, giving way to farmlands. They were following the road but so were the gévaudan. How long did they have before they were trapped between the packs?

"Azra, what should we do?" Cimree called out to him.

He suddenly left the road and headed toward the river, dodging through a copse of trees. Sweat trickled down Cimree's ribs. The soreness in her arms was becoming unbearable.

"This way!" he shouted.

"Are we going to swim across the river?" Perreta asked worriedly. "I don't think I can make it."

Cimree arrived next and saw what had attracted Azra. There was a logjam of dead trees that had been crushed by an ice floe in a previous winter. The limbs were bleached and devoid of pine needles, and many of the branches had been shattered off. It was a jumbled tangle of silver bark, all at conflicting angles. Azra set Cyrill down and hurried over to help Edwina. Perreta paused to gasp for breath, gripping a broken limb as she gazed at the scene in confusion.

Azra turned to Cimree. "It's not much, but it is some shelter. Clear some of the logs and try to make enough room for all of you underneath. I'll fight the wolves."

"Why not use our distaffs and fly away?" she asked.

He gave her a mocking look. "There are too many of us. If there were more help, we could."

Cimree nodded and went to work. She and Perreta began to shift aside the smaller trees. Suddenly, Cimree felt the presence of a serpent. Actually, more than one. They'd disturbed a nest and the snakes were preparing to attack them as intruders.

"Wait!" Cimree shouted. She saw an asp viper slither from beneath a log, heading toward Cyrill's legs.

"What is it?" Perreta asked. In the dark, she hadn't seen anything.

"There's a den of snakes here," she told Azra.

"I was counting on it," he said. "Enlist their help." His head jerked. "The howling stopped."

"Is that a good sign?" she whispered.

He shook his head no. "Get inside. Protect the children."

Cimree nodded and drew her distaff from her belt. She felt the threat from the serpents and used the magic of the grafting to soothe them. They instantly responded to her calming command, and the one that was readying to bite Cyrill's leg slithered past him instead.

"Snake!" he shouted fearfully.

"Where?" Perreta gasped.

"It's all right, they won't harm us," Cimree said coaxingly. She found the mother snake and grafted with it, bonding with its powers and taking them into herself. Her vision began to respond to the radiant heat from Perreta and her children.

"But will they bite us?" Blanka asked tearfully.

"They won't," Cimree promised. "They're our friends now."

She gave the thought command for the snakes to emerge from the knot of detritus and they responded. She was surprised to find several had responded to her summons, and not all of them had been in the woodpile. She felt venom tingling in her mouth, which she hadn't experienced earlier. Was it because these were asp vipers? Or because she was still so new at grafting with creatures she had affinity for?

Cimree finished clearing away a space among the logs. "Can you squeeze in there, please?" she said to Cyrill.

"Are there more snakes in there?" he asked, his voice quavering.

"No, they're all outside now."

"I'll go," Edwina said. She was the oldest, so the other children would look to her, and she hurriedly crouched and crawled inside the thick debris. Cyrill came next and then Edwina coaxed Blanka to come inside. She did so without fear. Perreta and Cimree were both too big to fit.

"Crouch down," Cimree told the mother. "Get as far in as you can and block the opening."

"What about you?"

"I'm going to stop any wolves that get past Azra."

"They're coming," Azra said in warning. His distaff was loose, and he was beginning to invoke the grafting magic, taking in the power of animals in the area. Cimree saw their glowing red spots loping in the woods. She could also see the gévaudan across the river too, standing out in bright oranges and reds against the blues and purples of the surroundings and the cool water of the Silver River.

Cimree instructed the snakes to guard them. They were small creatures but their bites were deadly. Most serpents fled from danger, but Cimree instilled them with courage and determination, as if they were protecting their own young.

Azra was a few paces ahead of her, choosing to stand in open ground so that the gévaudan could charge him from the front and side. But she'd seen him fight the grimalkin in Montheron and knew he wouldn't stay put once the fight began. He had a sword and a dagger, one in each hand, and prepared himself in a battle crouch.

The howling started again, filling Cimree's ears with noise and her heart with dread. She clenched her teeth, summoning the medallion's magic to defend them. She would use fear against them. When Azra glanced back at her, she saw his eyes glowing silver.

The gévaudan rushed at them, and Cimree used the magic of the medallion to try to scatter them, but they were coming fast, dodging and shifting. Locking eyes with one, Cimree was shocked to see the same silvering of its eyes as Azra's. But that was quickly forgotten as it snarled and barked at her, and she flooded it with the feeling of being helpless prey. It yelped in surprise and retreated, barking as it went.

Azra flew up and then landed in their midst, slashing with his weapons viciously. They leaped at him, aiming for his throat, and Azra impaled one on his sword before rising out of their reach.

Two were charging at Cimree, jaws snapping, slathered with drool. Cimree used the medallion again and caught the first one, scaring it away. The second one nearly reached her before the serpents began biting it, hissing in warning before coiling to jab with their arrow-shaped heads. The wolf was surprised by the attack but still it came forward. Cimree hefted her dagger and felt the quickness of the snakes in her. She stabbed the wolf in the skull, and it glanced off the bone, making the beast yelp in pain, while the snakes continued to bite it. She felt the taste of the venom in her mouth. Cimree caught its gaze and sent terror into it.

The wolf bounded away from the den but suddenly dropped to the ground, twitching, overcome with the venom.

Azra landed again, attacking the mass of wolves. Thanks to Cimree, he felt no fear and sliced his blades in unison, cutting and stabbing at the wolves. Another pack loped into sight, howling before joining the attack. Cimree's heart quailed with dread, but the medallion sucked it away from her so she felt only coolness, a sense of purpose. One of the wolves snagged Azra by the boot, trying to drag him off his feet, but he struck the snout with the sword pommel and leaped into the air again. Wolves jumped at him, and then several turned and charged at Cimree.

She gazed at them, flooding them with fear, trying to meet their eyes as the snakes attacked. The gévaudan snarled and one caught a serpent by the tail and flung it away. The other snakes hissed and struck at the wolves, but the balance of the attack was tipping, with more gévaudan joining the fray. She felt the pain of one of the snakes being bitten clean through, and she attacked the wolf who'd done it, to try to drive it off. Then teeth snagged her boot and a sudden tug knocked her off her feet. Another wolf came at her neck, but she managed to lock eyes and flood it with fear, causing it to whine and back off but not flee.

She kicked at the one tugging at her leg, ignoring the pain, and then Azra was on its back, slamming his dagger into its neck, killing it. She saw two jump on his back and he was nearly dragged down himself on top of her, but he managed to hold their weight before twisting and falling on them. His entire body was a weapon. She stood up, her leg bleeding, and sent another wave of fear against the gévaudan.

A yell from a man sounded, and then Andrin was rushing into the midst of the fight, swinging his sword and hacking away at the predators, allowing Azra to make it back to his feet. The snakes were fleeing, slithering back under the desiccated limbs to save themselves.

A wolf bit Andrin's arm and yanked, making him drop his weapon and stumble. It began to bite him as he flailed his arms to try to protect his face and throat. Azra launched at the gévaudan attacking Andrin and scattered them, the angel sworn's blade cutting through fur and bone. More were coming, drawn to the howls.

But finally, angel sworn descended upon the riverbank with spears and arrows. The gévaudan were pricked and stabbed as the defenders entered the combat. Uorsin was among them, the enormous blacksmith, and he scattered the gévaudan with a giant war hammer. Cimree felt a surge of gratitude as the defenders joined the fight, and soon the wolves were routed, loping into the woods and barking in their retreat. None of them seemed keen on facing the largest of the angel sworn.

Azra fell on his backside, panting for breath. She could sense the prickles of pain in his body from the magic. He'd been bitten several times as well and had new wounds.

Andrin was panting too, completely out of breath. Cimree was exhausted herself, but she went to Andrin and saw blood on his forearm, near the elbow where his leather bracers didn't cover. He squeezed the wound with his hand, wincing in pain.

"Let me help you," she offered. She quickly tugged off her backpack and began to render aid. The other angel sworn landed and some set up a defensive wall with their spears, the tips pointed toward the woods and the retreating gévaudan.

"Cimree? Azra?" the chief defender said, a striking woman that Cimree didn't recognize.

"Yes," Cimree said, trying to stanch the bleeding on Andrin's arm. "Did Trinati send you?"

"She did. My name is Lyssander. We're to bring you all to Clairvaux." She looked at Andrin. "Even him."

That was a welcome surprise. After binding Andrin's injury, Cimree went to Azra, who was still sitting on the ground. Uorsin approached and dropped to a knee by them.

"Wish we had come sooner, old friend," said the giant.

"I can bind your injuries," she said. "Where were you bitten?"

"They will heal on their own," he said. There was a distant look in his eyes. A sober look.

She crouched by him. "What's troubling you?"

"I feel strange," he said. "I don't understand what it is. It's unlike other injuries. Not the same as those vicious cats. Something is happening inside me."

"Then I hope they return so I can give them a proper grave," Uorsin said angrily.

"Come, we must go at once," Lyssander announced. "Help those children out of the brambles. We'll carry them back to Clairvaux."

The angel sworn helped clear away the wood to retrieve Perreta and her children. Andrin was still panting, his eyes feverish with pain as he clutched his arm to his side.

Azra reached out his hand for Cimree to help pull him up, and she did so, even while thinking it was strange because Uorsin was so much stronger than her.

"Keep your eye on him," he whispered to her, nodding at Andrin.

"What do you think is wrong?" she asked, keeping her voice low.

"I don't know. I will recover from the bite because of the fruit. He may not."

TWENTY-NINE
THE MADNESS

Cimree felt the breeze through her hair as she soared over the treetops of the valley of Clairvaux. Her shoulder blades tingled with the grafting magic, but she felt a surge of relief and gratitude to be back in the familiar embrace of the mountains. The stars and moon illuminated the cliffs, shone on the waters of the Silver River, and glistened in the mist coming from the numerous waterfalls. There were campfires burning throughout the valley with the addition of so many defenders from Montheron, and the windows in town were glowing gold due to the activity. The escorts directed Cimree and her companions to alight in the town in front of the high council building, and they were immediately greeted by Wegner, who embraced Cimree with relief. A surprisingly large number of people thronged the streets, even though it was the middle of the night.

"I've been so worried about you," Wegner said, a smile brightening his face as he released her. "You look exhausted."

"Who are all these people?" Cimree asked. She noticed Azra landing next, along with Andrin, Perreta, and their three children.

"They've been arriving here day and night. Most come from the interlake region."

"And the Queen Mother has let them? They're not angel sworn?" Cimree was surprised.

"She has invited all to enjoy the protection of Clairvaux."

Cimree put her hand on her heart. "I'm so relieved."

"I will send word to Trinati that you've arrived," Wegner said, gripping her shoulder. "Get some food and some rest."

"Is there room at the Silberhorn? Or should I go back to my cabin?" The thought of staying there without Milena worried her.

"Every home and dwelling in the valley is being used right now," Wegner said. "But we arranged room for you at the Silberhorn, yes."

"What about—"

"Those you brought with you as well," Wegner interrupted. "Trinati said they were coming. Go to Milton, and he'll provide what you need. I must send word that you've arrived."

Cimree thanked him and then went to Andrin and Perreta. Andrin looked feverish, and she saw blood seeping from the rags she'd bound his arm with.

"Come with me," she invited them and nodded to Azra as well. "There's a place arranged for us."

Perreta breathed a sigh of relief. "It's not as crowded as it was in Montheron."

"No, there is room in the valley. The Queen Mother is welcoming all."

Andrin grinned and scooped up Blanka to carry her. Cimree led the way from the high council building and down the street. The grafting magic trickled away, releasing her from the power of the bird she'd been bonded to. It had been a strain, but at least she'd made it the rest of the way to the valley. They took the side road leading up the little hill to the inn, pausing to get a drink from the stone trough along the way.

When they reached the Silberhorn, it was bustling with activity. Milton noticed their arrival with a look of anxiety, but then he recognized her, and grinning, he hurried over.

"I feared they'd sent another family, even though we're full," he said. "But I have two rooms left, kept aside for you folk. Welcome all to the Silberhorn! My name is Milton. Look at these adorable children. Are you hungry?"

"Very hungry," said Edwina.

In short order, they were crowded around a table, looking on as bread, fried cheese and honey, and skewers of meat arrived. Cimree's hunger surprised her, but the sizzling food began to sate her appetite. She noticed that Andrin had barely touched anything, focused as he was on making sure his children had enough to eat.

"There is plenty more," Cimree told him when she caught his gaze.

"I'm more tired than hungry," he said, grimacing. "The meat smells off to me."

Cimree didn't understand that. It was savory and delicious and as excellent as one could hope for. What kind of food was he used to?

More people arrived after them, and Milton, being a gracious host, encouraged those who had eaten to make way for those who were hungry. Cimree noticed the yawns and eye-rubbing from the children and slipped from her seat to ask Milton about the rooms. He explained where to find the two that had been reserved, and she went back to the table. Azra was eating another huge piece of meat, along with a platter full of buttered asparagus and mushrooms.

"Perreta, I can show you to the room. We don't have families here in Clairvaux, so it won't be what you're used to."

"We'll gladly accept anything," she replied. Cimree left Azra at the table to continue his meal while she took the family upstairs and helped them get settled. Two beds had been pushed together in the center of the room, and it took some time to arrange everyone, but the children were finally settled and quickly began to fall asleep. Perreta looked worriedly at her husband.

"I'd like to see how your wounds are faring," Cimree said to

Andrin. He nodded in agreement and approached her by a single lamp on a small table. She unbound the bloodied wrapping and was surprised to find the wound had almost healed. She used the pitcher of water in the room and a rag to wipe away the clotted blood and scabs. There were little silvery marks surrounding the bite, but the wounds had closed with no oozing or pus.

"How do you feel?" Cimree said, examining the little marks.

"They don't hurt, surprisingly," Andrin said. "I feel strange, though. I'm hungry, but not for cooked meat. I don't know what it is I'm craving. But nothing looked or smelled good."

That was concerning. He needed food to rebuild his strength. "Let's go down to the kitchen. Maybe we can find you something."

Andrin shook his head. "I'm exhausted. I just want to sleep."

"You'll need to eat something in the morning, then."

"Thank you for helping us," Perreta said. "For all the angel sworn have done." She gripped Andrin's hand and squeezed it possessively. "We're so grateful."

Cimree hugged her, gazed on the dozing children, and then went back down to the noisy common room. Azra had almost devoured the entire platter of asparagus.

She sat down across from him. "Andrin's wounds have nearly healed."

Azra lowered the fork, his mouth turning to a frown. "I'd have expected his wounds would be festering."

"I know," Cimree said. "He seems sick. Like you said. There were these little marks by the bite wounds."

"What kind of marks?"

"More a discoloration," she said. "Had a silvery cast to the skin. Like a burn that's healed but discolored. I've not seen it before."

"He may need a bite of fruit from the Gallows Tree," Azra said. "I feel normal again. You can see my appetite has returned. Earlier, I was craving raw flesh."

"Raw?"

He nodded. "I've had to eat that at times, during difficult journeys in the wilderness when we couldn't risk building a fire. You get used to eating anything."

"Andrin said the smell of cooked meat was repulsive."

"It's possible the gévaudan are carrying a sickness," Azra said. "A fever can make anything smell awful. I hope he recovers." He said this with worry in his eyes.

"I do as well. Are you tired?" she asked him. "I'm ready to faint."

"Go get some sleep. I'll stay here a while longer."

She felt something from him, an uncertain emotion she couldn't identify. His shifting moods always perplexed her. So she left the table, found Milton to thank him again, and went back upstairs. Cimree paused at the family's room and listened, able to hear that Andrin and Perreta were talking in low voices. She went to her room and saw the two beds on opposite sides of the space.

A feeling came over her. An urge to push the beds together like she'd seen in the other room. What would it be like to sleep near Azra? To feel him near?

A shiver went down her spine at the thought, which had been totally unbidden and nothing she'd imagined before. To be angel sworn meant to be celibate. She had not made the oath yet. And he had forsaken his. A little thrill went through her at her rebellious thoughts.

And they were dangerous. She shoved the thought from her mind and went to the bed by the window. She tugged off her backpack and set it on the floor, then went over to the bowl and poured some water into it to splash on her face. Her clothes were filthy and needed to be washed. Her body too. Thankfully the Silberhorn had an étuve, and she could have a hot steam bath and then a cleanse in the pool.

She lingered by the basin of water, confused.

What were these feelings wriggling inside her? Were they from the medallion? Were they Azra's feelings? She wiped water droplets from her face. She let out her breath and invoked the magic of the amulet to banish her feelings. Her heart became peaceful once again. That was better. She slipped under the blanket of the nearest bed and rested her head on her arm, facing the wall.

As she began to doze, she sensed Azra downstairs still. He was sitting at the same table, brooding. He didn't want to come up, even though he was weary as well. He was waiting for something. What was he waiting for?

Her eyelids drooped, and she blinked, trying to stay awake, trying to think. She'd heard a sound next door. The whimper of a child.

Cimree had always wanted to become an angel sworn. She'd been given to Clairvaux to become one, a rare privilege that would entitle her to live for centuries upon centuries. Some of the angel sworn were thousands of years old. Had lived many lives and learned many things. Like Azra. But he had betrayed his promises. Because of his feelings?

The terrors of Montheron intruded on her thoughts. The cat creatures that had attacked the people. The multilimbed monster that had stalked her from the rooftop. The Fear Liath who had descended on the valley. How many more had died since they'd left? Even though she was exhausted, she felt the stab of worry in her breast. She touched her hand to her chest, trying to calm her imagination down. She needed to fall asleep! Why couldn't she purge her mind of feelings and worries?

She wasn't sure how long she lay there, expecting Azra but he was not coming. Her thoughts became murkier as dreams began to impose themselves on her mind. She was picking mint from the little herb garden. And then she heard a wolf howl.

Cimree blinked, awakening in darkness. How much time had passed?

Azra bounded off his bed. She heard his blade snick free of the sheath.

"What's wrong?" she whispered in the dark, confused. It was still deep in the night.

"Didn't you hear that?" he said in warning. "The wolf?"

The mournful howl sounded again. A solitary howl. Coming from the town. Coming from nearby. Then she heard shouts of warning. Cimree threw off her blanket, hurried to the balcony door, and opened it. The cool air caused gooseflesh up her arms. Her heart pounded with fear at the familiar sound. There were no wolves in Clairvaux. Or, there hadn't been.

Then the screams began, coming from several streets away.

She looked across and noticed that the door to the family's balcony was ajar.

THIRTY
THE QUEEN MOTHER'S DOOM

Cimree listened at the door first, heard the whimpering children, then twisted the handle and pushed it open. To her relief, Andrin and Perreta were both there, trying to comfort them.

"I thought the gévaudan couldn't come here," Edwina said plaintively.

Perreta comforted her. "*Shhh*, we're safe here. There's nothing to worry about. The angel sworn will protect us."

Andrin noticed Cimree at the doorway and hurriedly stood. When he reached the light, he looked rested and steady. In perfect health. "Do we have to leave?" he whispered to her.

Cimree shook her head. "I saw your balcony door open and wanted to check on you."

"I was burning up with a fever," he said. "But it broke, and I feel so much better."

"Can I see your arm?" she asked.

He pulled up his tunic sleeve. The bite marks glistened, the skin still exhibiting a silvery cast. The swelling had subsided, though, and he looked stronger.

"Are you hungry?"

"Ravenous. But I'll wait until morning."

"I just wanted to make sure your family was all right," Cimree said.

"Thank you. We will be fine."

Cimree left them and went back to the other room. She shut the door, finding Azra on the balcony, listening. Another howl sounded, a mournful cry. It came from farther away.

"The family is all there," Cimree said, joining him at the balcony.

Cimree felt Azra's surge of relief as he nodded.

"You were afraid he was gone," she said.

"Did he still look sick to you?"

She shook her head. "He is well again."

Azra frowned. "That's ... unnatural."

"He had a fever earlier, he said, but it broke. That *is* natural, Azra."

He turned and folded his arms. "Some creatures go mad when they are sick. No healing can cure them. They must be killed. It's almost as if ... " He let the thought dangle, his eyebrows creasing with concentration.

"What?" She pressed for his concerns.

"I've been near wolf packs, Cimree. They fight for territory. They fight over food. They will attack us if they are hungry enough, but these gévaudan seem to be fixed on us as prey. Wolf packs don't cooperate with each other. How have so many come to the interlake region? It's like they are drawn here. And their numbers continue to grow."

"Maybe that strange monster has summoned them?" she suggested.

"Or maybe it has set them loose," Azra replied. "The madness I speak of, it can be transmitted from one animal to another. Even humans, if bitten, can die from it. That's why I asked you to watch over Andrin. I thought he might have a plague bite. That he would sicken and die unless we gave him some of the fruit of the Gallows Tree."

"He seems perfectly healthy to me now."

"We cannot always trust what we see. Remember all those cats at Montheron? There have *always* been cats at Montheron. But something turned them into something else. A plague bite but a different kind. What if the wolves aren't just sickened wolves? What if they are something else?"

She squinted at him and tilted her head. "I'm not sure what you mean?"

"I'm not sure of anything myself. I'm trying to foresee all the possibilities. The cats were already in Montheron. They transformed into larger, vicious animals. Say one became infected. Then it infected others. Now all the cats in Montheron are wild and vicious. There's a term I've heard the Queen Mother use, a description of what happens when someone becomes angel sworn. Their nature and whole substance changes from a past form to a new one. She called it a transubstantiation. A person's very essence has changed. It feels ... hauntingly like this. Only this is a transformation into something terrible."

Cimree leaned closer and whispered, "Are you saying you think *she* has caused this to happen?"

"No," Azra said curtly. "It would ruin her idea of perfect order. But remember that there was a First Man who was exiled from Clairvaux after partaking of the fruit of knowledge. He was her husband. Created to serve her, but he rebelled."

"But he is dead," Cimree said. "He died ages ago."

"Did he?" Azra said. "Does anyone really know for sure? There are rumors of lychgates and of beings that have surpassed the death of their mortal bodies."

"That cannot be true."

"The Vikander believe in them." He looked her in the eyes. "And I have been to places so evil that it felt wrong to even breathe the air."

She reached out and touched his arm.

A flash of anger came from him, and he jerked away. The sudden hostility and action startled her. "I'm … I'm sorry. Did I offend you?"

"No," he said curtly.

"I think I did. I'm sorry. What you said, what you've been through, it just made me want to comfort you."

He squeezed his eyes shut for a moment, then walked inside and crossed the room. She thought he was going to leave, but he paused, his hand on the doorframe. He bowed his head. He was struggling to subdue his feelings, which were so tangled with grief, rage, and pining that she wasn't sure what to do. She went back inside and shut the balcony door, just watching him.

"I could soothe you," she offered, wanting to take away his pain with the amulet's magic.

"Please don't," he said.

"I don't know what you've been through. I can't even imagine it. But it grieves me to see you suffering."

He turned his head, looking back at her. "You're the cause of it."

"How? I've not done anything—"

"Deliberately. I know." He turned and faced her. "You remind me … of her."

She stared at him blankly, confused.

He frowned and couldn't meet her eyes in that moment. His next words were halting. "Of Tirich Mir. Of that time I had with her. Our family. Our children."

"Your wife?" she whispered, understanding at last and feeling sorry for him.

He nodded and shuddered. "She was a healer." His expression constricted with remembered pain. "Everyone in those mountains was trying to kill me. But she showed me compassion and tended my wounds. Persuaded her tribe to protect me." His voice was so soft and yet full of anguish. "You must understand, Cimree, that this magic that tethers us together, it reveals *too* much. I feel a connection to you that is wholly unnatural. Unearned."

She stared at him, her feelings becoming more tangled in his. "I feel it too."

"It gives you power over me," he said. "I know you're not using it deliberately. I can sense when you resist it."

"What do you mean by that?"

"Earlier this evening. When you were trying to fall asleep. I had to stay downstairs because you were responding to *my* feelings. My memories. Memories you don't have or that we didn't share." He gripped the front of his shirt, and she saw the edges of the amulet beneath it. "This monstrous thing is drawing them out of me. Collecting them. It feeds on our feelings. It provokes them. I don't want to feel those things again. Not right now."

"From when you were married?" she asked, swallowing, wondering what he had experienced and confused by her own inexperience.

"I believe the Queen Mother sent you because she knew I would find you ... hard to resist." He said the last word with distaste. "She's the only one who knows my whole story. And I regret everything I confessed to her because she's used it against me over and over."

Cimree felt his rage begin to flare again, his internal inferno, which he used to protect himself.

She understood. "You're not angry with me, Azra. You use anger as a shield. You use it to burn away all other feelings."

"I have no other choice," he shot back, furious and frustrated. "She's given me no other course but to defy her."

"What does she want from you?" Cimree asked.

He chuckled darkly. "The same thing she wants from you and every other angel sworn. She wants—"

"Total obedience," Cimree broke in, knowing instinctively what he was going to say.

He nodded in agreement. "Yes. Complete submission. I gave it to her long ago. Blindly. But I've learned for myself that she was wrong to stay in Clairvaux. That she drove her husband away. That she saw he was given a second wife who bore him children that revolted and began to kill each other. So she's hiding from her failed marriage but believes herself justified."

Cimree's jaw dropped.

"I feel your shock, your surprise, your wonder," he said acidly. "I know her better than anyone. And I know her jealousy, although she disguises it. When I chose someone else above her, she broke me. She broke me in ways I cannot explain without shocking you further." His voice throbbed. "Hate is all I have left."

Cimree felt it. A core of heat in the center of Azra's being. A flame unquenchable.

He gazed at her with contempt. "You're just another torture. Another attempt to control me."

"I'm not," Cimree said, feeling her own rebellion stirred by his words. She'd always felt the burden of the yoke of obedience.

"Do you have any idea how old she is? How wise and experienced? Do you even know her name?"

"You know her name?" Cimree asked incredulously.

He nodded. "The origin story you've heard in Clairvaux is a twisted misrepresentation of what *really* happened. She's told me the true story. Ploys to win back my trust. My obedience."

"What if you are the one who is lying," Cimree said. "What if you've deceived yourself?"

"I've paid a dear price for it, then," he replied. "And she will pay a dear price for her pride. These wild things are coming to Clairvaux. They will destroy the angel sworn. If her greatest power, grafting magic, can be undone, then the only hope is to flee. To run from a place that she refuses to abandon." He held up his hands. "I'm right or I'm wrong. I submit to the judgment of the Oldknow if I'm wrong. We aren't any safer here than we were in Montheron. All we've done is bought a little more time."

"So you're convinced that leaving Clairvaux is the only way to survive. To hide away in that place you've been before. The place where you loved your wife. And where she healed you."

"I am, Cimree."

"But why? What makes that place any safer?"

"In these mountains, there are few if any caves. In Tirich Mir, there are thousands. The mountains are a fortress. No warlord has ever conquered them all." He gave her a fierce look. "I don't think any of us will survive what is coming if we stay here. But you tell me. Will others abandon the Queen Mother because I suggest it? Would you?"

She stared at him, silently brooding over his words.

"I didn't think so," he grunted.

"You didn't let me answer."

He took a couple of steps, bridging some of the distance between them. "Are you saying you're considering it?" She felt the spark of hope in his chest.

"I'm not sure if it's the best choice, or what may come, but you've been right so far. And you know a place we could go."

"*We?* I think everyone should be given a choice to survive."

"Like Andrin and Perreta's family."

"Exactly. And Wegner, and others like him, who could help make a new place possible. It would be incredibly difficult. At the first sign of suffering, half would want to come back."

Cimree nodded. "You're right. It would require a firm belief that where we're going is better than where we've been."

"*Are* you considering it?" He pressed.

"I've not made oaths by the Gallows Tree," Cimree said. "I am not fully angel sworn. I would not be breaking my word. But we would need to get a fruit from the tree. To heal Andrin." She tapped her own bosom. "To remove the stain in me. And I would set you free."

The look he gave her was full of promise and hope. She could feel it burning fiercely inside him. But then the flame withered. His countenance fell.

"She won't let us," Azra said. "She'd send them flying after us to stop us. And the tree has defenders too. The Morgarten. With mirror blades that turn every way. We *need* the fruit, but we cannot get it."

Cimree cocked her head. "I think Trinati still has one of the seeds. We could plant a new tree. In a new land."

She felt the urge to kiss him.

They were standing so close, the sky awakening outside with the dawn of a new day. She'd never even *thought* about kissing someone before. Was this thought from him or the medallion? The feelings were so embarrassing she lowered her head.

Azra touched her chin, lifting her face to meet his. His eyes were serious and intentional.

"I can't trust anything I feel until I'm not wearing this medallion anymore," he said to her. "And it is bound to me until Trinati releases the grafting."

Thirty-One
Fear Liath

The daybreak hymn echoed across the valley of Clairvaux, the shifting tones from the chorus of female voices sending a pleasing shiver down Cimree's arms as she walked along the footpath. She was making her way toward the trail leading up to the shrine to the Queen Mother, but she was still tired from the lack of sleep the night before. Azra walked in solemn silence next to her, and they were accompanied by angel sworn defenders, all led by Wegner, who represented the high council and had summoned them earlier. Trinati would meet them at the grove, he'd said, in the village overlooking the valley.

The hymn was finished before they reached the trailhead, but the melody still echoed in her mind. The rush of the waterfalls and the churning noise of the Silver River awakened memories. She wanted to savor them, to commit to her mind the sounds and sights of the waters, the rugged cliff walls, the beautiful trees, and the farmlands. Even her breakfast had been a delight to partake of. Because she knew, in her heart, that she would be leaving Clairvaux forever. That idea caused a premature pang of homesickness.

After grafting with some mountain-dwelling animals, they hiked up the rugged slope where the opposing cliffs nearly intersected. As she walked, she said farewell to the different waterfalls she saw. Mist still clung to the edges of the cliffs, though it was a beautiful day. But despite the beauty, things had shifted inside her. Her decision to leave Clairvaux weighed heavily, yet it still *felt* right.

She was stronger this time and the grafting lasted until they reached the village. It was not nearly as crowded as the one in the valley below. The sheer cliff at the base of the Queen Mother's citadel loomed on their right. They made their way silently through town until they reached the wooded edge, and soon the shrine appeared. Trinati was standing at the entrance by the sculpted stone pillars, a few scattered leaves at her feet. Standing near her was Captain Jodocus of the Morgarten and four other men wearing light armor and carrying weapons. They were gazing at the new arrivals with stern expressions. One of the men sneered in contempt when he saw Azra. It made Cimree bristle with anger.

Azra's emotions were subdued. The night before, they'd discussed at length how they could leave the valley undetected. How to guide Andrin, Perreta, and their family out as well. And any others whom they'd trust with that knowledge. She'd wanted to confide in Wegner that morning, but the presence of the defenders had restrained her.

The shrine opened to a beautifully gardened area with stone benches for contemplation and a slew of terraced walls with a variety of plants and flowers.

Trinati wore an inscrutable look as they approached. She eyed Wegner first. "Was the wolf caught and killed?" she asked him.

Wegner frowned. "Caught. Not killed."

"Why not?"

"Because our weapons do not harm it permanently. Even the iron ones. It heals incredibly quickly. And at daybreak, it transformed into a man."

Trinati did not seem surprised. She nodded to him and then

shot a look at Azra before turning back to Wegner. "What did he say for himself?"

"He was surprised to awaken naked and chained. Claims to have no memory of the night before. There was a bite mark on his calf, just behind the knee. Not a wound—it had healed. But the indentations were still visible and had a discoloration."

Cimree swallowed. A man bitten by a wolf had transformed *into* a wolf.

Trinati turned to Captain Jodocus. "I want every newcomer searched for such markings. We need to weed out the gévaudan from among the flock."

Jodocus nodded, and Cimree felt coldness seep inside her. Andrin had those markings. She wondered how long before the bite plague would affect him.

"The fruit of the Gallows Tree can reverse it," Cimree said. "Azra was bitten as well, and he no longer has the marks."

Trinati looked at Cimree and narrowed her eyes. "That's unfortunate. You see, the Fear Liath has established a den in Clair-vaux. It's claimed the Gallows Tree."

Cimree gaped.

"It seems to prefer areas frequented with mist," Trinati continued. "The Gallows Tree is near one of the waterfalls. It killed all the members of the Morgarten who defended the tree. It's killed everyone we've sent there thus far." Her eyes shifted to Azra. "The Queen Mother wants you to destroy it."

"I don't think it's possible to destroy it," Azra said.

"This creature causes fear," Trinati said. "And with Cimree's help, you will be immune to its most dangerous effect. The Queen Mother wishes you to do this. That is why she's summoned you here."

"The Queen Mother is here?" Cimree gasped.

And there she appeared, as if by magic. Maybe she'd been half-hidden by the defenders. The Queen Mother's snowy hair and studied smile made Cimree's knees begin to tremble.

"Without the tree, we have nothing," the Queen Mother said. "Wherever this monster came from or whatever summoned it has become our greatest threat. Our survival depends on destroying it."

Azra's whole body tensed the moment she'd begun speaking. His heart was full of hate and fury, and he clenched his hands into fists. Not out of violence, but Cimree felt it was to keep him from crying out in pain. His tormentor. His nemesis. They were face to face again at last.

"Hello, Azrael," the Queen Mother said with a look of kind compassion.

"You took that name away from me long ago," he replied, his voice shaking with emotion.

"If you rid us of this beast, all the past will be forgiven. You may go wherever you wish. I will command you no longer. That is my offer, Azrael. Help us. Please."

"What if I cannot kill it?" he said bluntly.

"You are my destroying angel. The Oldknow will empower you to do this. Have faith in that. As I believe in you."

Cimree felt a surge of disbelief. Of disdain and mockery. He bowed his head. "I submit to you willingly." He was lying. Cimree felt it plain as day.

"Captain Jodocus. See that he is given everything he needs. You will accompany them to the edge of the woods and see my will is done. If the beast is slain, then he may leave unmolested."

"As you command, Queen Mother," the captain said, bowing his head.

Azra lifted his head and looked into Cimree's eyes. She felt compassion for him. He was being offered what he'd always desired. But he didn't believe it would be given to him. He didn't trust the Queen Mother. Nor did he believe he could win against the Fear Liath. He felt he was being consigned to death.

"Cimree. Walk with me." The Queen Mother offered an

inviting smile and gestured, with her open palm, to enter the shrine.

Cimree nodded and looked at Trinati as she neared her. The other woman looked rested and healed. Younger even. Had she bitten from the fruit herself? Trinati made no gesture, gave no indication of what was to come.

Cimree passed her and fell alongside the Queen Mother as they entered the garden. It was the same path that Cimree had walked earlier when Trinati had taken her to see the Queen Mother. That had been a brief walk through the garden, which had a variety of side paths and stone structures that Cimree had only glimpsed before. This time, the Queen Mother took her into a shaded glen with wisteria and climbing roses. The path was soft turf with flat square stones embedded in the grass.

"He still hates me," the Queen Mother said with a sigh. "I wish it were not so."

"He's embittered by all he's suffered," Cimree said cautiously.

The Queen Mother glanced at her and smiled thoughtfully. "The Tanaquil medallion connects you to him. I've shared that bond with him too. Before he was so angry."

Cimree felt she was being lured into a trap of sorts. That the Queen Mother would try to pry from her things she didn't want to say.

The Queen Mother came to a stone bench built on legs crafted to look like lion's paws. She sat down and patted the seat next to her.

Cimree obeyed and sat down, feeling worried and confused. The Queen Mother acted like nothing was amiss, even though she'd just confirmed that the Fear Liath had claimed the Gallows Tree.

"Has he told you about Delara?"

"Do you mean his wife?"

She smiled and nodded.

"I didn't know her name."

"But he told you she was a healer? Like you?"

"Yes."

"I think you can heal him, Cimree. In time. Do you see what hate and revenge has done to him? How they fester like poison in a wound. I want him to be whole again."

Cimree turned her head and looked at the Queen Mother. "Weren't you the cause of his hate and longing for revenge?"

"Did he tell you what happened to her?"

Cimree shook her head no.

"Well, she died, Cimree. And I allowed it to happen. I permitted it. Those tribes in the Tirich Mir have a corrupt belief. They suppose that women and men are equal. But that is not so. That is not how the Oldknow created things. They have polluted and corrupted the very fountains of life. Azra was allured by them. I can see why. He saw something different and exciting there. He wanted to change the natural order of things." She pursed her lips and shook her head before patting Cimree's leg. "You would not understand these things. You are innocent still. But I understand them. I had a husband long ago. And he rejected me and was banished from Clairvaux by the Oldknow for his disobedience."

She fell silent, and Cimree watched her as she gazed into the pleasant trees ringing the little secluded garden before continuing with her story. "This was our home. This was our kingdom. We would walk these gardens unrobed, with no shame. *He*, my husband, introduced shame into the world, Cimree. All because he was seduced by our enemy who whispered to him in the guise of a serpent. He believed in a lie over the truth of the Oldknow." She sighed and swiped some snow-white hair from her ear.

"What was the lie?" Cimree asked.

"There was another tree in the valley back then. A tree whose fruit makes one mortal. I've since cut it down because I saw its capacity for evil. The Oldknow said that if either of us partook of the fruit of that tree, we would die. My husband tried to persuade me to leave Clairvaux with him. But I remained obedient to the

Oldknow's command. I refused. I would rather remain alone than be disobedient to the Oldknow."

Cimree wrinkled her brow. "But if you were alone, how are there so many people?"

"The Oldknow fashioned for my husband another wife. Havah. But in the eyes of the Oldknow, we are still married. My state has been a celibate one. And I've found much joy and purpose here." That didn't contradict what Azra had told her. "I've seen what happens in the fallen world, Cimree. I've witnessed the transgressions of all mortal kind. The pain and suffering they cause each other." She shook her head. "I do not regret my choice. I maintain the title the Oldknow gave me. But it is just a title. I have a name, a past, and I have memories of countless ages of disobedience." Her voice became more firm. "I will not forsake this valley. It was given to me. The Oldknow told me that the hills would be removed and mountains would depart, but His kindness, His *everlasting* kindness, would not depart from me. I will stay here. No matter what happens."

Cimree felt strange. Not angry or confused, just perplexed. She knew the Origin story of the creation of the world, of the husband who had chosen to depart and abandon his wife. She even knew of the infamous serpent, which is why snakes had been driven out of Clairvaux.

"What happened to Delara?" Cimree asked.

"She was killed by the angel sworn I sent to liberate Azrael," the Queen Mother said. "He had lived among them for some time before we discovered him. He had children with her. He'd become a father."

Cimree felt a stab of pain in her heart. "You ... you killed them?"

"It was my command that he be set free. I did not know, at the time, how deeply his heart had been corrupted by the experience. All the adults were killed. But not the children. Children are innocent."

"What became of them? Of Azra's children?"

"That was a long time ago, Cimree. They were given to other families to raise. They were nurtured and protected and taught our ways. They lived joyful lives, which would not have happened in those warring mountains. I thought he would heal in time. I thought he would understand from his experience the evil of what he had succumbed to. But he nursed his hate and revenge instead. Maybe now, at last, he can be at peace once again. I will not compel his obedience any longer."

She reached over and smoothed some of Cimree's hair. "And I won't compel yours either."

The Oldknow said to the husband, "This thing you have done by partaking of the fruit of knowledge—for what cause have you violated my commandment?" And the man said, "The serpent deceived me in the first cause. And I ate." And the Oldknow said to the Queen Mother, "Behold, the man has become like one of Us. Knowing good and evil. Lest he put out his hand and take also of the fruit of the Gallows Tree and eat and live forever, I will send him out of Clairvaux to till the ground, to hunt beasts, and to multiply and replenish the earth. He has rebelled against thy rule and seeks his own dominion. A fallen world have I ordained for him. That he may learn to judge good from evil. Thou shalt not compel his obedience or that of his posterity. But thou shalt invite and entice him to do good always. He shall never return to Clairvaux, lest it be destroyed. But of his posterity thou mayest approve if they swear fealty to thee and to Me."

— Origin, the Tale of the Queen Mother
of Clairvaux

THIRTY-TWO
REBELLION

Cimree and Azra walked deeper into the vertex of the valley. The cliff walls rose steeply before them, a wedge shape that was unpassable. The noise of the waterfall they approached became louder and louder, as did the inner feelings of turmoil in her heart. As soon as they had left the boundary of woods leading to the Gallows Tree, where Captain Jodocus and his escort waited for them, she'd told him all the Queen Mother had revealed to her. The promises of freedom. The gentleness of the words. And she awaited his response.

"She can be very gentle when she wishes to be," Azra said flatly. He had been given the weapons of his choosing to face the Fear Liath. He'd chosen two mirror blades, a hunter's bow and quiver, and a brace of knives. He knew the way to the Gallows Tree and which waterfall it was near. The two of them had been sent alone to face the Fear Liath.

"I'm not sure what to make of it," Cimree said. "She not only offered you freedom; she offered it to me as well."

"I know her. She did not offer us a gift. It was a threat."

"In what way?"

He glanced at her, his heart bubbling with anger. "Everything she told you was meant to manipulate you, Cimree."

"But what am I to think, then?"

"I can't think for you. Nor should I. Don't you see it? She put us on this path to achieve her ends. She's lost the tree. She will do anything to get it back. Even risk our lives."

"So what do we do? We cannot just walk away. The hunters are watching us. And what about Andrin and Perreta and the children? What about the people coming to Clairvaux? If we fail to destroy the Fear Liath, they're all going to die."

Azra shook his head and sighed. "I don't know what her plan is. But she's desperate. If we make it to the tree, she will not deliver on her promise. That much I know."

"You think she's lied to us?"

He snorted. "She's lied about everything."

"Like what?"

He turned and looked at her skeptically. "The Origin story. The tale of the first husband. The serpent and the fruit. It did not happen that way."

Cimree blinked in surprise. "But those words, that lore, it is part of the valley. This valley is proof that it's true. The Gallows Tree is proof."

"The tree is real enough. So is its fruit. But the story isn't."

"But how do you know?"

He stopped walking. "Because I've heard her share different versions of it."

"When?"

"When I was Azrael. I listened to her share a version with Trinati that was different than what was told to others. The version you know is a simplification. It is missing elements. The serpent, for example. There is more to *his* story than what is in Origin. Over the centuries, she has stripped away bits of it. It barely resembles the version I learned when I came to Clairvaux."

"Why would she change it?"

"To stop people from questioning it. To make it a sort of mystery. To be clung to for security. The truth is that the Oldknow wanted her to leave the valley. And she refused because she was afraid of what lay beyond."

"I don't understand anything of what you're saying." She felt frustrated but also interested.

He started walking again, so she hurried to catch up with him.

"I cannot tell you," he said. "If I do, I must suffer myself to be killed in a gruesome manner. That is a consequence of being angel sworn. I violated my covenant, but I did not reveal anything improper. I just refused to obey her. And I can see why the first husband did the same. She is too stubborn."

"You are calling her stubborn?" Cimree challenged.

He paused again and turned on her. "I came from a brutal and evil kingdom. Under the boot of a warlord who despoiled everything he touched. Who knew no boundaries nor accepted any authority above his own. The depravity, if you knew it, would make you weep. I escaped. Barely. And I came to Montheron. It was such a contrast to the horrible realm that I'd lived in. I was but a child then. No more than eight. But I saw the difference."

"Did Captain Odeon take you in?"

He laughed. "I was there long before Odeon. I became a hunter. I joined the angel sworn. When I met the Queen Mother, I told her about the brutal kingdom that I'd fled from. She sent the Long Patrol to study it, to see if what I'd said was true. And when she learned that it was, she destroyed it. You cannot imagine how I felt. How vindicated. I believed everything she taught me. I trained and learned and mastered every skill, despite the injustices deliberately imposed to test our loyalty. I obeyed every word of her command with exactness." His voice throbbed with loathing. She could see the memories in his eyes. Could feel the mixture of emotions in his chest. The feeling of pride. Of horror. He'd been the destroying angel. And he regretted it.

She touched his arm, another instinctive gesture. This time he didn't pull away.

"She told me that men and women were incompatible," he said softly. "That men would always vie for dominance. She used the warlord's brutal example to offer proof. When men rule, the people suffer. I believed it. I was convinced of it. I felt there was a part of me that was always to be feared, distrusted, even loathed. And then I found another way."

"When you found Delara," Cimree said, lowering her hand.

"I didn't believe it at first," Azra said. "I refused to believe the evidence of my own eyes. I made up every possible reason why what I was seeing was wrong. But I could not, in the end, help but be convinced. What does Origin teach? 'It is not agreeable for the woman to be alone.' Well, Cimree, it is not agreeable for *men* to be alone either." He pointed at her. "All creatures have mate bonds. I don't mean to be simplistic, but there is a natural order to things. And since the beginning of this world, she has defied it because of what happened in the garden with the serpent. She's created this myth, this elaborate lie, to justify her fear of attachment and belonging. She will not leave this valley. Even if everyone is going to die."

From the misty trail ahead, a figure emerged from the trees. It was Trinati, wreathed in mist. How much had she overheard? Cimree felt her stomach lurch with dread.

Azra turned around and scowled.

"You're talking so loudly I can't help but wonder if you *wanted* me to hear you," Trinati said with a devious smile.

"How long have you been there?" Azra asked coldly.

"I brought a snake back with me from our journey," Trinati answered. She had a pouch attached to her belt that was different from what Cimree had seen before. Immediately, Cimree felt the bond of the serpent, which was being tethered in grafting magic.

Trinati opened the pouch, revealed the listless reptile inside, then settled it into Cimree's hand. Trinati's nostrils flared with disgust.

"They're quite adept at camouflage," Trinati said. "Which is how I concealed myself from you. I could see you both quite well. A disgusting creature, to be sure," she said, gesturing to the creature in Cimree's hand. "But your affinity made me curious to see what gifts they had that might be useful on our journey."

"Our journey?" Azra asked with a tone of curiosity.

Trinati's lips grew firm. "I tried reasoning with her. But I've come to accept that your judgment of her is correct, Azra. She will not leave. And she will not allow anyone else to leave Clairvaux."

"She just promised us freedom," Cimree said, confused.

Trinati shook her head. "No, you're a ploy in a desperate gambit. She believes these abominations have come for the tree. She intends to destroy it. In the hope that if it is gone, the abominations will leave as well."

Azra shook his head and snorted. "So she was sending us to our deaths."

Trinati nodded. "She does not want you leading us anywhere. None of the angel sworn have been able to prick this creature. Make it bleed. While you engage it, the rest of us are to douse the tree in oil and set it afire. That is our mission." She gave them both a calculating look. "I'll fulfill the mission. I don't want the tree to fall into enemy hands. But I still have the seed, and I intend to plant it elsewhere."

Cimree felt a surge of relief and hope. Trinati had been making plans all along. "How many have you persuaded to come?"

"Uorsin. Wegner. Several other members of the high council are in on it." She looked at Cimree and then at Azra. "I've persuaded those that I'm telling that this is a secret mission for the Queen Mother. To establish a new tree and colonize another valley. But it will only work if you are part of it. Azra is the only one left who has been to Tirich Mir."

Cimree smiled. "And to think we were already considering it."

"So she was intending to kill us all along," Azra said. He didn't sound surprised. "I want you to gather that family I rescued. They're going too, or none of us are."

"I thought you'd make that demand. I've already arranged it. One of my trusted lieutenants will lead them to Netherwind Pass. I've stationed only those I can trust there."

"I'm relieved, but can we not save more?" Cimree asked. "Others should be given the chance to decide."

"If word gets out, then the Queen Mother will block our effort. I can't risk it. Not yet."

"So we just need to make a show of fighting this thing? To give you time to burn the tree?"

"Exactly. You'll head to the pass, and we'll meet you there."

"How do you know the Queen Mother hasn't already anticipated your rebellion?" Azra asked.

Trinati gave him a scrutinizing look. "Because she's too entangled in her own self-deceit. She wants to believe people are loyal to her." She paused. "When the fire is burning, that is your chance to flee. Fly away. Meet us at Netherwind Pass."

"I'm still stunned," Cimree said. "That she was going to send us to our deaths so ... spitefully."

Trinati shook her head. "It wasn't out of spite, Cimree. It was out of caution."

"Caution? How so?"

"Because you wear the Tanaquil medallion. It will continue to corrupt you. And we need another fruit or another tree, or it will twist you further. It was never her intent that you wear it this long."

Cimree's heart fell. "I didn't want this."

Trinati nodded in acknowledgment of Cimree's feelings and then gripped her arm. "We must each do our part. Now be ready. Watch for the flames and then get away from the tree."

Azra drew his distaff and pointed it at Trinati.

Thirty-Three

Betrayal

Cimree stared in disbelief as Azra invoked the grafting magic on Trinati. She watched as Trinati slumped to the earth, listless. Her eyes were open, her jaw slack. She was utterly helpless.

"Wait ... why?" Cimree demanded.

Azra put the distaff back and approached the indolent form of the archangel. He began to search her.

"What do you think you are doing!" Cimree said.

"Looking for the seed," Azra replied. He found it wrapped in a packet of cloth in her pocket. He unfolded the cloth and looked at the seed. He rubbed his thumb across the thready texture. Then he brought it to his nose and sniffed it.

"It's the one," he said and then folded it up again and offered it to Cimree. She was still so surprised she couldn't speak. "Take it!"

"Why did you do that to her? Are we leaving now?"

"Of course we are!" Azra snorted. He stood, approached her, and thrust the package into her hand. "I don't want to fight that thing. And I don't want to be under Trinati's control any more than I wanted to be under the Queen Mother's. We're not taking the Netherwind Pass. I already gave Andrin directions to another meeting place."

"But what of Wegner and the others?"

"They're loyal to Trinati. I don't trust her, and I don't want to be bound to her. We are going. Now! While we still can. Without the seed, it was useless trying to flee."

"What did you do to her?"

"I grafted her to a tree grub," Azra said with a haughty smile. "It will wear off soon enough, so we can make our way. And now we have that serpent too, which will help when we leave."

"Azra, are you sure?"

"I suspected that Trinati was going to rebel. I haven't said anything. I know the Queen Mother. And Trinati was far too reckless. This was her first disobedience. I'm an expert at it. I know without a doubt there will be enemies at Netherwind Pass. Someone has already betrayed her." He took her by the hand. "This is our chance, Cimree. Let's get out of Clairvaux while we can!"

She looked down at Trinati's vacant eyes. A little trail of drool leaked from her mouth. It felt wrong to leave her so helpless. But Azra was right. It might be their only chance to flee the valley before the more dangerous foes arrived. She thought of Andrin and the bite mark on his arm. He would not be given fruit from the Gallows Tree unless he foreswore his marriage.

"Why do you hesitate?" he demanded.

"I'm sorry. But you are right. Let's go." She gave an apologetic look to Trinati, and then the two of them began to walk briskly hand in hand. She wasn't sure when their hands had touched or who had instigated it, only that it felt natural to do so. She stuffed the bundled seed into her pocket. They no longer walked toward the falls but toward the Silver River. They were near its origin, the base of a massive waterfall—the Wilderswill. The other waterfalls in the valley joined with the Silver River as it traveled toward Lake Beatriz. Mist from the falls lingered day and night, along with the omnipresent rush that was so noisy Cimree doubted even the hymns of the angel sworn could have overpowered it.

Still holding her hand, Azra tracked his way through the trees until they reach the banks of the river. There were boulders lodged in the silver waters, and trees were interspersed along both sides. On the other side of the river, a trickling waterfall cut a ribbon down the cliff face opposite them. They were at the wedge of the valley, near the point where cliffs would block any way forward.

Azra came to stop at a cluster of larger, moss-slick boulders and studied the area. He released her hand and drew his grafting wand again. There were some blackbirds in the trees, and he snagged at them, imbuing himself and Cimree with the power to fly. The speed and strength of flight depended on the kind of bird bonded with, but for this short purpose the blackbirds were perfect. Instantly, she felt the tingles in her shoulder blades, and they glided over the river to cross it. The Wilderswill's thunder began to ebb as they followed the meadow.

"We'll find cover in those trees," he said, pointing to the growth of aspen and pine ahead.

They never made it that far. She felt the thrum of anxiety in Azra's heart.

Captain Jodocus arrived with a patrol of hunters, coming from the heights of the cliffs and landing in a circular pattern around them. Their weapons were drawn. Azra pulled his twin blades out. He was determined to fight, even though they were vastly outnumbered.

"You can't win this challenge, Azra," Jodocus said. "There are more of us watching from the cliffs."

"I'm not going to fight that thing," Azra said. "It's all a sham anyway."

Cimree counted eight of them. Eight hunters. Her nerves were raw with worry. She could sense Azra's fierce determination. Fight now or fight later. He'd known all along there was no leaving Clairvaux without a fight. He was putting it on his terms.

"Where's Trinati?" Jodocus said. "She didn't come out of the woods with you. I half expected her to, since she's turned into the betrayer."

"We didn't want to go along with her scheme," Azra said.

"Does she still have the seed?" Jodocus said. "The Queen Mother suspects she does."

"It was given to someone you wouldn't suspect," Azra answered. "Trinati doesn't have it anymore. She wouldn't tell me what she did with it." His cunning and deceit were impressive.

The angel sworn began advancing. "Don't make me destroy you, Azra. I know what you're capable of. You can't win."

"I like my chances," Azra said. "Why don't you come with us, Jodocus? This valley will be destroyed soon enough."

"Well, I like *our* chances," Jodocus said.

Cimree wondered what to do. She could use the amulet on everyone. She could drive them away. That was probably their best hope.

She began to summon its power, focusing first on Jodocus. She reached out and snatched his emotions, tethering her to him with the power of the medallion. She'd felt real fear in the mountains when she'd discovered Damion's dead body. That sense of fear, of panic, of—

"Cimree," Jodocus said in warning. "I have archers aiming for you. Do not use the Tanaquil against us. Azra—lay down your weapons or we kill her right now."

She felt Azra's heart cringe with fear and worry. He looked back at her, gazed at the men surrounding him. He felt defiance too. He didn't want Cimree to die. Not when he could prevent it. Frustration roiled inside him.

"Azra, I won't warn you again. You will face the Fear Liath and free the tree. Or she will die right now, and then you will face it unarmed. Either way, you are going to the Gallows Tree. You think the Queen Mother didn't foresee this? That the girl wasn't brought for this reason? Think man! You cannot outsmart her!"

Azra looked into Cimree's eyes. She felt the gushing disappointment. He dropped the mirror blades into the meadow grass.

Cimree unclenched her control of the magic. She could see her own glowing eyes reflected in his.

"Bind his arms. Take his distaff too."

"You think I can defeat it without grafting?" Azra said in a hollow voice.

Cimree watched as the ring of hunters tightened around them. They were looking at her and Azra with disdain. Cimree swallowed, feeling sick to her stomach. The Queen Mother had promised them freedom, but she had only intended their deaths. The sting of the betrayal was bitter to taste.

Azra did not resist when the hunters bound his hands behind his back. His swords were confiscated from the grass. Cimree worried they might search her and discover the seed in her pocket. She looked at Jodocus until he glanced her way.

"You weren't at Montheron," she told him. "You don't know what's coming."

"If I had been at Montheron," he answered defiantly, "I would have defended her to the last warrior! Like Captain Odeon did. Obedience is the first law of heaven."

Azra snorted. One of the hunters raised his hand to smack Azra on the mouth, but Jodocus gave him a warning look not to.

"I tell you, Jodocus," Azra said, "this valley will be desolate. Its streams will turn into fire. Its dust into brimstone. Its smoke will last for a generation or more. No one shall pass through here. No archangel, no mortal man or woman. Nettles and brambles will come up in this wasteland. It will be for jackals and vultures. The night witch will have no place to rest."

"How dare you say that," Jodocus said, his voice throbbing with rage. "How dare you use her name that way!"

Azra looked at him incredulously. "Those aren't my words, Jodocus. The Oldknow sent a messenger with that warning ages ago. A thousand generations ago. She wrote it down. She *knew* this doom was coming. And she's done nothing to prevent it."

"You're a liar."

"Am I? Ask her yourself. You *know* her true name means *night witch*."

Jodocus drew a dagger and looked like he was about to plunge it into Azra's chest. Cimree stepped in front of him since he could not defend himself. "Blasphemer."

"Put down your blade, Captain," Cimree said, summoning the magic again. Trying to dispel the anger and rage.

"I speak the truth, Jodocus. Ask her yourself. Ask her about the messenger. Ask her about the warning. I am not lying."

"But you deceive, just as Asmodeus did in the garden. Just as he tricked her husband!"

"Oh, Jodocus. That story is false. You cling to shadows. The Queen Mother was supposed to leave Clairvaux. It was the Oldknow's will that she do so."

"Apostate!"

Cimree increased the magic, trying to siphon the dangerous feelings away. Jodocus turned on her, bringing the blade to her throat. She felt the edge against her skin.

"I warned you not to use your magic against me!" he threatened.

"I'm trying to stop bloodshed," Cimree gasped. "Captain. You did not have orders to kill us. We're defenseless. Put aside your anger."

His lips twitched. She released the magic again and was gratified when tempers began to cool. She did not feel any deceit coming from Azra. There was no false motive at all. What he said, he believed.

Jodocus slid his dagger into its sheath and glared at Cimree then at Azra. "You are both going to the Gallows Tree. Defeat the Fear Liath if you can. But if you try to leave the mist again, my archers will strike you down. Do not trust in false prophecies. Now, fulfill the Queen Mother's will, you brute." He gripped Azra's tunic front, his face deadly serious. "Or the next time, I will not stay my hand." And he looked at Cimree to imply that he would cut her throat himself.

THIRTY-FOUR
KILLING FOG

Cimree's heart sank with despair as she and Azra were marched toward the waterfall near the Gallows Tree. This was the heart of Clairvaux, it's most sacred precinct. Her agitated mind grasped for some way out of the situation. Angel sworn would be watching like eagles from above. And even though their assuredly keen vision could not pierce the mist, they would know if Cimree and Azra attempted to escape as soon as they left the boundaries of the mist. Going to the tree brought death. Retreating from it did as well.

Captain Jodocus called a halt. Cimree gazed up at the mountain wall and the thunderous Wilderswill cascading off its face, breaking apart into a thousand rivulets. A thick growth of trees lay before them, wreathed in mist from the falls. The pit of dread in her stomach sank deeper.

"You will go face this doom," Jodocus said curtly. "Dispose of the Fear Liath, and you will live. The Queen Mother may show you mercy still, despite your unworthiness. If the monster cannot be destroyed, then the tree must be burned. We stand ready to fulfill that order. Now … depart."

Azra gave him a look of loathing and contempt. "My weapons?"

"I give them to you freely. Raise them against me or any of mine, and you will be brought to ruin. This I vow." He nodded for one of his sentries to return the mirror blades to Azra. Finally, they returned the distaff. They had weapons ready, including one man with a dagger poised at Cimree's neck. She swallowed nervously.

Azra sheathed his swords and then extended his hand to Cimree. Anxious to put their captors behind them, she accepted his hand, and they both walked away.

"What are we going to do?" she whispered to him.

"We prepare for a fight," he said in a low voice, using his free hand to draw his distaff. He began to weave a pattern of graftings, quickly and efficiently, drawing on the woodland animals nearby. She felt, as she had at Montheron, his resistance to pain, or more accurately, his willingness to suffer, to take on more than most could bear. It grieved her that he hurt himself that way, but he knew what he could endure, and great strength came from his surrender to agony.

Cimree drew her distaff and bonded with the serpent that Trinati had brought. This was an easy bond, a joining of power that wasn't forced but freely transferred. The snake lay coiled in the bag Trinati had given her. She felt her senses enhanced, the ability to see heat would be helpful. Reflexes. Venom. And not just that. An ability, if still, to be unseen, to blend in with the surroundings in the natural world. She had not experienced this in Montheron because a town was not a serpent's habitat. But the woods, this misty grove, would enable her to be more invisible. Hiding from the Fear Liath would help her survive. And it felt so natural that she wondered whether that desire to be still and blend in had played some part on the mountain when she'd first encountered the Fear Liath.

The grafting felt natural and comfortable, with hardly any pain or discomfort involved. The serpent *wanted* to be part of her. Was this the nature of having an affinity? She remembered Wegner's previous warning that even a Beesinger could be stung. It felt almost laughable in that moment. She wished there were other serpents nearby so she could control them as she had at the logjam and use them to scout their prey.

The farther they walked into the mist, the more nervous she became, and she felt a similar sense coming from Azra.

"How far to the tree?" she whispered to him.

"It's at the base of the mountain. There is no trail leading to it. The woods are guarded by the Morgarten day and night, to prevent mortals from stealing the fruit."

Even though it was day, the mist engulfing them diluted the sunlight. There were no more sounds of other woodland creatures. Just the cracking of twigs as she passed. She noticed that Azra's footfalls were nearly silent. He was walking in a different way, a stride that was purposeful but wary of making noise. She didn't understand what he was doing, so she could not mimic it, but she was determined to ask him about it if they survived this encounter.

Images came to her mind. Of Damion. Of Milena. Both savaged and destroyed by this creature. Her breathing quickened with fear.

"Use the medallion to calm yourself," Azra said. "I can feel what you feel."

She nodded and invoked the amulet. Again she felt the sweet rush of power as she silenced her fears. Azra's eyes began to glow silver. She imagined hers were glowing too.

The beast suddenly cried out, the frightening roar just as Cimree remembered from her mad flight off the mountain, and it was coming from directly ahead. Had it sensed her use of the magic? It seemed possible.

"Have you heard that sound before?" she asked. "This is the sound it made."

"No," Azra answered. "But it is just as it was described to me in Tirich Mir."

"I hope you can kill it," Cimree said with determination.

"I will try."

The ground became steeper as they ventured deeper into the waterfall's fog, and the noise of the water came violently to their ears. She stared into the mist, trying to see the heat of the beast's form. Her fear was gone, siphoned into the amulet. She was walking to her death and yet felt calm, as if nothing in the world were wrong. The fear of heights kept people from walking too close to the cliff's edge. And the absence of fear gave them the idea that they were infallible. But the danger was the same either way.

She heard a snuffling noise in the woods. Azra released her hand and gently drew his mirror blades. They gleamed in the mist, radiating light from the source of their forging.

"Do not confront it," he said to her. "Keep as many trees as you can between you and it. And keep me free of its terror."

"I wish we didn't have to do this, Azra."

"If wishes were horses, beggars would ride. If I can find a way out of this situation, I will call out to you."

"Just be careful," she said, touching his forearm.

She felt the jolt it caused him, the remembered pleasure of having an intimate companion. He didn't jerk his arm away, but she sensed a flicker of disapproval from him.

The snuffling noise had gotten closer. Cimree felt no fear. Every emotion but determination had been drained from her.

Azra marched ahead of her, swishing the blades. She infused him with confidence and courage.

"Come, you devil," Azra said in challenge. "You will not find me weak with fear."

A smudge in the mist announced its arrival. The beast was taller than a man, taller than an ordinary bear. It stood on its hind legs and let out another roar that promised devastation and death. The amulet absorbed the terror of it, and Cimree felt the peculiar urge to giggle.

Just beyond it, she sensed a powerful magic. A tree with roots as deep as the underground rivers within the mountains.

The Fear Liath dropped down to four paws and shifted closer. Its aspect was like no bear she knew, save for a scarred snout and slathering fangs. Its eyes were milky white and crazed, and a fetid smell came from it, making her gag. Dagger-long claws jutted from its paws, and when it reared again, it revealed an arm coming from the center of its bulky chest and yet another protruding from its back. Multilimbed. Everything about it shrieked of corruption and ill creation.

With a terrible snarl, it suddenly rushed at Azra.

He leaped over it, but the crooked appendage from its hunched back swiped at him. Azra cut at that unnatural limb with the swords, and the metal struck fur with a thump. The Fear Liath pivoted and vaulted at Azra, but he jerked away with a hummingbird's reflexes, then slashed at the beast. The creature's fur was the color of soot and coals, and its quick movements blurred in the shadowed woods. It swiped at him and missed again, the claws effortlessly ripping through a tree trunk instead, spraying fragments of wood.

Azra landed in a crouch behind it, stabbing at where its heart should be. But his blade could not pierce its hide.

Quick despite its bulk, the Fear Liath swiped at him yet again, and Cimree heard the grunt and felt the pain as it connected. Again the blades whirled, stabbing the monster in another vulnerable spot, this time aimed at its throat, and Azra danced back out of reach when the blow proved ineffectual. The Fear Liath, treating the weapons Azra brandished as insignificant, charged at him, trying to maul him, but the warrior flew up, remaining just out of reach of its claws. It howled in frustration and then shifted, charging at Cimree.

"Behind a tree!" Azra shouted at her.

Cimree quickly retreated behind the nearest one, but the Fear Liath swung a large paw at it, breaking the trunk and knocking it to the side, and she gasped, then darted into a thickly wooded area, to a tree with three branches shooting up from a single trunk.

"Fly!" Azra warned her.

Cimree drew her distaff and tried to find a bird, but there were none within the mist. Nature had abandoned this place that the Fear Liath had claimed. She heard the splintering noise as another tree was broken through, but she whirled and faced the beast, unafraid. The Fear Liath loomed over her, jaw open, revealing its horrid teeth.

Cimree felt the magic surge through her in a familiar response.

"Stop!" she commanded it, holding out her hand. She felt a wind at her back, a rushing of power that tossed her hair.

Impossibly, the beast halted, panting, snarling, raging at her power over it. The medallion controlled a force she didn't understand. She could sense the maddening fury of the Fear Liath, its desire to rip her to pieces as it had done to so many others. But she defied it, hand held up, and it could not resist her. Their wills clashed. She drew on the power of the amulet again, striving to reach its depths.

"Go!" she commanded it, her voice raw with emotion, the wind rushing behind her like a storm.

The beast grunted, defiant yet daunted. It dropped down on its forepaws again. The limb that bulged from its chest like some grotesque deformity slashed at the earth. It huffed at her, spitefully, and then sauntered away. She realized she could not see any heat from it nor had she seen any before. It was living but it was not living and the air around it shimmered with iridescence. Again, the abhorrence of its nature twisted inside her stomach.

Azra approached her, a look of relief on his face. His eyes were glowing silver still as they shared the magic of the medallion.

"I thought ... I thought it would kill you," he said, shaking his head. "But you stopped it. You commanded it! How?"

"There's something about the medallion," she said in confusion. Spots began to dance before her eyes, and a weakness stole over her, making her shake. She swayed, but Azra dropped his blades to catch her.

"I feel faint," she whispered, her knees turning to water. The magic had left her, abandoned her, and she felt it was all she could do to keep her chin up.

"Cimree!" he shouted, his voice sounding farther away. She felt his hands digging into her arms near her shoulders.

The roar came from the mist again. The Fear Liath ... had it sensed her weakness?

"It's coming back." Cimree panted, fear sparking in her chest. She tried to quell it, but the medallion had become inert. She looked in Azra's face and saw the silver drain from his eyes.

The medallion had halted the Fear Liath, but it had taken a cost from her, a sapping of her strength and energy just like it had in Montheron. In consequence for its use, she would be helpless.

Azra set her down in the leaves and picked up his weapons. She felt his heart quail with fear and tried to snatch the feeling from him, but there was only a void where there had once been power. Her own heart began to quicken with dread as the darkness closed around her.

She fainted, her ears ringing with the roar of the falls before she lost all consciousness.

THIRTY-FIVE
THE GALLOWS TREE

Pain. Hopelessness. Death. Those were the feelings Cimree encountered when she regained consciousness. Her mind was fogged by weakness and incapacity, but she roused herself only to find she was in an unfamiliar place and covered in leaves. She felt the agony of Azra's wounds and realized he'd been attacked by the Fear Liath. He was lying nearby, bleeding to death.

She heard the snuffle of the Fear Liath in the mist. It had to be close or she wouldn't have heard it over the rush of the waterfall. As she blinked fully awake, she found herself sprawled out, covered in foliage and withered leaves. How had she gotten there? Azra must have carried her away. He'd set her down—that was the last thing she remembered before fainting. And he must have tried to hide her in the brush when the Fear Liath caught up with them again.

As she lifted her head, she caught a glimpse of the creature's bulk in the fog. Her heart began to quail with fear. She reached for her distaff, making noise in the process, and heard it grunt. She grit her teeth and carefully drew the scionwood from its sheath at her belt. She sensed the serpent in the bag Trinati had given her and used the wand to graft with it again. The joining was immediate and effortless. Although she could not see any heat coming from the Fear Liath, there were ripples in the air that flashed in and out of sight. But she could smell it once more, and the stench was unbearable. Her reflexes quickened, and she could taste venom in her saliva. But what she wanted at that moment was camouflage. To blend in with the woods so well that the Fear Liath could not see her.

She summoned the power of the Tanaquil amulet to smother her fear. The snuffling noise was coming her way. Cimree lay perfectly still, gripping the distaff in her hand tightly. The Fear Liath materialized from the fog, the odd-angled appendages of its extra arms giving it a menacing look. Dagger-like claws dripped blood, and the awful snout was bared, revealing its hooked teeth.

Azra was dying. He was lying nearby, breathing shallowly and painfully. Like Milena and Damion. And all the other victims of this creature.

It did not come directly toward her. It was searching, using its senses to try to track her. From the mist behind it, she saw the glow of flames and white heat on the blue of the surrounding woods. Something was burning. She realized instantly it was the Gallows Tree. Captain Jodocus and his men had doused it in oil and set fire to it.

The Fear Liath was a dozen paces from where she lay. It growled and lifted its head, then bellowed its fearsome roar again. The sound was deafening and frightening, but the amulet subdued her feelings.

Leave, just leave! She thought at it.

The Fear Liath bounded toward the burning tree. As soon as it was out of sight, Cimree scrabbled from her hiding place and rushed to where she felt Azra. Without the bond, she would not have found him easily. His armor and clothing were in tatters. His bow was broken on the ground nearby. A dagger protruded from a nearby tree trunk. One of his swords had broken in half. He lay on his side, one arm outstretched. His eyes were open, his mouth a rictus of pain as he panted.

Cimree knelt next to him, gazing at the devastating injuries. No healer could save him. Let alone a novice one. There were too many wounds. He'd lost too much blood already. Even with his accelerated healing, he was going to die.

"T-Take ... the ... amulet," he said, his voice quaking in pain.

"I can't. Not until Trinati unlocks it." Her heart panged with the loss of another ... friend? When had he become her friend? Tears stung her eyes.

"You'll ... need ... it. When I'm ... dead."

"Where can I go? You're the only one who knew the place."

"You have ... to try," he whispered. He closed his eyes, shuddering.

"Azra," she groaned, touching his shoulder. She felt something else inside him, something more than pain. He was remembering when his wife touched him. He was clinging to that memory as he died.

Cimree began to weep. She'd lost everything. Her mentor. Her valley. She had no one to turn to. Nowhere to run. Hopelessness seeped into her but was held at bay by the mysterious amulet that Azra still wore around his neck. It drained her emotions, preventing her from being overwhelmed by them.

She looked up at the mist-shrouded sky, feeling racked with grief and loss. In her mind, she recited a desolate prayer to the Oldknow. Like the chorus of hymns that sang from the heights of the mountains each morning. Each night. The idea to seek aid from the Oldknow was all she could think of.

What is to become of us? I thought we were Thy children? Why? Why have Thou forsaken us?

She wrestled with her feelings of despair. She released her hold on the magic, allowing herself to experience the sorrow. She heard the Fear Liath roar again, heard cries from men who were still near the tree. In her heart, she knew they could not kill such a creature.

Cimree gazed down at Azra, watching him struggle against death. Each breath was a battle. A battle he was losing. His thoughts clung to his memories to comfort himself in his dying hour.

Is there something I can do? she thought, feeling not rebellious but another feeling. What was it? Submissive? *Is there a way I can save him? If I can save him, we can bring others to Tirich Mir.*

She heard a snap of twigs behind her. Someone was approaching.

Do not look.

The impression flitted in her mind. Cimree squeezed her eyes shut. She smelled someone. The smell was gentle, like the subtle aroma of edelweiss. She heard another snapping stick. Cimree felt an intense curiosity to look.

A cry of pain from farther away made her lift her head, but she didn't open her eyes. The smell of edelweiss was close. She felt a leaf being pulled from her hair.

"Who are you?" Cimree asked, still squeezing her eyes shut. Not quite afraid but not reassured either.

Silence. No one spoke. But she could still smell the other person, could sense she was no longer alone with Azra.

"Can you help me?" Cimree pleaded.

She heard the snap of twigs again, could smell the person as they left her side and knelt by Azra. The curiosity to look was overpowering. But she did not yield to it. Her stubbornness prevented it.

Another smell. A flowery smell.

"What are you doing?" Cimree begged.

Then she felt what Azra felt. A soothing magic began to envelop him. His wounds were shriveling, the skin knitting together impossibly fast. It was not the purple fruit of the Gallows Tree. It was something else. Something powerful and sweet-smelling. It suffused Azra, taking away his pains, his injuries. It washed through him, making him gasp and breathe and groan with delight instead of agony.

Cimree opened her eyes, unable to resist, and started in surprise at the little girl kneeling by Azra, holding a bit of flowering moss to his chest. The girl wore a simple tunic and probably nothing else. No trews or boots or cloak. However, there was an ankle bracelet shaped like a serpent. The girl was probably eight years old. Just a little girl with dark hair.

The girl turned her head and looked at Cimree. There was a frown of disapproval on her mouth. Or was it disappointment? She could not sense the girl's feelings. They were completely blocked from her.

"You healed him," Cimree said in wonder, gazing at the rested look on Azra's sleeping face. The scratches and marks were all gone. He looked significantly younger. She turned her gaze back to the girl.

"He's my father," the little girl said.

And then she blinked and Cimree forgot everything.

"Cimree, wake up!"

She opened her eyes, finding herself on her back. Azra bent over her, his face near hers, his look worried. The youth and vibrancy in his face startled her. Normally the rate of the transformation slowed down after a while, but his had seemed to accelerate. He was startlingly handsome.

"Where are we?" she asked, grunting, trying to sit. Azra took her by the arm and pulled her up. There was a strange little girl kneeling in the leaves nearby, gazing at them. There was something familiar about her. But Cimree could not remember having met her before.

Azra helped pull Cimree to her feet. His clothes were tattered and spattered with blood, but he looked hale.

"What happened!" Cimree gasped, gazing at him.

"I don't know," Azra said. "I awoke, roused by that girl. She won't speak. We have to get out of here."

She turned and saw the flames of the burning tree. "They lit the tree on fire!"

The girl frowned angrily, her eyes flashing with fury.

"We have to go," Azra said. "They'll kill us if they know we survived."

"But what happened?" Cimree said. "Your clothes—"

"I know," he said inexplicably. "Maybe the fruit is still working in me. We have to go."

Azra turned to the girl. "Come. It's not safe here."

The girl nodded and rose, brushing leaves from her bare knees. Cimree noticed the ankle bracelet shaped like a serpent.

"What's your name?" Cimree asked the girl.

The girl just stared at her soundlessly.

"Do you understand me?" Cimree asked.

The girl nodded.

"She could be afraid," Azra said. He began to gather the remains of his weapons. His bow was broken. So was one of his swords, but he took up the pieces. Then he yanked the dagger out of a tree trunk.

A roar sounded. The Fear Liath was coming. The little girl turned and looked toward the blazing tree. Then she walked up to Cimree and took her hand.

"Where can we go?" Cimree whispered to Azra.

"Where I sent Andrin and Perreta. There's another way out of the valley. Follow me. Hurry!"

They began to jog through the mist, heading away from the burning tree. Cimree was still shocked that the Queen Mother had fulfilled her aim to destroy it. The flames were displaying livid color in the mist. They hurried along the upward slope toward the mountain face. The sound of snuffling came from behind them.

"It's getting closer," Cimree said worriedly.

Azra turned and hoisted the little girl over his shoulder and began to run. Cimree struggled to keep up with him, but soon they reached the edge of the woods and came to the valley. The clouds overheard were pierced by the sun's rays. It felt good to enjoy the warmth on her skin. Azra gazed skyward, examining the cliff face.

"A little farther," he said, ambling over some boulders that had dislodged from the mountain and gotten stuck on the slope. They were going higher still, and Cimree felt her breathing getting more and more labored. Azra seemed tireless, even though he was carrying someone.

At the nexus of the valley was a boulder field. There was no path, just a collection of boulders that had tumbled down the mountains and piled up together. Azra jumped from rock to rock, as surefooted as anything, while Cimree paced herself to avoid losing her footing. Higher they went, ambling up this boulder field, until her chest felt like it would burst. Rugged pines clung to the unforgiving terrain. They were too high for aspen to grow. Even higher they went, until they had passed the mountain's debris and began to trample through vegetation and growth.

Just when Cimree feared her heart would fail from the effort, she saw a placid little lake that had gathered at the base of several mountain crags. She'd never seen this grotto before. The waters were even greener than at Lake Beatriz. Large boulders, some the size of cottages, were scattered around the rim, some cleaved in half. More signs of avalanches revealed the dangerous nature of the place.

And then she saw little Blanka poke her head around one of the boulders on the right shore of the lake. She squealed with delight and pointed at them.

Then Cyrill and Edwina popped out next, followed by Andrin and Perreta. Cimree felt a surge of relief when she saw the family together. Azra, breathing hard, set down the little girl and walked across a makeshift bridge of rocks to reach the other side and embraced Andrin.

"I was afraid you weren't coming," Andrin said. He gaped at the bloody costume that Azra wore. "That monster roaring. Did it get you? How did you survive?"

"I don't know," Azra said.

Cimree felt the little girl take her hand again as she looked shyly at the other children. Blanka approached first and hugged Cimree's legs.

"This is Blanka. That's Edwina. And the brother is Cyrill," Cimree said, introducing the children to one another.

"Can't she speak?" Edwina asked, giving the little girl a look of interest.

"She hasn't spoken yet," Cimree said. "We must help her be brave."

An arrow clattered against the boulder next to where Cimree was standing, the shaft snapping to pieces on impact.

"To the boulders!" Azra barked, gazing up again.

Angel sworn hunters were hovering above, bows in hand.

Had they missed on purpose? Or were they trying to kill Cimree as Jodocus had promised?

Thirty-Six
Memory's Quickening

Cimree crouched in the space formed beneath two large boulders resting against one another, her heart beating frantically. The nameless girl huddled next to her. There was no fear in her eyes, but she wore a somber expression. Azra had helped Andrin's family get shelter elsewhere. She could see the children cowering in a cleft of rock. Azra's back was pressed against the stone. The determination in his heart burned into her own.

Three angel sworn came down from the sky and landed near the shore of the lake. Each held a majestic bow with celestial-iron-tipped arrows already nocked. One of them was Captain Jodocus, and his face was twisted with menace.

"You cannot leave Clairvaux," he said with resoluteness. "The Queen Mother forbids it."

From her vantage, Cimree saw the children trembling with fear as Perretta tried to calm them. Andrin had his sword readied, and Azra pulled out his distaff and began weaving with grafting magic for the two of them.

"You did not accomplish the task you were given," Jodocus said. "The Fear Liath is still there."

"Yes, and the tree is on fire," Azra shot back. "There's no reason for any of us to stay now."

"But you took one of the seeds. They must all be burned. Bring it to me, and I will escort you back."

"I'm not going back to a cell," Azra said angrily.

"You accepted that consequence when you betrayed us," Jodocus said. "We have you pinned down, Azra. And I have more angel sworn on the rim. You cannot get free. Now come out before those children get hurt."

Cimree swallowed. They were on the verge of escaping the valley and the destruction that was coming. All that stood in the way were Jodocus and his hunters.

"I know you're very capable of hurting children," Azra said. "But I will protect these."

"There is no need for further violence," Jodocus said warningly. "Bring us the seed. I cannot return without it. I know you have it."

"I do not," Azra said.

"Then Cimree has it," Jodocus snarled in frustration.

One of the hunters was eyeing Cimree's position. She was covered by the boulder's bulk, but if they flew to the side, she'd be exposed, along with the silent girl.

She sensed Azra getting ready to fight and saw Andrin clench his sword hilt. The two were going to charge the angel sworn. But that's what Jodocus was expecting. And they'd be cut down with arrows before they reached them.

Cimree invoked the magic of the medallion and watched as Azra's eyes turned silver. The girl crouching near her squeezed her arm suddenly and shook her head no.

Surprised, Cimree released control of the magic.

"Validar, you take Cimree and the child. Arriest and I will take the others."

A shadow swooped overhead and suddenly plunged. Trinati

arrived, swinging her sword to attack Jodocus directly. With the sound of her sword striking the captain's quickly raised bow, Azra charged at the others. One lifted his bow and sent an arrow, but Azra dodged the shaft and it clattered harmlessly against the boulders. Andrin leaped into the fray as well, yelling in fury as he brandished his sword. Cimree was taken aback by the change of events and came out from the beneath the boulder, pulling out her dirk.

Trinati went after Jodocus with a vengeance, her sword cutting through the bow once again when he used the broken weapon to block her for a second time. He dropped the piece that remained and pulled out his own blade to counter hers, but Trinati pressed him hard until they were both splashing in the water.

Azra launched at the nearest angel sworn, who had drawn another shaft and pulled it back. Azra caught the man's outstretched arm and deflected the shot, then kicked the fellow savagely in the knee, making him shout in pain. Andrin rushed the third person, who shot an arrow at him, but Andrin's reflexes had been enhanced from the grafting magic and he jerked to the side, the missile sailing harmlessly past him. Cimree gazed up at the mountains surrounding the upper lake, expecting to see other angel sworn joining the fight. And then she saw Wegner and Darcia and others floating down from the heights, each gripping their own weapons.

Trinati knocked Jodocus down in the water and aimed her sword for his chest. "Yield, Captain," she said in a warning tone.

At the same time, Azra struck a blow with his dagger hilt to the one he'd maimed with a kick, knocking him unconscious. He then turned on the man Andrin fought so that it was two against one.

"Captain!" shouted the man suddenly fighting both Andrin and Azra.

"You're the archangel!" Jodocus shouted at Trinati. "How dare you do this!"

"You weren't at Montheron," Trinati answered with an edge in her voice. "We are going to leave Clairvaux and start anew. Any who want to come with us are welcome."

Jodocus still had his sword, but he hadn't raised it to try to protect himself, since Trinati was standing over him, leaving him in a precarious position. Cimree saw his body trembling, whether from rage or the coldness of the water she didn't know.

Wegner, Darcia, and the others landed nearby.

"The pass is clear of the Morgarten, Trinati," Wegner said. "Your defenders are holding it, and Uorsin is there with his hammer."

"This is treason," Jodocus snarled.

"The Queen Mother chooses not to leave the valley herself," Trinati said. "I tried to persuade her. And she's persuaded you that Clairvaux will not fall. But it will. And we will go far away, where these creatures cannot follow us."

"Heretic!" Jodocus shouted at her.

"Captain?" the other defender said, his voice quavering. He clenched his bow, an arrow on the string, but the tip was lowered, aimed toward the ground. Both Azra and Andrin had their blades pointed at him, but they did not fight.

Cimree came to stand next to Trinati. She felt inconsequential holding the dirk after seeing Trinati's fighting prowess.

"She's deceived you," Jodocus said to Trinati, casting a look of contempt at Cimree. "I know she wears the Tanaquil amulet. She's manipulating you all!"

"I have not. We're just trying to survive, Captain Jodocus," Cimree said. "Please don't stand in our way."

Jodocus looked at Cimree with fury. "The medallion is corrupting you."

"I don't know if that's true," Cimree said. "It does not control me. I'm not using it now to influence anyone. Including yourself."

Jodocus gave Cimree a baleful look. "Does she even know, Trinati? Have you told her?"

Cimree felt a throb of distrust in her heart. She frowned and then shocked herself when she blurted, "Go, Captain. Or we will kill you."

She felt Trinati stiffen at her side in surprise, but she knew this was the only way. Maybe she'd been influenced by Azra for too long, but she felt in her core that a man like Jodocus would not respond to any lesser threat. And especially not one willing to be acted upon.

"Shoot her!" Jodocus snarled.

The final angel sworn lifted his bow to aim it at Cimree. In a flash, Azra had jabbed forward with his dagger, piercing the man beneath his raised arm before he could loose the arrow. The angel sworn grunted in pain, his eyes looking confused before he fell backward and landed in the shallows of the lake. A ring of crimson began to spread from him. Azra turned and looked down at Jodocus menacingly. Only Cimree could feel the regret in his heart despite his icy stare.

"Go, Captain," Cimree said again even more purposefully. "Or we *will* kill you."

"They'll send hunters after us," Trinati warned.

"Azra, how much time do they have before Clairvaux is over-run?" Cimree asked.

"I don't think the morning hymns will be sung," Azra said flatly.

Jodocus's eyes widened with surprise. "That cannot be!"

Azra shrugged. "Believe what you will."

"They cannot breach her mountain fortress," Jodocus said. "We can withstand a siege for months!"

Azra snorted. "The grimalkin of Montheron were turned against us by a creature that severed our graftings," he said. "I think it led the Fear Liath to Clairvaux. You think it can't turn the birds against her in the Eyrie? However or whoever created it, there is no fighting it. All we can do is run."

"I will go back," Jodocus said firmly. "I am loyal, even if I'm the last."

Trinati looked questioningly at Cimree, as if unconvinced that letting him go was a good idea, but she didn't argue when Cimree nodded purposefully and said, "You may go."

Trinati stepped back and Jodocus slowly rose, his breeches and tunic dripping. He was trembling with the cold. He bent down and picked up his sword from the water.

"Celestial iron doesn't hurt them," Azra said.

"I'll take my chances," Jodocus said with fury.

He backed away from them, gazing at the dead man in the lake. The other, unconscious. Then he floated up and began to soar back down into the valley.

"We should have killed him," Trinati said.

"I was prepared to," Azra replied.

"We've seen enough death," Cimree cut in. "He'll learn for himself soon enough that he's wrong."

Andrin's family crept out from the cleft in the boulder. Cimree imagined that the boulder had broken in half while tumbling down from a greater height. The debris in the area made her wonder what the mountain lake had looked like in a previous age. The voiceless girl came up and looked at Andrin curiously. Andrin tousled his son's hair, then noticed the girl staring at him.

"Who's she?" he asked, looking confused.

"We don't know," Cimree answered. "But she's fixated on you."

The girl approached and pointed to his arm. His elbow actually.

"What does she want?" Andrin asked.

It was where the wolf had bitten him. Where the silvery mark was. "Roll up your tunic sleeve," Cimree said.

Andrin sheathed his sword and tugged up his sleeve, revealing the half-crescent bite mark. The girl stared at it, then touched his arm with her palm. When she removed her hand, the mark was gone.

Andrin gaped in surprise.

Cimree grinned with relief. "She cured you."

Azra looked at the girl, and a relieved smile came to his mouth. "Thank you," he told her sincerely.

She just looked at him. It was a significant look that seemed as if it should mean something. But Cimree had no idea what. She had no memory of this girl or where she'd come from. But Cimree believed she had also healed Azra somehow. What kind of magic did she possess?

Wegner approached Trinati. "My lady, we should depart at once. I've no doubt the Queen Mother will send hunters after us."

"I can stay behind a little while and watch for pursuers," Darcia offered.

"We should stay together as a group," Trinati said. "We're not out of the mountains yet. And Tirich Mir is a long way away." She gave Azra a meaningful look.

He folded his arms. "You are not the archangel anymore," he said. "You lost your rank when you challenged her authority. The same happened to me."

"What are you saying, Azra? That you won't show us the way to Tirich Mir?"

"I'm saying you are no longer in charge," Azra said bluntly.

"Someone needs to lead," Trinati said. "That is what I've been trained for."

"Perhaps now is not a prudent time to establish a new hierarchy," Wegner suggested. "We should go while we still can."

"I agree," Cimree said. The tension between Azra and Trinati didn't abate.

"Are you going to tell her?" Azra said to Trinati.

Trinati's eyes flashed with fury. "We should go."

"If you don't tell her, I will," Azra said. "She should know."

Cimree's stomach quivered with dread. "What should I know?"

"Azra," Trinati warned.

Azra turned his gaze to Cimree. "Another thing I've figured out without being told. This isn't the first time you've rebelled against the Queen Mother." He turned back to Trinati. "How many lives has she lived before this one?"

THIRTY-SEVEN
FORGOTTEN

They'd crossed the ice-choked pass and had started the steep descent on the leeward side, where Azra led them to a massive cave blocked from view by scree and scrub. A valley lay at the mountain's base far below, but beyond that was another teeming range of mountains stretching as far as Cimree could see in both directions. Each mountain in the range displayed a snow-packed labyrinth of craggy rocks and cliffs. As Cimree turned back to the cave entrance, she noticed a river cascading from the opening down to the valley. The cave entrance formed an inverted triangle and was very tall at the entrance, with narrow ledges hemming in the river, but it flared wider and even higher once they were fully inside. Cool air blew from it as they gathered together, survivors from Montheron and Clairvaux, to rest from the arduous hike, which had taken the rest of the day.

Cimree had been pleased, on arrival, to see Uorsin quickly building a fire to warm them and how he and Azra had spoken as genuine friends for the first time since their escape. Azra and he had been friends before his captivity in Montheron, and she'd overheard them chuckling about a shared adventure they'd once had. Seeing Azra laugh had startled her at his capability for being familiar in such a way. And she admired him for it.

"Do we have some food?" Edwina asked Cimree when she came by to check on the family. Many people were laying out blankets, but others shivered in the dark cold of the cave.

"Azra is going hunting," Cimree said. "Did you save any of the huckleberries we found earlier?"

Edwina nodded and coaxed over the nameless girl, then started to braid her hair. The poor waif's tunic had ripped in places, and her feet were tied with rags since there weren't any spare boots for her. She hadn't uttered a word the entire time.

Cimree continued to where Andrin and Perreta were sitting together. Andrin had carried Blanka much of the way and looked exhausted. When Cimree approached, he gave her a nod in welcome, then looked behind her to where his daughter talked gently to the other girl.

"You found the girl by the Gallows Tree?" he asked her. "And there's no idea where she came from?"

"No one has recognized her," Cimree said.

"She healed my arm," Andrin said gratefully.

"I asked Edwina to befriend her," Perreta said. "Poor thing. I wonder whose she is."

"So do I," Cimree said. "It'll be dark soon, so try and get comfortable. Azra said no fire tonight. We don't want the smoke to give away where we are."

"He thinks of everything." Andrin chuckled. "Wegner assigned me guard watch at midnight. I'd best try and get some sleep now."

Perreta smiled at her husband and brushed her hand along his face. As Cimree watched the tender gesture, she felt a surge of something. Was it jealousy? It was a complex feeling, but she felt the power of the medallion as it yet again snatched away her strong emotions.

Cimree looked toward the front of the cave and saw that the daylight was fading fast, and it made her wonder how long it would take for Azra to find an animal to kill. She sensed he was not far away, somewhere on the downward slope. She noticed Trinati talking to Wegner at the side of the entrance, and the unease, anger, and curiosity the medallion had managed to keep locked away during their trek bubbled up, so she made her way over. The murmuring of the river and rushing of the nearby waterfall made it impossible to hear the two of them until she was standing right next to them.

Trinati gave her a wary look. "Has Azra told you how to get to Tirich Mir?" she asked.

Cimree shook her head dismissively. "He's the only one who knows the way."

"How convenient," Trinati said. "Wegner and I were discussing what lies beyond the mountains. Marshes and bogs and a few settlements. It may take months to reach Tirich Mir."

"We may not reach it until next year," Wegner said. "We may have to find a place to winter."

"Hopefully somewhere warmer than this cave," Trinati said.

"May I speak with you?" Cimree said abruptly.

Wegner started to leave, but she caught his arm. "Both of you." She trusted Wegner. He'd always been gentle and kind to her. He wasn't the fastest climber, but he had made the journey with his huge pack of supplies and had never fallen behind once. She appreciated his sense of sacrifice for the whole.

"What is it?" Trinati asked.

"Earlier, you said you didn't know how many lives I've lived. We were pressed for time and the need to leave, so I didn't insist on knowing then. But I am insisting now. What do you know about me? And how long have you known?"

"I imagine you're upset and think I've concealed things from you deliberately," Trinati said defensively.

"I know you have. But then you were obedient to the Queen Mother's orders. She's not giving the orders anymore."

"It seems that *you* are," Trinati scoffed.

"I'm not trying to usurp your authority, Trinati. Please just answer me. I'm still struggling to comprehend that I'm not who I thought I was. That I never was."

"What I said earlier was the truth. I don't know how many lifespans you've lived."

Cimree turned to Wegner. "Did you know about me?"

He shook his head no. "I didn't. I believed you were a foundling and were given to Milena to raise. We'd never met until then."

"But *you* know more about it," Cimree said, turning back to Trinati.

"What I know won't satisfy your curiosity," Trinati said. "The Queen Mother kept secrets from all of us."

"Tell me what you do know, then."

Trinati sighed. It was clear from her bothered expression that she wasn't used to people demanding information from her. As the Queen Mother's archangel, Trinati had been the one who made demands.

"You were the Queen Mother's spy," Trinati said flatly.

Cimree blinked in surprise.

"It was hardly common knowledge," Trinati said. "You've always been good with people. With persuading people to divulge things. A good listener. You were never part of the high council. Just someone the Queen Mother would send when a situation required ... discretion."

Cimree still couldn't believe it. "Did Milena know?"

"Of course not. No one knew. I was her archangel, and I knew very little about you or what you did for her."

"But to be the age I am," Cimree said, "I would need to have eaten an entire fruit from the Gallows Tree. Maybe eighteen years ago? I have no memory of that past life. None at all. Why would the Queen Mother rob me of that?"

"Because you rebelled," Trinati said.

"Over what?"

"I don't know. I was never told. The Queen Mother gave you to me when you were a baby. I was told to find you a home in one of the villages in the interlake region. And that you'd be coming back. You were already angel sworn. And she needed you for a purpose."

"Was that purpose to reclaim Azra?" Cimree demanded.

"I don't ... know," Trinati said hesitantly. "You may have done it willingly. I can only guess what happened. But I knew who you were when you were a child. Everyone else treated you like an ordinary foundling. But you've always had a rebellious streak. Remember the day your clothes got carried away?"

Cimree did, and the memory still embarrassed her. "I was a child."

"And you have none of your past memories and I know nothing further about you."

Cimree felt a pit of disappointment and frustration growing in her stomach. The Queen Mother knew the answers she sought, but there was no way for Cimree to get them. She would have to go the rest of her life without knowing.

"Cimree," Trinati said gently, "I've trained for this moment. If anything were to happen to the Queen Mother, I was to take her place. You are not prepared to lead these people. Any faulty decision made could have disastrous consequences. Surely you realize this."

"What do you want me to say, Trinati? That I agree with you?"

Trinati frowned in frustration. "I know you agree with me. I also want you to agree that *I* should be the leader of this mission."

"Azra doesn't agree," Cimree said.

"Well, you can *make* him agree," Trinati suggested.

"I'm not going to make anyone do anything," Cimree said. Then she felt Azra's presence nearing the cave and looked over Trinati's shoulder.

Trinati frowned and turned to look at what had caught Cimree's attention. They both saw Azra carrying a stag on his shoulder, climbing up the trail leading from the fertile mountain valley below.

"That was quick," Trinati said, sounding impressed. "Will he make us eat it raw, I wonder?"

Cimree glanced at Wegner and saw a troubled look on his face. He was used to deferring to Trinati since she led the high council. But that didn't mean he always agreed with her. She'd have to talk to him separately. To learn about his true loyalties.

Cimree stepped past Trinati and Wegner on the narrow ledge at the entrance. She had known he was close, knew he was fatigued at carrying a burden, but the conversation with Trinati had so engrossed her attention she hadn't sensed his approach until he was nearly there.

She climbed down the trail and then gazed back at the opening of the cave. It was dark enough that she couldn't see Trinati and Wegner anymore.

It was a beautiful buck across his shoulders, and she felt the grafting magic at work inside him, allowing him to bear the burden more easily. He had the bow and arrows he'd taken from the hunter he'd killed on the other side of the mountain.

Azra paused at the edge of the stream and then sloughed off the buck, laying it on some nearby rocks. "You have answers. But you're not satisfied with them," he said.

"I have answers that only give me more questions," she said. "I was the Queen Mother's spy apparently."

Azra pursed his lips. "Your affinity for serpents is more explainable now."

She'd released the serpent from the bag Trinati had given her after they'd crested the pass and returned to dry ground, but she'd sensed serpents in the mountains, skulking beneath boulders, lying in wait in bushes for prey. They were clearly out of Clairvaux as she sensed them everywhere.

"I haven't tried to deceive you," she told him. "I didn't know."

"I can tell that you're being truthful," he said. "I suspected you were more than you seem. But it makes no sense that she'd rob all your memories."

"Trinati also said I was rebellious," Cimree said. "That I've defied the Queen Mother before."

He folded his arms and gazed at her. Much of his youth had returned, and the fruit no longer seemed to be working. It usually took a fortnight to restore all the lost time but his had sped up and concluded. "Maybe that's what made you valuable to her."

She looked at him incredulously. "How so? She *hates* disobedience."

"True. But more than that, she hates being wrong. She would encourage some of us, those in her inner circle, to challenge her thinking. To question her decisions. She wanted to be able to prove to us that she was right."

"That sounds annoying," Cimree objected.

"For someone who values people's feelings, I imagine you would not have enjoyed it. She was not arbitrary. Well, other than deliberately."

"Oh?"

"Injustice is a feeling that prompts immediate and harshly negative reactions—anger, contempt, feelings of revenge. During our training for the Long Patrol, she authorized our leaders to treat us unjustly in order to provoke that reaction. We might be told to tie a knot a certain way, and we would do so only for them to say we'd done it wrong and punish us for it. Or we'd be awakened in the middle of the night to be told we'd failed in a duty we'd never been assigned."

"That sounds miserable," Cimree said with sympathy.

"Ah, but it served a greater purpose. As members of the Long Patrol, we go out into the lone and dreary world. We face man's injustice to man. And by learning how to endure it patiently, it made us stronger, more resilient, more clever in our deeds. I didn't enjoy the training, Cimree. But I learned wisdom from it."

"As much as I would have abhorred such situations, I must

admit that I'm glad you endured it. Without you, we wouldn't find Tirich Mir. How far away do you think it is? How long will it take to get there?"

"Three years," he answered bluntly, rendering Cimree momentarily speechless. "Don't tell the others."

"Why ... so long?" she asked.

"I'm being pessimistic," he said. "Which I've been trained to be. We haven't begun to endure hardship yet. Climbing this first mountain was easy. Wait until we have to cross the steppes. Then a desert. Cold, wind, hunger. Some of them aren't going to make it. Some will want to turn back. Some will be killed by those who block the way."

Cimree's courage begin to wilt. "That's not very hopeful, Azra."

"Well, that is where you come in, Cimree. You will need to keep us all hopeful that we'll get there someday. That's why *you* will lead us there."

And she felt something stir in her heart that surprised her. That his confidence in her meant something. It meant a great deal.

EPILOGUE
THE GOLEM

The kobold jabbed the spear into Captain Odeon's already lacerated back. He grit his teeth and kept marching, with heavy chains binding his wrists. He was exhausted, half-starved, and the only reason he'd survived so far was because he'd been given some of the fruit of the Gallows Tree before the nightmare had begun, and he was younger and healthier. His reptilian captors were marching him through the valley of Clairvaux. And he saw, in despair, their ranks had already savaged the buildings and structures. Stumps of stone and scorched beams showed where the violence of fire had ravaged the town. Carrion birds were squawking noisily as they fed on the carcasses of the dead. The sky was filled with such birds.

Onward he marched, knowing with dread the destination his torn boots were bringing him to. The kobolds spoke in a guttural language he didn't understand. He only called them that because it was similar to the sound they made most frequently. Their communication was primitive, but there were legions of the scaley reptilian creatures, and they walked on hind legs with long tails and wore battered armor that looked like it had rusted at the bottom of a lake and gripped weapons with claw-like hands. The fleshy bulbous orange eyes with slitted pupils were disgusting yet contained a canny intelligence as did the grinning snouts. Knobbed horns crested their heads. Some only reached his waist and others were even more diminutive. But they had wicked temperaments and were quick to punish.

They followed the trail along the Silver River that met the trail leading to the higher village, the one that led to the Queen Mother's fortress. Another jab in his back made him nearly cry out in pain. Once Montheron had fallen to the grimalkin, the creatures had suddenly vanished back into the town, transformed again into simple cats.

Odeon and the others had barricaded themselves inside the fortress, where provisions had run out swiftly because of the great numbers gathered within. Fear turned the mortals against each other. Odeon and his men had tried to persuade them to listen, to cooperate and ration food, but eventually the angel sworn were rounded up and imprisoned by the half-crazed men who rose up to lead. Their distaffs were taken and violently snapped in half. And then Odeon and his compatriots were locked away and given no food.

He didn't know what had happened next, but he heard the skirmish when the kobolds arrived. Talking to kobolds had proven unwise. The mortals were collected and put to work on the island. From his cell, he could hear the noise of hammers and chisels on stone. The kobolds continued searching the fortress. They *ate* the cats first. Like they were a delicacy. The sounds through the barred windows were awful to hear. The angel sworn prisoners were found, days later, delirious with thirst and ravaged by hunger. And they had been brought in chains to the great hall, where they met the awful being who had triumphed over the angel sworn.

A being communicating in guttural growls and clicks. A golem, made of muscle and translucent skin. Its flesh was completely diaphanous, so that its skeletal and muscular systems and its variegated blood vessels were all on display. It had body parts Odeon had never seen before, and its visage was so gruesome, so horrific, that his every instinct told him to revolt in disgust. It was huge, over eight feet tall, and clambered about like a spider with its multiuse appendages and great strength.

There was, in the book of Origin, the mention of a creation half-formed, a golem. *I will praise thee, for I am fearfully and wonderfully made. Marvelous are thy works. My golem was not hid from thee when I was made in secret and curiously wrought in the lowest parts of the earth. Thine eyes did see my golem, yet being unperfect. And in thy book all my members were written. How precious are thy thoughts to me.*

The ancient word "golem" meant *half-formed*. A creation in progress. But this thing, this monstrosity, had a grafting wand. A bit of bark from the Gallows Tree. And it used it, in Odeon's presence, and clutched it in its six-fingered hand as it descended from the wall and came up to him and his men. The defenders had trembled in horror at the beast who had defeated them. Trinati had told him of this thing climbing rooftops. He turned away as it took one of his defenders by the arm and then he squeezed his eyes shut when the man screamed in agony only to have it silenced with an aftermath of incoherent sounds. Odeon turned back, confused, and found a mist of pieces oozing on the floor near the golem and a new arm grafted onto its own body.

Odeon had stared in shock and terror at the power of the golem. It spoke but in a language that was strange and choking.

"Work! Work!" the golem had barked at them. "You—will—work!"

THUS ALL THE survivors had been made to dismantle Montheron. The kobolds were their taskmasters. The workers were given raw fish to eat and lake water to drink. Odeon was forced to obey or be killed. Every mortal and angel sworn on the island had been pressed into labor, beaten with whips if they didn't comply, and the structures that had been built generations ago were erased. Odeon's grief consumed him as he was forced to wreck what he had helped to build. There was nothing so painful to him as this great and sudden change that had overcome his life.

And then, weeks after being enslaved, the golem reappeared, and commanded the kobolds to drag Odeon from Montheron.

"Queen—Mother!" it growled before flying away with wings like a bat's.

And Odeon found himself, away from his comrades, on the lonely road back to Clairvaux. Hungry, sore, discouraged, disheartened. The village at the valley's entrance had been razed. The cottages and homes had all been burned. He walked because he had to. Because he knew no other way to survive but to obey the worms that had become his masters.

Fog had settled over the deepest part of the valley. A fog that stank and made his skin crawl. He climbed the path leading to the upper village, which had also been desecrated. He'd heard no hymn that morning. Had seen no sign of life except his kobold companions and the carrion birds. His heart nearly burst with despair.

The long march ended at the lonely and quiet mountaintop. The highest tower had been sheared off. The roof was gone, deformed and turned into cinders. He had imagined he would cry to see it thus befouled, but he had no tears left to weep. His bones ached even though they were the bones of a younger man. The lacerations in his back stung and festered. The magic of the fruit was no longer healing him, so he would continue to suffer wounds as any mortal might.

The kobolds marched him to the shattered gate. Carrion birds had stripped away the flesh of the defenders, leaving nothing but bones and broken armor and swords. The marbled stone was pitted and pocked. He gazed helplessly at the ruin of the halls as he passed them, watching the reptilian tails swish as the creatures led him in. They looked uncomfortable. Fearful even.

At last, Captain Odeon was brought to the great hall, where he found the Queen Mother chained to the floor. On her throne sat the golem. The broken roof lay in pieces around them. The Queen Mother's robe was ripped and tattered. Blood had dried on her face. She lifted her head and weakly turned it to him. Surprise registered. She had her distaff in her bleeding hands.

"Odeon," she panted.

He tried to go to her, but the kobolds put a wall of spear tips in his way and snarled at him.

The golem clicked and hissed with some sort of gleeful response. Its eyelids were invisible, and its orbs operated independently of each other. One eye fixed her. One eye fixed him. The tongue lolled over its teeth.

Odeon had no weapons. No armor. His tunic and trews were threadbare and ripped. Thankfully he still had his boots, but they were scarred and torn.

"Cim-reeee," the golem hissed again. It pointed its distaff at the Queen Mother.

Odeon licked his lips. "What does it want?" he asked the Queen Mother. There were bones scattered throughout the audience hall.

"It wants the Tanaquil medallion," the Queen Mother said. "It wants Cimree."

"Cim-reeee!" the golem shrieked, bouncing up and down on the seat. It dropped from the throne and began to prowl. It approached the Queen Mother and pointed the distaff at her.

"I don't know where she is," Odeon said. "They left weeks ago."

"You must find her, Odeon. For my sake. You must find her and bring the medallion."

"Cim-reee!" the golem hissed again. It wrenched the distaff from the Queen Mother's bleeding hands and offered it to Odeon. "Cim-reee," it said once more, almost cooing like a dove.

And the Oldknow made tunics and trews for the First Man, Lan, and his second wife, Havah, and clothed them and sent them out of Clairvaux to till the ground, to raise flocks and herds, and by reason of use have their senses exercised to discern both good and evil. And Lan and Havah were each given a distaff of scionwood from the Gallows Tree to tame all creatures and to make thread and clothing for their children. And the asp viper followed after them. And it bit the woman's heel.

— Origin, the Tale of the Queen Mother
of Clairvaux

AUTHOR'S NOTE

The first time I heard the story of Lilith as part of the creation story from the Bible was in a book series by Piers Anthony I read while in high school. It is an ancient Hebrew legend that Lilith was Adam's first wife who refused to be subservient to him and was expulsed from the Garden of Eden for being willful. According to the derivatives of this legend, she's suffered a pretty negative reputation since then and is generally known as the mother of demons. Her Hebrew name was used in Isaiah 34:14 and has been translated as *screech owl* or *night hag*. And this was part of the inspiration for the Angel Sworn series.

I've long been fascinated by the stories of creation, whether in Mayan legend, the Bible, Milton's *Paradise Lost*, or Tolkien's intricate Middle Earth. When my wife and I went to France and Switzerland to celebrate our thirtieth wedding anniversary in 2024, we were inspired by a visit to Lauterbrunnen. That picturesque setting didn't just inspire Tolkien to create Rivendell, it also inspired Clairvaux. I've never been to a place that reminded me so much of Yosemite Valley until we went there and took the ski lifts up to some of the highest mountains in Europe. Those exhilarating rides gave me so many creative ideas for the magic system in this book.

You have undoubtedly also noticed some very significant cross-over elements to my other books as well. These aren't just Easter eggs (as many readers like to call them). This story is an origin story to one of my worlds, but I will hold off disclosing which until a later book. For now, you will have to be satisfied with the web of clues I've been carefully strewing about and try to make connections on your own. But I will reveal things, I promise, as you proceed.

Many years ago, a local high school did a production of *The Sound of Music*. It began with a choir of nuns coming on stage, holding candles, and singing a Gregorian-style chant with a backdrop of the Alps. Just that opening scene caused me to pull out my cellphone and begin tapping in the dark an email to myself: *"Idea —musical order that sings to drive away evil spirits. The singers are killed one by one to stop the barrier which keeps them out."*

It was just the germ of an idea. A tiny seed. I had no idea how much this seed would sprout and grow after that.

In this version of the creation story, the First Man partakes of the forbidden fruit and is driven away from the garden.

In book two, *Tyrant Queen,* you will learn more about the serpent in the tale.

About the Author

Jeff Wheeler is a Wall Street Journal bestselling author of over thirty epic fantasy novels, including the *Kingfountain* and *Muirwood* series. His stories captivate readers with strong, moral protagonists, complex characters, and richly detailed worlds. Known for clean, compelling fantasy, Jeff's books explore themes of integrity, loyalty, and growth, with interconnected series that keep fans eagerly turning pages. A husband, father of five, and active in his faith community, Jeff draws on his life and history to craft uplifting tales. Discover his worlds at jeff-wheeler.com or through his online classes at Writers Block (writersblock.biz).

www.ingramcontent.com/pod-product-compliance
Lightning Source LLC
Chambersburg PA
CBHW050522110726
47899CB00005B/1561